COAST TO COAST

Frederic Raphael

COAST TO COAST

ORION

Copyright © 1998 Byronic Investments

The right of Frederic Raphael to be identified as the author
of this work has been asserted by him in accordance with
the Copyright, Designs and Patents Act 1988.

First published in Great Britain in 1998 by Orion
An imprint of Orion Books Ltd
Orion House, 5 Upper St Martin's Lane,
London WC2H 9EA

A CIP catalogue record for this book is available from the British Library

ISBN 0 75280 456 1

The characters and events in this book are
fictitious. Any similarity to real persons, living or dead,
is coincidental and not intended by the author.

Printed and bound in Great Britain by
Clays Ltd, St Ives plc

for Beetle

Open House

'Know what I like right away,' the woman said, 'about it? It feels like people have been really happy here. Have they?'

'And through here is the living room,' Marion Pierce said.

'It certainly feels so. Is it all right if we check it out upstairs?'

'That's what we're having an open house for,' Marion said.

'I don't know why anyone would want to sell this house, do you know why they would, Bradley?'

'Let's go upstairs, if you want to go upstairs,' the man said. 'While it's still daylight.'

'It's still going to be daylight for hours yet.'

'I know,' he said.

'You have to say something to people,' the woman said.

'But you say *everything*,' the man said. 'I mean, do you have to like make lifelong friends with everyone you meet? All she's wanting to do is sell the house.'

'*Marion!*'

'Hi, Paula.'

'She should cut and run, don't you think so? The way he talks to her. Those people just went up the stairs.'

'Or *he* should,' Marion said. 'She's a pain in the ass. From way back.'

'I hate a man talks like that to a woman. I can't believe you're really doing this. The Pierces selling 5746, Hillcrest? I cannot believe you're doing it.'

'Maybe we're not. We didn't exactly have an offer yet.'

'So listen, I brought you these. Farewell offering, but that doesn't mean you have to go. Non-returnable. My mother's recipe. All the way from the old country. St Louis yet! If all you are is hungry for reassurance, take the cookies and say it ain't so!'

'Give them to Barnie. He and your cookie jar go back a long way. All good things come to an end.'

'I *know*, and here I am still waiting for them to begin. Hey there, Grimond! Hey there, pal! He still jumps up at me.'

'He jumps up at everybody,' Marion said. '*And* slobbers.'

'He's a wet lover,' Paula said. 'If you like them it's fine. How does Barnaby feel about selling? He loves this house.'

'He wants it, he can keep it,' Marion said. 'The kids've gone. I get tired keeping their rooms just like they remember them when they come by a coupla times a year.'

'Is it true,' Paula Hobday said, 'he's really going to marry that girl?'

'Who's that?'

'Benjamin. Your son. Who's that! Who else have you got? The one we heard about at Thanksgiving? What's her name?'

'Put it this way,' Marion said, 'he'd better. Because we're going all the way to LA for the wedding. Imogen.'

'I'll bet you something.'

'For instance?'

'Barnie is out all day today, am I right? Leaving you to smile at the people. I bet you he's got urgent business on number one court with Jack Piper. Men are such cowards. They pretend they want change, but do they?'

'How much did you bet? Because you just lost it. He's actually lending me moral support, and hating it. He's skulking in the den, tearing up letters he'll be asking me where they are in a coupla weeks' time.'

'Did you ever have the IRS do an audit on you? Nick Shaffer had them do an audit on him and he had to produce bills from wives he'd forgotten he ever even had, or face penalties!'

Barnaby was frowning at a script for a pilot that never got made and which was a lot funnier than he remembered. He was starting to get outraged, all these years after the event, that the Network had not liked it or even called him back on it. Maybe he could change the names of the main characters and turn the law office into . . . what? Could the couple be vets possibly? They could possibly be vets or they could conceivably be personal trainers, unless someone had already done personal trainers.

Paula said, 'Barnie, you're not seriously doing this?'

'I don't seem to be getting a lot of laughs, so I guess it has to be serious.'

She kissed him as if someone might be watching. 'Have a cookie. I hate to think of you leaving the neighbourhood as slim as you arrived. I hate to think of you leaving, period. But am I ever going to say so? I very nearly have too much pride, don't I?'

'Excuse us,' Bradley said, 'if we look . . .'

'Go ahead,' Barnie said. 'This is the den. It's small and not particularly well lit, but you know where you are in it. Cornered.'

'You're Barnaby Pierce the comedy writer, aren't you?' the woman said. '*The Stinkinsons*? Am I right?'

'You know he is,' Bradley said. 'We established that.'

'Because that was my totally favourite soap for a while. Especially the first series. You should nevera killed Evgenny. She was some character. What are you doing now?'

'Actively thinking about suicide,' Barnaby said.

'What's that, another comedy?'

'The way I do it,' Barnaby said, 'probably.'

'Suicide is killing yourself, Bernice. He's thinking about killing himself.'

'These are shelves,' Barnaby said, 'and that's a Compaq. Not the latest model because, rightly or wrongly, I don't need that. I lose enough files using this one.'

'I was going to say,' Bernice said.

'He knows that and he doesn't want you to. Is that the dining room through there?'

'Table and eight chairs round it,' Barnaby said. 'How did you guess?'

'Let me tell you something. You were right not to be a salesman,' the man said. 'You definitely made the right decision there.'

'Dining table's got a great big burn in it,' the woman said.

'Dining table's not for sale.' Barnie was looking at Paula when

3

he called out, and she was looking at him. Then she picked up a framed photograph from a collection on the imported rotatable bookshelves with their freight of useful reference books and old scripts. 'I am; it's not, is how I feel.'

'It's still got a burn in it,' the woman said.

'Benjamin's getting married. I can't believe it.'

'That's Christopher,' he said, 'you're looking at.'

'I know that,' Paula said. 'I remember Christopher so well.'

'That's right,' Barnie Pierce said.

'How long is it now?'

He took the frame and put it back where it had been.

Paula said, 'So when do you fly out?'

'We're driving.'

'Have you looked at a map? You'll find Los Angeles is still situated right the other side of the country. *Driving?*'

'In the red E-type Jaguar.'

'There and back?'

'There. We're giving it to Benjamin as a wedding gift. He always loved it.'

'So did you, didn't you? You took me out in it once. Remember that?'

'I remember everything,' Barnie said.

'*Driving*,' Paula Hobday said. 'You and Marion, or what?'

'That's the plan. We have people we want to see on the way.'

'And after that you're seriously going your separate ways?'

'We're just doing things one at a time.'

'Are you really? That'll be a first for you, won't it, Barnaby?'

'OK, Paula,' Barnie said. 'OK.'

'Are you saying OK to me? Remember who I am? You remember everything, so I guess you don't.'

'Isn't that water under the bridge I see down there?'

'And it's *cold*! I don't want you to go.'

'Paula . . .'

'And then comes the little cough. Paula . . . Don't forget the little cough. Just don't tell me how great Graham was. I know how great Graham was, and is, but don't remind me; I know. You never told her, did you?'

4

'Why would I?'

'And she never guessed? She never told you she guessed. Because Marion . . .'

'Would you be in this house right now,' Barnie said, 'if she'd ever guessed? Would you subsequently ever have been about to be the trusted recipient of our tropical fish?'

'She probably had a fling herself.'

'Marion doesn't do those things.'

'No? And here I always feared she was human.'

Jayney Biebel, the realtor, was wearing jeans and a ruffled white shirt. Her high heels made her look shorter. 'Hi, Mrs Pierce,' she said. 'Sorry we weren't here sooner, but this is Mr Reid and Ms Reinhardt I told you I was bringing.'

'Barry and Tanya,' the girl said. 'We're Barry and Tanya.'

'Come on in,' Marion said.

'Hey, Barry, listen, welcome home! Know what I mean? Because this is truly it for me. Lust at first sight!'

'Could you work here, Tanya? Is this a place you could work?'

'I'm a graphic designer. I think I could work here. Did you work here, Mrs Pierce?'

'I raised four kids,' Marion said.

'I want kids,' Tanya said, 'but I don't want to stop working.'

'Have four,' Marion said, 'and you won't.'

'You should see the upstairs,' Jayney Biebel said. 'You have four children? I didn't realise that. How great!'

'Had,' Marion said.

Barry and Tanya went upstairs and Jayney Biebel winked at Marion. 'I took them someplace else first because I knew they'd be knocked out coming here after this other place which was . . .' She paddled her hand. 'If that.'

'You know how to sell.'

'I know how to try.'

'I threw my cookies at Barnaby's feet,' Paula said, 'and he spurned them not. He did not spurn them in the least. And now I have to go. You're not seriously driving to California?'

'He wants to.'

'You can *fly* the car out, or have someone else drive it.'

'He wants to drive it.'

'He doesn't want to let it go,' Paula said.

'I know that, Paula.'

'Or you. He doesn't want to let you go either. Neither do I.'

'I'm Jayney Biebel. I'm the realtor.'

'Hullo. And goodbye. Because . . . Graham and I have to go to some fund-raiser *chez* Polunin. How come you weren't asked?'

'We were,' Marion said. 'But first things first.'

'I never seem to work that. We'll see you before you go, won't we? I have the fishes to collect, if nothing else.'

'Hullo, Mr Pierce. Jayney Biebel.'

'Oh hullo.'

'I'm the realtor. Are you going upstairs?'

'Do you not advise it? Is there something I should know?'

'You may find some people up there. Their names are Barry and Tanya. Who are very interested in the house. So . . .'

'I don't tell them about the roof, is that it?'

'The roof?'

'He's kidding,' Marion said.

'It's a living,' Barnie said. 'Sometimes. All I'm going to do is get me a sweater. Will that shake their resolve?'

'I knew a writer once,' Jayney Biebel said. 'He was a little like your husband.'

'Really? What did he write?'

'Uh-huh. Principally T-shirts. He wrote principally for T-shirts and bumper stickers. They were bigger then. A bigger market. He worked on the last Reagan campaign so you can see how long ago this was, unfortunately.'

When Barnie went into the bedroom, Tanya and Barry were on the bed. They had not taken off the Thai silk quilt, but they were right on the bed.

Barry said, 'OK, I'm sorry. This was an impulse thing. You ever do something on an impulse?'

'Not a lot,' Barnie said. 'I usually wait till I'm asked. Would you kindly put your clothes on and leave this house?'

'We like it,' Tanya said. 'We might make you an offer.'

'My offer is you get out before I throw you out.'

'You don't want to sell your house, don't sell it.'

'You don't have to be aggressive,' Barry said. 'For the same money, you could be polite.'

'Is it polite to fuck in other people's houses? Is that polite? And another thing: where's the money?'

'I don't need to take this. I said I was sorry.'

'Come on, Barry. I don't actually like the shape of the bay window too well. And I also *hate* what they did to the bathroom.'

'And *and* also,' Barnie said. 'How many strikes is that?'

'You should see what somebody did in there. Especially the lights, which are truly such a mistake.'

There was the sound of sudden loud Beethoven from downstairs: the Milstein. Then it was as abruptly turned down. Barnie watched Tanya and Barry finish dressing and go towards the door.

Barry said, 'You walk into bedrooms, you're liable to find people doing things. Something you might like to remember.'

'We never needed a house this big,' Tanya said. 'I didn't realise how big it was. This many rooms?'

There were people Barnie had not seen before walking through the hall and others checking out the kitchen with Jayney Biebel. He went into the living room, where the LP of the Beethoven violin concerto was playing for a bearded man who was pulling out other old LP's from the floor-level shelf next to the fireplace. Barnie said, 'We're taking those with us.'

'You have some great pressings here. Would you be insulted if I made some kind of an offer for some of them?'

'There could well be an ugly scene,' Barnie said.

'You have the Tortelier Dvořák for instance.'

'Yes, I do.'

'Which has been unobtainable for at least ten years.'

'It still is,' Barnie said.

'Mr Pierce. Mr Pierce, would you show me and this gentleman how the pass-door works from the garage? We don't seem to be able to work the lock.'

'You punch in the code, 2468, and then you swipe the card through it, is all. You also turn the knob.'

'I'm sorry, but it doesn't seem to happen. I'm probably stupid.'

Barnie went and punched in the code, 2468, and swiped the card through, kicked the bottom of the door and it opened. The red 1967 E-type was in the garage, alongside Marion's GTI VW and the '78 Buick which Barnie never found time to get rid of.

'You also have to kick it, Mr Shapiro,' Jayney Biebel said, 'is what we didn't know.'

'While you're here, how do you operate the doors to outside?'

Barnie pressed the button and the wide doors began to yawn upwards. As they rose, Barnie saw the bearded man marching towards the street with a loaded briefcase under his arm. He looked back at the house and then he was out of the gate and Barnie was ducking low under the slow garage door, even though it was almost up already, and calling out, 'Excuse me . . .'

The bearded man gave a very good performance of a man walking casually away from the house and not imagining that anyone could possibly be calling to him.

Barnie said, 'Hey! Excuse me.'

'Oh, were you calling me just now?'

'May I see something?'

'Now wait a minute . . .'

'That's all it'll take,' Barnie said. Then he said, 'You know what I should do, don't you?'

'OK,' the bearded man said, 'I'm a little bit of a fanatic.'

'And also,' Barnie said, 'I think you're a little bit of a thief you omitted to mention.'

'I told you it was a rarity. It was stronger than I was.'

'And so am I, I would guess, which is probably all that's stopping you knocking me down and . . . Get out of here.'

'I'm sorry. Truly.'

'Go home and think about yourself,' Barnie said. 'Because you're disgusting taking other people's property.'

'I bet you haven't played that pressing in fifteen years.'

'And won't again,' Barnaby said, 'but you're still not getting it, on a bet.'

When he went back into the garage, Mrs Biebel and Mr Shapiro had already left. He pressed the button and the wide doors started back on down. He had his hand on the long hood of the cold E-type as he watched the doors dock on the floor. Christopher had wanted to know why he couldn't take the Jaguar to go to Colorado. They had a Chevvy in those days and Barnie said he could take that. They used a lot of salt on the roads to Aspen; he didn't want the Jaguar to come back with ulcers. Christopher didn't smile; he wanted the E-type, because it was cool. Suppose he had let him take it, would it have made any difference? What made any difference to what? Did Marion think about him and Paula? Did she possibly have something current of her own that had made her not make more of it?

When Mrs Biebel finally went, after telling them that a lotta people had expressed interest, and one or two seemed really serious, Marion opened all the windows she could reach and it still seemed stifling and unhealthy in the house. 'That was a truly hateful experience, wasn't it?'

'Wasn't it?'

'What happened upstairs exactly?'

'What happened upstairs? Oh! What happened upstairs was Tanya and – what was his name?'

'Barry, wasn't it?'

'Tanya and Barry is right were filled with affectionate feelings for each other. They were communicating on our bed. Without taking off the spread.'

'I don't believe you.'

'Fine.'

'They were seriously . . .?'

'They were officially engaged,' Barnie said. 'In the prone position. The lady superior, if that helps you picture the scene.'

'You know something funny?'

'Unfortunately; many things. Not all of them saleable. That's probably what's unfortunate.'

'I never saw anybody else doing it.'

'You've seen blue movies, haven't you?'

'Have I? When have I?'

9

'The Talbots that time.'

'I never saw anybody doing it in the flesh. They weren't *that* blue.'

'How often does anyone?'

'I think a lot of people must. Was he actually . . . like, *in* her?'

'She was riding 'em, cowboy.'

'And what did you do exactly?'

'I thought about the bedspread. Exactly. I thought about you and the Thai silk bedspread and what you would say if . . . something . . . happened to it. *On* it. Which it didn't, because – although I didn't want to – I checked, and it didn't.'

'I talked to Hal, did I tell you, on the telephone?'

'You're telling me now. When?'

'Yesterday.'

'And you're telling me today.'

'You said I should call him. I called him.'

'Is he going to be around when we hit Seattle?'

'When else did you see people doing it?'

'I thought we were through that one. I never did necessarily.'

'You did. I can tell.'

'I never saw you with Hal at least.'

'That was twenty-four years ago.'

'I know that. And I never saw you with him. OK, I saw a couple in a motel when I was working with Leslie Mickey down in Atlantic City when you were . . . busy with . . . the kids.'

'Christopher,' she said. 'I was having Christopher. And?'

'We were working out of this motel, trying to lick a pilot, and this couple walked into a room kinda down and over from where we were working and . . . I don't think I woulda . . . oh, I don't know, maybe I would, but Leslie being there, it became kind of a dare, if you like, so we . . . watched them. They were quite impressive. Did all kinds of stuff you might not have heard actively discussed at length on TV at that time.'

Marion said, 'Sounds like I owe them something, do I?'

'That's silly.'

'Hal said he's going to be around. He'd like us to stay with them for a coupla nights, if we feel like it. I don't think it's silly.'

'He was a black guy,' Barnie said. 'I guess she was somebody's wife.'

'It was your idea we go see Hal and . . . Erica.'

'No one's going to see Erica, and you know it, Sweets. *You*'re going to see Hal.'

'He used to be your best friend. He wants to see you again just as much as he wants to see me.'

'It's all part of the same deal and you know it. "Used to be" means he isn't. "Used to be" means he fucked my wife, as you may know.'

'You told me to call him and now you act like it was all something you just found out about, just so you can have the pleasure of looking at me like that. You fucked Paula, didn't you, in this house?'

'We weren't going to ever have this conversation again.'

'And she was *my* best friend, supposedly, and have you noticed how nice I've been to her all these years?'

'That was your pleasure.'

'I look at her mouth and I see your dick in it. Is that my pleasure?'

'It must be, or you wouldn't.'

'Was it there ever?'

'You want a divorce, we'll have a divorce. I'm not going into details.'

'I have my answer. You seriously think I'm going to drive with you all the way to LA?'

'I'm giving the Jaguar to Benjamin for a wedding present. How else are we going to get it there?'

'Why are you?'

'Because he wants it.'

'And because you don't want to.'

'Possibly. That's possibly true. And totally irrelevant. I don't believe in motivation. I don't believe in *examining* motivation especially.'

'How many times did you use our room? You and Paula?'

'You bitch sometimes, Sweets, aren't you? Okay then, one time. Just the once. And you drove up. I probably should've said never and not given you the satisfaction. Just don't tell me that's the only satisfaction I ever did give you.'

'Don't script me, Barnaby, will you please?'

'Fuck it,' Barnie said. 'Fuck it, fuck you. I'll drive the car across to LA and you can fly. You can walk. You can do what you want. I never should've told you shit.'

'All this because I called Hal Pfeiffer. At your suggestion.'

'Some people pick scabs. I'm one of them.'

'You went to motels with her, is that what you did?'

'Have I ever asked you what you did?'

'I hate those trousers with elasticised waistbands she always wears. Never trust a woman who wears elasticised waistbands. They do it to make things easy for guys to get a hand in.'

'They do it because they're fat, and you know it. This is such old ground, Marion, I can't believe we're fighting over it.'

'All the best battles are fought on old ground. That's what battles are about. You could perfectly well put the car on the train and we both fly to the coast and pick it up there.'

'We have to take Grimond to your sister's. How are we going to get Grimond to your sister's if we fly?'

'We can take a trip upstate and then catch the plane.'

'You don't want me to drive that car, do you? Is what this is all about. Not even alone.'

'Maybe I don't want to be alone myself.'

'You want a divorce,' he said. 'And you don't want to be alone?'

'What did she do that was so special?' Marion said. 'Paula? Did she do something I didn't? I bet she yelled. I bet she called you Barn. Did she? Did she call you Barn?'

'We're talking about eight damned years ago.'

'She climbed up and bounced, didn't she? She has the chest for that *and* she knows it.'

'Sweets . . .'

'Why can't we enjoy this? Why can't we revel a little bit?'

'You don't like to revel and you know it, in this particular field. You're finding reasons to be angry. You're finding reasons to justify yourself, retrospectively, because of Hal.'

'Beef up the script, Pierce; it's not working.'

'Did I ever ask you what you did or didn't do with Hal? Paula appealed to my vanity is what Paula did principally.'

'Which became twelve inches long the minute she did so.'

'Talk dirty,' Barnie said. 'It's fine by me.'

'Did you ever give her cystitis?'

'You don't give people cystitis. They get it. Men aren't responsible for women getting cystitis.'

'I'd quite like to drive,' she said. 'It's one of the things we never did, isn't it, from sea to shining, polluted sea? So now it's too late, let's do it.'

'Do you think we could shut some windows now?'

'Sure. Why didn't you ever tell Paula that you finally had to tell me about you and her?'

'I guess I still wanted *something* to be secret. Also . . .'

'Yes?'

'Also I think I'd've wanted to tell her about you and Hal. I don't know why; but I know I didn't want to.'

'I know why,' she said, 'and so do you, of course. She called you Barn, didn't she, Barnaby?'

'You know the funny thing about marriage, Sweets? You both agree you'll forgive and forget. You sign the goddam peace treaty. And then the war begins.'

'She called you Barn, and you liked it. And that's the woman we're selling up and giving our fish to. Put that in a new series of *The Stinkinsons* and people would laugh and laugh.'

'Possibly,' Barnie said. 'It would have to be done right.'

Coffee Break

'You drive and you drive in this country, and you never seem to be any further away from where you started.'

'Or closer to where you're going,' Barnie said. 'You are though. That's how they turned it into the United States: by making all suburbs the same and then making the whole country into suburbs.'

'Except for the war zones.'

'Of which,' he said, 'this car threatens to be one.'

'Who's making threats? I'm not.'

'Who else do we have? Grimond, did you growl?' The dog on the back seat looked at each of them in turn, and back again. 'Grimond is making like a tennis fan.'

'Now you're backing away. You make a threat; then you smile; and I'm supposed to think it's all a joke. But if I ever say it *is* all a joke, and not a particularly good one, you go sour on me. So let's leave Grimond out of this, why don't we? Because, are you aware of that?'

'We have a long way to go,' Barnaby said, 'so why open our wounds this early? Ask yourself why we're making this trip.'

'You wanted to.'

'I wanted to give Benjamin the Jaguar because – between ourselves – whatever the hell desert distances that involves – I didn't want to. I wanted to keep it *and* I wanted to give it to him. I wanted to punish myself, if you want to put it that way, for being a lousy father by not being one. Apparently at least.'

'I don't want to put it any way. You want to give him the car, give him the car. You don't, don't. Why not give him something else? And fly out?'

'When you loved me, you knew damn well. Or understood. Or pretended to. Actually, you know damn well now. Only you don't love me, so you pretend not to. You want me to say things that can't be forgiven because you've decided I'm unforgivable.'

'You deliberately say things in a way I don't understand – that you hope I don't – and then right away you turn into side-eyes Pierce, those blip-blip glances of yours. Blip, blip, blip. Laser treatment. I was looking for maybe a truce while we crossed the continent. Fat chance. Like the ancient Greeks went in for, didn't they, when they were on their way to the Olympic Games? Before they gouged each other's eyes out in the wrestling.'

'You know the trouble with us now, Marion, don't you, ever since this thing came up between us? Truces are only threats in their best clothes. I feel like I'm always in court. I feel like I'm in court after I didn't wash a dish or wipe my hands and left a dirty mark. I feel all the time – and here's something you can despise in me – on the verge of rage or tears, tears of rage, tears of self-pity, you know the range. I feel pathetic and, pathetically enough, that's what makes me . . .'

'I've said this before, Barnaby, you're afraid of wanting what you – I'm not going to say *want* – at least furtively like to think about, toy with. And always have. I don't blame you. You so want to be the innocent party that it makes you feel guilty. And rightly so, because in your heart – if that's the operative organ – you've been imagining what it would be like not to be married, not to be married to *me*, just not married period, like – OK – ever since we got married.'

'I'm a comedy writer,' Barnaby said. 'If I don't see the tears in laughter and the laughter in tears, where do I go for honey? Or should that be "money"?'

'You see what I'm up against? The capper.'

'A slightly clever man who made a pact with the devil. Who also looked like the Welcome Lady. Not you. When he agreed not to be too clever in office hours, which got longer and longer until he stopped being clever at all. Until he became the funny man who wasn't funny. Anything along those lines?'

'You think I don't like you. You think I don't respect you. You think I'm not grateful for a hundred and one things you did, we did, down the years. And at the same time – no, listen, because we have *days* of road ahead of us – at the same time, you know that I *do* feel those things – '

'Intermittently. May I say intermittently intermittently? Because it just could be the adverb of the month.'

'You want to have a grievance that's so manifestly – '

'There's another useful one.'

' – *justified* that nothing else I say weighs a single ounce in the scales against it. One thing you want to be, if nothing else, that's the guy who never wanted any of this to happen. And that's a lie, Barnaby. It doesn't matter; I don't blame you; but that is what it is. I haven't invented, or cooked up, this situation between us. And, no, I'm not saying you have. It's something like weather; you can talk about it, but you can't argue sunshine into being rain, or vice versa.'

'You still get rainbows,' Barnaby said. 'But I don't see any in our situation.'

'What you really dread isn't losing a wife. It's – '

'Dividing the books and the records.'

'There you go.'

'Is what you were going to say.'

'Is what you did say.'

'I was cutting to the chase. And now you think I was doing the chasing. I dread the whole damn thing.'

'But you haven't categorically said to forget it.'

'You're my wife. Who I have learned not to be categorical with. Whom I respect and whose decisions, especially the ones that aren't the ones I want to hear, always seem more likely to be right than my own. Like when I didn't buy those tartan pants.'

'Tartan pants.'

'In Tucson, Arizona, when people were wearing tartan pants.'

'Those were terrible. You woulda looked terrible.'

'Did I buy them? One curl of the Marion lip and .` .`.'

'How about me and Bermudas?'

'True. You have the legs for almost anything, but not for

Bermudas. Bermudas were designed by someone who hated people to have legs.'

'They're a kind of a dare. No one looks good in them, so how do I look? Kind of a thing.'

'"Do you love me?" in other words, is what you're saying.'

'Do you love me in extra-silly clothes? Exactly.'

'I agree,' Barnaby said.

'You don't really want to sell 5746.'

'Does anyone?'

'I don't want to be the prisoner of a house. It's ignominious, Barnaby. You do see that, don't you?'

'If I'm going to give up everything that's merely *ignominious*, how am I going to make a living? How would I ever?'

'You didn't need to do those things.'

'Oh. Which ones were those? Remind me.'

'See what you're doing? Hear what you're doing? It's my fault you wrote *Sergeant Bimbo*.'

'You *are* Sergeant Bimbo,' he said. 'Where else do I get my inspiration?'

'Blip blip! Take a look how it's going. Smile smile, blip blip.'

'You really hate me, Marion, don't you?, is what it comes back to.'

'I know you is what I really do.'

'To know is to hate. We only love what we don't get too close to. Tall dark strangers. Kids with big eyes and legs like sticks. Singapore. Rain forests. English TV.'

'Paula.'

'We did this already. We did this before. Let's not do it again, unless you seriously need it to motivate whatever ... What's the matter with you, Marion? We were almost having a good time together, is that the problem now? It happened; it stopped happening. I never loved her. You know that.'

'I was trying to be philosophical.'

'Philosophers don't ... Stick to the One and the Many, how about we do that?'

'Wasn't I?'

'I teed that up for you.'

'And I actually made contact. Has to be a first time.'

'Is that what you still hope for?'

'Could be. I don't know that I *hope* for anything.'

'Did you ever wonder about a black man?'

'I don't do those things really.'

'Ever ask yourself why?'

'Line's busy. I never get an answer.'

'Busy with what?'

'I guess I'm afraid. Afraid I won't measure up. Afraid he'd be too hot for me.'

'Is that it?'

'You know better.'

'Maybe you don't want to be punished. Or mastered. Is that it?'

'*Mastered?*'

'Enslaved.'

'Is that what black men do?'

'I have no experience. He said that to you, didn't he?'

'Who said what?'

'Routine prevarication.'

'Sounds like a medical procedure.'

'And that's more of the same. Hal.'

'I don't remember.'

'I do. The poisoned chalice. You do too remember. He wrote you that letter.'

'Which you opened.'

'Which you showed me.'

'Because you'd already torn it.'

'It was in the stack. I tore it, then I saw it was for you. Cute of him to address it to the house.'

'It was all over. We'd all said everything that had to be said. You said he could write to me; he wrote to me. Then you started crying foul.'

'I thought I just started crying. He said that one day, if you got the chance, you should try fucking a black man. He talked a lot more . . . directly to you than I ever thought I could.'

'You have your problems; Hal had his.'

'Have and had,' Barnaby said. 'Do you want to stop for something? You want some coffee and a donut or something?'

'You want to fatten me up? For what? I could use some coffee before we get there.'

'My version of an answer might run along the lines of "Sure, why not?" Sucker for simplicity, right? Hal advised you to make it with a black guy before you died so you could know what you were missing and you know it.'

'How much did that say for him finally?'

'Am I or was I ever in the business of saying things for Hal Pfeiffer? I don't remember being.'

'You did when you were best friends.'

'That was a long time ago.'

'Everything was,' Marion said.

'Fort Plain. Sounds fancy. Let's pull in here. *Mueller's Coffee Academy*! Let's hope we can learn something to our advantage.'

'It says something else to me, but why would you want to know that?'

'For instance?'

'That . . . Probably we should not get into this right now.'

'Let the wound fester. Always a sound principle.'

'You think he was trying to make trouble.'

'Hal?'

'I think he was afraid he hadn't been, OK, the lover I wanted him to be.'

'We'll leave the car here,' Barnaby said, 'so we can see it from inside the Academy. I don't want to lose it to an enthusiast after all these years. He was thinking of you, was he?'

'I don't know what he was doing.'

'You told me how great he was.'

'I didn't mean . . . in that department. You know that.'

'Do I?'

'I came back, didn't I? Why do you suppose I did that?'

'We had kids. Is what you told me. I'd already noticed, because I can be very observant, especially when left alone with them for a period of days, but it was good to have confirmation.'

'You used to be away for days sometimes.'

'In the fucking studio. You never had to bother with the studio part, did you? Men's work. Which is what you now want to do. I hope it makes sense to you. It makes sense to me only because . . . why would you want to have done what I did?'

'Barnaby, Barnaby.'

'Go do it,' he said. 'Go find a black man and do that too, while you're at it.'

'I dreamed I did once.'

'You did? You said it didn't appeal to you. Being enslaved.'

'I said I dreamed about it once. I didn't say it appealed to me.'

'Then why dream about it?'

'Please. We don't choose our dreams.'

'Don't we? What's the latest thinking on that? Do we know? How do we get to have them?'

'They're like mental garbage, isn't that what I read someplace?'

'Mental out-takes. Unwanted footage. I read that. Think there's anything in it?'

'Probably a buck or two for the author.'

'What was his name?'

'OK, it was Clifford.'

'Clifford. And who was he?'

'I don't know. A black guy supposedly.'

'*Supposedly?* How is someone supposedly somebody in a dream?'

'They're supposedly something in real life; they can be supposedly somebody in a dream. Why not?'

'What I mean is, how did you know that he was supposed to be black? In what way wasn't he?'

'Are we going to have this coffee?'

'In what way was the guy in your dream . . .?'

'He was meant to be black, but I wasn't convinced. He was meant to be kind of, OK, masterful. But I wasn't convinced there either. He was sort of . . . nice.'

'And you were disappointed?'

'I was, OK, slightly pissed. I didn't think I wanted him to be, all right, violent with me . . .'

'But then again you did.'

'I had this feeling that the dream wasn't going right. It was kinda miscast, I think you'd say.'

'Except that you did. Did you recognise who the guy was who was pretending to be black? Was he really called Clifford – it wasn't Clifford Vittorini, was it? – or was he pretending to be Clifford too?'

'It was definitely not Clifford Vittorini. I think he was somebody I made up. But I have no facility for fiction apparently, so he was this like *apology* for a black man.'

'We never knew enough of them. Aside from some actors, I knew one at NBC at one time, Alphonse LeBrun, who was a sound man, that I liked quite a lot. He was a bridge player. And there was a warden I met one time, up at Sing-Sing, when they asked me to maybe adapt that British series, remember, about people in jail. He was a terrific guy, I thought. Introduced me around. We had this script conference with a bunch of no-hopers. Funnier than I was, a lot of them, a *lot*. He told me that this one guy was the head honcho in the drugs field and I said, "How do they *get* drugs in here?" And he was like . . . I don't think I ever got a bigger laugh. Certainly not from you. There was Clifford that painted the house that time.'

'He was white.'

'You liked. Are we ashamed of that, not knowing more black people? Marion, Jesus! This is incredible. You know something funny – this *is* funny – because I think this guy, no, I'm positive, his name *was* Clifford. The pusher. Clifford Macnamara, because I couldn't believe it. He was tall and he wore the shades and he was very, very handsome and he told me like how he was getting out in a year, which would give us time to set up the series so when he got out, he would like to be in it. He gave me his day and night numbers. In Sing-Sing! Clifford Macnamara.'

'I had your dream,' Marion said. 'Like you had my letter.'

The Academy had round dark wood tables, polished till they seemed to have puddles in them, and ladder-backed chairs. A waitress in cap and apron brought their coffees in earthenware mugs on brown saucers like big cookies.

'Nice,' Barnaby said. 'He wanted to leave you wanting something, is the truth, even if it couldn't be him. He wanted it to be him, ideally, but . . .'

'Do you know how many years ago you're talking about?'

'Oh absolutely. Have you noticed something? The further away things get, the more people like to think about them. First anniversaries are nothing, but . . .'

'I think it's pathetic.'

'You always were a critic with bite.'

'That smile,' she said.

'Is what you're divorcing me for. Sorry. My dad used to say that if you didn't smile, you couldn't expect to sell. I think Arthur Miller probably taught him that.'

'Dale Carnegie.'

'Who probably wrote the most evil book of the century. *Mein Kampf* at least *raved*. And was unreadable. Not unbuyable, I didn't say, but . . .'

'That's OK, Barnie. You don't have to cover yourself. We're only drinking coffee in Fort Plain, NY.'

'You always . . .'

'Barnaby, quit this what I always do stuff, can you possibly? Because I don't, and if I do, I don't want to hear about it. I don't. Evil, do you really believe that?'

'Oh yeah,' he said. 'I think Dale Carnegie was evil. I think he ruined America. He made Babbitt – and I don't mean Irving – seem like a national hero. Him and the guy did the road signs coast to coast all the same, all like suburbia. If we had a just justice system, those guys would have been indicted and the history of the Republic woulda been . . . OK, it wouldn't. Still and all . . .'

'Barnaby,' she said, 'you don't really want to be with me, you know.'

He pushed away his saucer and the almost finished coffee and reached for a napkin (dark blue floral one side, white the other). Marion's image was softened and then he held the napkin to his nose and eyes and he was going to sneeze. He held it there for a while and then he didn't know what to do with it and finally he crumpled it and put it on the saucer and it slowly unfolded itself, like the flower which it seemed, on one side at least, that it wanted to be. Finally, it fell off the saucer and Barnaby left it there in the shiny puddle on the table and pushed back his chair. He looked at her then and it should have been love, but it wasn't.

So when they were in the car again, he said, 'You really don't mind about it, do you? Selling 5764.'

'I'm the heartless one,' Marion said, 'isn't that what you'd like to be the truth?'

'I'm just making an observation.'

'You know what it is about people who just make observations? They *never* just make observations. A famous comedy writer told me that.'

'I want to meet him. Or her, or her. Sounds an interesting person.'

'You want me to tell you you're interesting, Barnaby? Did I ever say you weren't?'

'I hate it,' he said. 'I hate it so much I don't know what I want to have happen.'

'To the house.'

'Is that a meaning glance you just sent across towards the jury? Remember that, well, mark that well, ladies and gentlemen, because he cares more about his *house*, as you will just have heard, than he does about his wife and family. Rest your fucking case, Marion. Give your case a fucking rest.'

'And we're into rage again. How about you put me down in Albany or someplace like that with an airport and I'll fly on out to LA and I'll see you there, maybe, and we'll be the nice people they all think we are, for the wedding at least?'

'At most.'

'Whatever. I *hate* selling 5764 and if you don't know that, you don't know anything.'

'Which would be my usual score.'

'You want to know what I'm tired of, Barnaby? *That's* what I'm tired of. Your self-pity, which is really vanity wearing old clothes to attract pity. I like you better being a sonofabitch, if you want the truth.'

'If it'd make me free, I would. But it doesn't. Because what you're saying is – '

'No, no.'

'Yes, yes, *what you're saying is* – you have only ever liked me for infinitesimal periods of time, because – '

'I didn't like you *that* much when you were.'

'God dammit, Marion, we're talking about our whole lives practically and . . . I would never say anything like that to you.'

'And why? Because most of the time you don't even notice what kind of a bitch *I'm* being.'

'You know the hell of it?' he said. 'I really love you, and it doesn't do a bit of good, does it?'

'And you hate me,' she said.

'And even that doesn't do any good either.'

'Two pins,' she said, 'and I'd go right back and kill that Mrs Biebel and take down that sale sign and move right back in.'

'We haven't moved out,' he said. 'That's the hell of it. We've quit on it, but we haven't moved out, and I don't think I ever will.'

'But you will,' she said. 'Frankly, how much time did you ever spend there compared with me?'

'I love my den.'

'But you have an office.'

'You didn't like Jason. I started working with Jason Mason, it was only a matter of time.'

'Jason Mason. Imagine being his mother.'

'I pass,' Barnaby said.

'And deciding to call him that.'

'There are writers,' Barnaby said, 'they never *say* their dialogue, aloud, and I guess she was one of them. Jason Mason. Maybe she thought it was cute. Some people think alliteration is cute. Maybe she thought, give the little feller a cute name and he'll never run into trouble. They'll always smile. *He* always smiled.'

'I guess every comedy writer needs a partner does that. He called me "dear". I could never like a man who called me "dear" all the time, even if he did smile at the same time. He smiled at the same time he *died*, I shouldn't wonder.'

24

'You really hated him.'

'I'm sorry he's dead.'

'I'm not,' Barnaby said. 'I couldn't stand the guy and I didn't know what to do to get rid of him. He was invaluable. He had the common touch. Everything he touched turned to shit and they couldn't buy it fast enough. If you want to feel real rich, and be going downhill all the while, Jason Mason was your ideal partner. I *hated* doing *Sergeant Bimbo* in case you have any lingering doubts in that department. Hated it; the first series, the second series, the third series. I got richer and richer and I felt worse and worse. Maybe that was why . . . I never really liked her, you know.'

'Who was that, dear?'

'You know damn well. I never *liked* Paula. She pretty well embarrassed me, if you want the charmless truth. It's the only brand there is, very often. I don't mean I didn't . . . enjoy having her, but . . . she was never a rival, as far as you were concerned. She was something I could afford to have.'

'She *charged*?'

'Of course she didn't charge.'

'Like the Light Brigade she charged.'

'Like the Light Brigade, she did charge.'

'She was Jason Mason's fault, was she?'

'She was my fault, if we're into faults. I was trying not to be.'

'Did you fuck her in the ass?'

'No. Marion, no.'

'You didn't? Or you aren't going to tell me?'

'I'm not going to tell you *anything*. Correction: I've told you everything I'm going to tell you about me and Paula. You don't want to know those things.'

'You did.'

'I mean it, Marion.'

'I would have.'

'I don't know what that means. Or how you could possibly know.'

'She has that kind of an ass. Large and firm and inviting. She works it like that was something that was in her mind some of the time. Admit it, Barnaby; I was a hitch-hiker and I sat here and said, "Did you ever want to or, if you like, *actually*, fuck that neighbour of yours in the ass?" would you be outraged like this? Would you be sulky and . . . affronted? I mean, how can a man do the things with a woman, his *wife*, that you did with me for thirty years and still pretend to be a fucking *virgin*?'

'Depends on the wife,' Barnaby said.

'That's funny, but not very; OK, not at all. Because doesn't this, to be serious, tell us something about ourselves at this point?'

'Shall I tell you what it tells me, that you won't like it telling me? It tells me that you're still accumulating evidence. It tells me – I didn't think you'd like this – that I can't and I don't trust you not to tell the world whatever I tell you. It tells me that . . .'

'Know the trouble with your case, Barnaby? You *never* rest it. You're in court all the time.'

'You were really insightful, really *deep*, Nolan, you'd just possibly reconsider what you take to be my attitude and guess that maybe I want you to . . . just once maybe . . . before we . . .'

'There's something else you're good at: summoning up the unwanted tear. That angry little shake of the head that says "Now look what you've done to me!" That's quite a talent of yours.'

'It doesn't pay residuals though.'

'I never wanted you to do *Sergeant Bimbo*. I used to sit there and every laugh I gave was something I had to make myself do before I did it.'

'There were some good laughs in *Bimbo*. There were some true laughs. Jason had a tonight's-special-laugh for things that were really funny. He thought of quite a few too. He was really into the character; he'd come up with things that were really *her*.'

'He was in love with you, wasn't he, little Jace?'

'You're coming with a late rush, Sweets.'

'Fuck you,' she said. 'For the "late" bit.'

'Jace had a girl, librarian worked in the Widener.'

'No further questions.'

'I'd thought he was in love with me . . .'

'You'da what?'

26

'OK, I'da been embarrassed.'

'And understanding.'

'And gotten rid of him. I couldn't have worked with him. He was *never* in love with me. I don't appeal to those people.'

'Oh, oh, oh . . .'

'One of them once said to me, in college, that I was one of those people wasn't attractive to either sex.'

'That was Rex.'

'That was Rex.'

'Which only goes to prove it. Rex Tischman, who was a very pretty guy, I have to admit that.'

'Money written all over him.'

'Suits were made of it. Great haircuts. Everybody else looked like they wanted to be rock stars. He had to be Cary Grant.'

'Cary Grant wasn't, you know; there were rumours, but they were envy-tipped, or so I was promised.'

'Rex Tischman,' Marion said, 'was the dish from hell.'

'I didn't know anything about this,' Barnaby said.

'Neither did he.'

'So what was I? Second best?'

'I feared him; I despised him; what the hell was he doing in a second-rate school like . . .? Did he ever tell you?'

'He told me one thing that I remember.'

'You always get hurt by the things, you had one ounce of controlled reflection . . .'

'Controlled reflection? Me? Where would I get stuff like that? I wouldn't even know where to get coke. I must be one of the only people of my entire generation – never mind profession – wouldn't know who to ask for shit. I asked anyone, you know who he'd be? An undercover agent.'

'They can get it for you same as anyone.'

'You know where to get drugs in Ipswich?'

'Ask Paula. She'll know. There isn't anything that pretty baby can't get you tickets for.'

'As long as it's full already.'

'Rex Tischman,' Marion said. 'He made you a declaration of love.'

'Those people don't love.'

'And you're someone thinks I'm accumulating evidence? Because that's evidence if anything is evidence. Those people! You'll have a hell of a time in the slammer when that grace note gets read into the record. I get in the witness chair, I'll adjust my fucking microphone before I cough that one up.'

'Rex Tischman was a narcissist in a class of one. He musta been fulfilling some stipulation in his rich uncle's will or something, hanging out with us when he shoulda been where? Harvard. Princeton. Princeton.'

'He'd told you what he felt about you right out, how would you have reacted?'

'There's no evidence,' Barnaby said.

'There's evidence,' she said. 'Silent witnesses talk louder than words. What he didn't say is what he said. People don't just go up to other people and tell them they're not attractive unless they mean something by it.'

'I think he was just feeling mean and . . . said what was in his head. People can be shitty and truthful. In fact . . .'

Marion said, 'Wait a minute. Was this after you and I . . .?'

'I get it,' he said. 'Where this line of questioning is leading. To the greater glory of Marion Nolan. Why not? I'm going to stall and say, "I don't know when it was", which is the truth, but not the whole of it, of course.'

'I was almost certainly in the same class in Rex Tischman's eyes.'

'Same class?'

'He put you in.'

'Except that on your account, according to your deposition, that *isn't* the class he *really* put me in. So are you too in the class of not being in the class that I'm not in either? This could give us an unexpected lot in common, belatedly.'

'I hardly exchanged two words with Rex Tischman.'

'You can't even call him just plain Rex, even now, because you feel that would be . . .'

'Presumptuous. Yes, I do, I guess. He was kind of an aristocrat, wasn't he?'

'By which you mean he'd been rich for a full twenty minutes.'

'He had those eyes, smooth as pebbles.'

'Most eyes are not smooth?'

'Like they'd been smoothed under clear water for centuries. Like they were in the family.'

'The guy's family made its original money as morticians, did you know that?'

'I didn't know that.'

'Morticians. Those eyes probably belonged to some other entirely *different* aristocrats . . .'

'That's enough, Barnaby. Don't go getting jealous on me at this remove, please.'

'Princeton plain-stitch,' Barnaby said. 'Do you know what that is?'

'Excuse me? Is this a knitting question suddenly?'

'It's something they do, or did. Gays. Princeton plain-stitch. I saw in a book about Auden. W. H. Auden, the poet.'

'I know who W. H. Auden is.'

'In a book about him. It was something he said people did. Like it was something basic. Like it was the equivalent of a standard forehand in tennis terms.'

'I can imagine,' she said.

'Princeton plain-stitch?'

She made the repeated motion for him. 'Isn't that what it would be probably?'

'Oh, OK,' he said. 'OK. That's probably it. They probably don't do it any more. They've probably moved on.'

'So,' she said, 'you're telling me that you never did anything like that? You never had any experience of that kind.'

'Do you think less of me?'

'Your mother told me you were fastidious, did you know that?'

'Mother said that? When?'

'When I came to visit for the first time. She said it as if it was something I'd be pleased to hear.'

'And were you?'

'I was thrilled. Proved there were things about you that I knew, she didn't.'

'Plenty,' he said. 'And then some.'

'That was a funny visit. She looked at me a lot. I mean a lot; all the time I was there. Scrutinised me, is what she did. Slightly puzzled, not disapproving but, yes, puzzled. Any ideas?'

'About?'

'Why I puzzled her?'

'You do,' he said.

'I do, that's right. I think she was puzzled what it was about me that you could possibly want.'

'Come on, Marion. You were a good-looking girl. Not even Alice wouldn't have *some* idea what a man might see in you. But I'll tell you what *really* puzzled her, if it doesn't dent your self-esteem too deeply, which it shouldn't: what *you* could possibly want with me. She was looking for the flaw which would account for why you would want to settle for her son.'

'You don't know your mother.'

'Who do I know? I coulda known Rex Tischman, but he killed himself, so it's a little late.'

'He killed himself?'

'In Italy. He killed himself very, very dead, on his forty-fifth birthday.'

'You never told me.'

'I know,' Barnaby said. 'It was something I didn't tell you. How about that?'

'Mean,' she said.

'I didn't even know you knew him. *And* it was probably mean. You don't know how tempting it's been, at various times along the line, to know something – however trivial or irrelevant – that I know you don't.'

'Irrelevant to what?' she said.

'Is very much the question,' he said.

'Irrevelant to what?'

Good People

Silence had turned into *a* silence, something each dared the other to break. Grimond watched them, open-mouthed, from the narrow bench behind the seats. His lolling tongue was silvered with saliva. He seemed thirsty for someone to speak.

When Barnie said, 'Fuck it,' he was letting slip whatever delicate thing was suspended between them. He was damned if he would keep up his end of it any longer. 'And please don't act surprised or ask me what the matter is as if you didn't know.'

'You have to do this, don't you?' Marion said. 'For some reason.'

'I blinked,' Barnie said. 'You wouldn't; I did. You win. Congratulations.'

'Haven't you ever noticed how whenever we go to visit anybody you don't want to visit, you always do this?'

'I leave noticing those kinds of things to you,' Barnaby Pierce said. 'You're so *damned* good at it. I mean, what would we need duplication for in that department of all departments?'

'What are you so *angry* about suddenly?'

'It doesn't feel sudden to me,' he said. 'I don't think it's sudden. Do we go left up here? I'm not so sure it's anger either.'

'You know damn well we go left. And it is too anger.'

'Almost anything I ask you . . .'

'Don't finish that one, Barnie. I know you're quick, but there is such a thing as too quick.'

'Let's not get personal now,' Barnaby said.

'You can ask me anything you like,' she said.

'And you'll answer? *Anything?*'

'Not things I don't know.'

31

He was driving up a side road now between wired and numbered lots of young pine trees. Then there were sycamores and then the woods ended and there were white-fenced fields and cattle and they could see the Carroways' farmhouse and the barns and the new gleam of an aluminium silo. One of the cows was humped, gushing a leak.

'Did you ever masturbate?' he said. 'There's a question you have to have the answer to.'

'That's something you really need to know?'

'No one stipulated *need*,' he said. 'I'm curious. What? Thirty years we're together and I'm curious about it. Translate those years into air miles and then tell me if I'm not entitled to a little bonus.'

Marion leaned back into her silent position. She might as well have shut a door in his face, except that he could still see her and the way she shut her eyes and let them come open slowly, as if the world were not worth seeing any more but she would give it one more chance.

'Fuck it,' Barnaby said.

'Again?'

'Absolutely again,' he said.

Nessie came out of the house in big-seated painter's dungarees and a pair of those same blue-black New Mexican sandals she always wore. Her dark brown hair was roped in an untidy bundle on top of her head. A couple of fawn Yorkshire terriers, one with one ear cocked, the other with both, skittered on the porch and dived to tangle with Nessie as she embraced Marion as if they were really close.

Marion said, 'How are you, sis?'

'As is obvious,' Nessie said. 'Rich and powerful. Hi, Barnaby.'

'How are you, Vanessa? You look great.'

Calvin Carroway came into the yard from the direction of the chicken run. He was carrying a basket of eggs over his arm. A handful of beets dangled, as if held by the veined ears, from the same fist. He was wearing a jeans outfit and rubber boots like a regular countryman, but he was freshly shaved and he had the air of someone who had chosen to be happy not doing something which might have made him happier. His modesty was both becoming and accusing: he had done the right thing and look what it meant he had to do all the time.

Grimond finally flopped down from the car, diving to the dirt yard after a long, long look, like a bad swimmer committing to an element not his own. The country was a little too full of scents and possibilities to suit a suburban dog. He went and his low rear-end wagged nervous pleasure at seeing Calvin.

'Place looks just great, Cal.' Barnaby shook Calvin's spare hand and held him, briefly, by the elbow.

'God is good,' Calvin Carroway said.

Marion was just saying, 'How's Randolph?' when, as if someone had been waiting for the question, they heard the sharp jolt of a shot, and then another, together with breaking glass.

Randolph sauntered into the yard carrying a .22 rifle. His cropped hair did not fall over the plastic strap of his back-to-front black cap. It bristled brightly, like a mushroom brush. Randolph was fifteen years old and bigger than boys used to be at fifteen. He wore assault boots and fatigues.

Calvin said, 'Come say hullo to your Aunt Marion and Uncle Barnaby.'

'I already did,' Randolph said. 'Last time they were here.'

'Look who's come to stay with us.' Nessie was holding Grimond between her legs, both hands dry-shampooing the dog's head.

Randolph nodded and then walked on into the house.

'Lunch in ten minutes.'

Marion said, 'Is today not a school day?'

'Randolph . . . quit,' Calvin Carroway said.

'*Quit?* At fifteen?'

'Nessie and I are working with him, which is much better. They weren't equipped for someone like Randolph in Reading.'

'Great-looking new silo you have there,' Barnie said. 'What do you keep in there?'

'I'll show you,' Calvin said. 'Though it's more what we will than what we do.'

'What we will *if* we ever do,' Nessie said to Marion. She was leading the way into the kitchen round the side of the house where the washing was out to dry. 'I've got bread in the oven.'

'You're still baking bread!' Marion said.

'Name something I'm not still doing,' Nessie said. 'Name one thing.'

'Smells good too. I love this kitchen. The old Aga.'

'You can have it.'

'Come on, Nessie. You have a beautiful life here.'

'And what about you?'

'I told you in my letter.'

'What was "separate lives" meant to mean exactly?' Nessie said. 'In other words, you're getting a divorce.'

'It means what it says. It means finally I feel like it's now or never. A girl can get wrinkled being slept in. I want to see what else I can do possibly. Divorce is not the main point.'

'You have such an enviable life. Not being grateful is part of it, I guess.'

'You can't take comfort in other people's envy, Ness. I don't *want* comfort.'

'Seems you must've had an awful lot of it.'

'So,' Marion said, 'how about you?'

'You're kidding.'

'Randolph still cello-crazy?'

Nessie was tasting beans for a moment and apparently had to think about whether they were done. Then she said, 'Music seems to . . . bother him recently. Calvin thinks maybe he's *too* musical; it disturbs him.'

'You mean he quit that too?'

'He's doing something different temporarily.'

'Which is?'

'He's into welding,' Nessie said.

The boy did not come when he was called to lunch. Calvin waited and then he bowed his head and thanked the Lord for this and all His other mercies and they sat down. They were eating their homegrown salad, when Randolph came and stood in the doorway. 'Anybody know anything about acting schools?'

34

Barnie said, 'What do I do? Press my buzzer if I do? I know something.'

'Because I think I could be a great actor.'

'You could for instance act coming and sitting down like a civilised person,' Calvin Carroway said.

'Know the best quality an actor can have? Which I've got.'

'I know it can't be timing then,' Barnie said.

'Menace. Which I do have. Nessie will confirm that. In abundance. You can't ever quite tell which way I'm about to jump. Can you, Cal? Ever. Do I mean it? Don't I? Who knows? I'm someone you have to watch.'

'All the time, I imagine,' Barnie said.

'Turnips? You're actually serving them turnips?' Randolph sniffed and sat down next to Marion and looked at her as if she had a low neckline. 'Your sister is really scared of you, Marion, in case you didn't know that. She thinks you're so well dressed, so soignay. And see how shiny *his* face is? Think it's always that way? Uh-huh! He's afraid you despise him because, despite all the evidence to the contrary, he believes in Him. Like I do, don't I? And also possibly because – this could be crucial – he can't make babies like you, Barnaby, evidently can. Or could.'

Marion said, 'Your mother says you're into welding these days.'

'You spoke to my *mother*? When was this?'

'While we were getting lunch.'

'Oh, you mean *Nessa*. Nessa says I'm into welding? I am too. It frightens her, doesn't it, dearest? The naked flame. The hot tip. The mask. The rush. They're afraid I'll burn the whole place down. They're not sure if they dread that or they can't wait for it. Have you seen the silo? It set them back, and for what?'

'He's right,' Barnie said. 'This guy's going to be one hell of an actor.'

'Screw going to be. I already have the first fifteen years of my career behind me. You're an actor too, aren't you, Uncle Barnie?'

'I'm a writer, of a kind. I guess you have to act a little bit to write the kind of crap I do. In that sense, right, I am.'

'You underestimate yourself. Because here you are, as I understand it, for the very last time before you go solo, both of you, and you're acting like you were still part of a couple. You're passing things at table and everything! You're truly exemplary. I mean you act like families were forever and, hey, you'll be back to see us again real soon. Who would guess that you were here strictly to dump the pooch and be out of here in, oh, two hours flat, if that's possible?' Randolph looked at his faintly haired wrist, on which there was no watch. 'Hey, is that the time? Gotta go myself!'

He put a slice of ham in his mouth and stood up. He was almost out of the doorway when he turned round and said, 'Oh Marion, one thing, OK?'

'Careful of those last-minute questions on the way out, kid. Too much Columbo can weaken your impact. *Déjà vu*, you know?'

'If you ever do speak to my mother – my mother-mother – check out whether she really is a triple murderer, as is often alleged. Unless that was my dad. I kinda hope against hope maybe he was some kind of a performer. Tap-dancer maybe, who does a little gigolo work on the side. Someone I can look up to.'

His boots thudded more than they tapped, but he did a little number.

'You never know what's in the blood, do you? The talent in the corpuscles, working quietly away until one day you maybe, for no good reason anyone can think of, all of a sudden sing like Placido Domingo.' He made a cute face. 'Or maybe you wind up shooting a perfectly good dog.' His forehead rumpled at them. 'Timing OK?'

'How do we live with it?' Nessie said. 'We live with it.'

'I remember going through it,' Marion said, 'with . . . with ours.'

'He's not ours, is he?' Nessie said.

'He is too,' Calvin Carroway said.

The Pierces drank their coffee and ate Nessie's excellent oatmeal cookies as slowly as they could. They had to stay well over the two hours that Randolph had predicted, didn't they? The boy had gone out of the house again, which was a comfort and a reproach. Barnaby walked with Calvin down to where he was thinking of a possible piggery, although people in the neighbourhood were against pigs. Calvin's willingness to endure hostility seemed to be of a piece with his Christianity; the man had an appetite for isolation that might have impressed a stylite.

Nessie started crying while she and Marion were talking about Marion's plans for the future. It did not stop her from speaking quite sensibly, but the tears kept rolling down her face and pinking her chin and she tried to catch them now on the back and then in the palm of her hand. Marion knew she was meant to go on talking, so she did, about her plans to maybe teach and about the apartment she had looked at in Boston, not far from the Commons, which she always liked. Nessie was sane and lucid about the problems and charm of a woman living presumably alone in the city, and she also cried. Was that shooting Marion could hear?

Nessie said, 'If you and Barnaby are seriously not going to be together . . .'

'What?'

'It doesn't matter. You don't suppose he'd do something for me, would he?'

'I'm sure he would if he could.'

'Because, OK, how is his sperm count these days?'

'Excuse me?'

'His sperm count.'

'How would I know?'

'I shouldn't have asked. I shouldn't have asked. Assume I didn't.'

'You shouldn't have asked me,' Marion said.

'What difference would it make to anybody? You're right. The right moment, when's that, you know? Never!'

'You're serious.'

'Don't you know what it is to want something and be never going to have it?'

'Nessie . . . I know what a lot of things are.'

'Listen, all I thought was, as he's all set to leave us his dog . . . But you're right: I shouldn't have. Don't tell him, OK? I asked.'

'Why don't you ask him? He'd maybe . . .'

'I couldn't,' Nessie said.

'And I could?'

Randolph had not come back to the house by the time they were ready to leave. Marion had Barnaby open the narrow trunk of the E-type and get out a bone-shaped number which she had bought to sweeten the moment when they were parting from Grimond. She whistled and whistled for the dog and Barnaby called 'Grim? Grim!' a few times, but he did not come.

'He wants you to see that pemmican is no way to his heart. It is though.'

'Grim? This isn't like him.' Barnaby took the phoney bone and walked towards the big barn.

Marion said, 'Randolph likes animals, doesn't he?'

'He doesn't have too much to do with them,' Nessie said.

'He doesn't hurt them at least, does he?'

'He doesn't hurt anything,' Calvin said. 'He has problems, but for me that's not one of them, thank God.'

Marion said, 'I do appreciate you doing this.'

'Our pleasure,' Calvin said.

Marion put her arms round Nessie, who was still very pale for someone who lived so much in the open. 'I'll be back, sis,' she said. 'I'll come back, when I'm settled, if I am, or you could maybe come and spend some time with me.'

'That should make things worse,' Nessie said. 'I'd like that.'

There was a big saw-horse in the barn, made of unshaved wood, and stacked billets of timber, ready for the stove, right up to the planks of the platform where baled hay waited for winter. Chickens kept busy around the bellied sacks of feed against the long wall.

'Grim? Come on, Grimond! Don't be *that* at home already. Grim, come on, boy, come on out here.'

One of the Carroways' Yorkshires came slinking towards him,

straws in its back, as if it expected something. Barnaby walked right through the barn and was on his way out to where an axe was stuck in a stump of raw wood when, in a corner, he saw flecks of the afternoon sun gleaming on varnished wood. The body of the cello was punctured and splintered where the shots had gone in, but the sweet, mute curves of the sound box were still intact.

Barnaby took some breaths of the good air. He did not know what he thought. He didn't even know what he felt, except that shame and pity and rage and relief (that Randolph was none of his business) were all mixed in a sour brew which stirred an imagination that did not want to think about the Carroways. He was glad that he never wrote about certain kinds of things and he sure never would.

Finally, Marion said maybe it was just as well and evidently Grimond had made himself at home, so she and Barnaby embraced Nessie and Calvin Carroway, as if something slightly amusing had happened which made them all closer despite everything, and then they got into the E-type and were more glad even than they imagined to be leaving without any further problems.

They were near the wide gate out of the property when Randolph jumped out from some laurel bushes and stood in front of the car with the .22 and a hold-it-right-there expression on his face. 'You didn't say goodbye.'

'You forgot the stetson, kid. Were you there to say it to?'

'Have you seen Grimond anyplace?' Marion said.

'Not recently. He was around. Are you seriously driving to California?'

'Eventually that's where we hope to wind up.'

Randolph was looking into the car. He was looking at the space behind the seats where Grimond had been. 'Take me with you,' he said. 'Will you do that? I promise not to sing or dance.'

'We can't even take Grimond,' Barnaby said.

'Look at it this way, Aunt Marion: you could well be helping to avert a rural tragedy.'

'You know what you should do, don't you, Randolph? You should go back to your cello. I remember the way you used to play, which was seriously promising.'

Randolph was looking at Barnaby. He was looking and he was smiling and Barnaby felt the heat in his cheeks and couldn't look at Marion. 'I want to go to California,' the boy said. 'Better for me, better for them probably. With you.'

Barnaby said, 'Tell you what, Randolph . . .'

'I don't think so,' Randolph said. He leaned and took a white rock from the edge of the drive. 'I'll tell you what. Take me with you or I'll smash this rock right through your windshield. Or at least I'll mark your paintwork with it. I'll start with that.'

'Don't get mad,' Marion said. 'Whatever you do.'

'Who's mad? I'm nowhere near mad.'

'Well, don't be,' she said, 'with him.'

'Because here's the thing,' Randolph said, 'and you both know it: they can't handle me. I'm ruining their lives and I'm not having too much of one myself. They're good people. I don't say they're not, but they're not good for *me*.'

'They love you, Randolph, more than you can guess.'

'I can guess. And it's killing them. It's killing me. Love, love, love. Imagine I'd lived with you and not them.'

'So right away I'm old and grey and considering suicide,' Barnaby said. 'Is that seriously all you want for Christmas?'

'I love it,' the boy said. 'You see what I mean? You could write a part for me. We could work on something together. I'll go to school if you want me to.'

'I think it's a very good idea,' Barnaby said. 'Go to school, graduate high school, maybe go to college, and we'll see what we can maybe work out together.'

'You don't like me, do you?'

Barnaby looked at Marion and then he opened the car door.

'I don't like that gun,' Marion said, 'one bit. Be careful of that.'

'Believe me,' Barnaby said. 'Listen, Randolph . . .'

'Should I really? Should I?'

'It's not a matter of whether we . . . like you. It's more a matter of logistics.'

'Is it really? Is it really, Uncle Barnaby?'

'No, not really,' Barnaby Pierce said. 'We have a small car; we're going a long way; our marriage is maybe breaking up, maybe not; and we don't want to travel with a strange young man who thinks he has bigger problems than we do, and maybe has.'

'But?'

'But. OK, you're really serious about acting, I'm sure I can help you. Eventually. If I live so long. Maybe in New York more than in California, because that's where my basically despicable contacts are. Lower the gun, OK? I have home-grown turnips on my stomach. What happened to Grimond, do you happen to know that?'

'He's around. He's checking out the cows and they're doing likewise. He's fine.'

'You know what they say? Learn to act with a dog and you can act with anyone or anything.'

'Camels are next?'

'Good! I like you fine,' Barnaby said. 'I think you're going to be fine. But let me tell you something, let me dispel one illusion in case you seriously have it: no one *suddenly* sings like Placido Domingo. And that includes Placido Domingo.'

Randolph thought about that and then he took the hand Barnaby was holding out. The boy's eyes were moist and he almost hated Barnaby for seeing him like that, and being the reason for it, but all the same he threw the rock down and kicked it into the side. 'You know what, don't you?' he said. 'You'll drive away and you'll stay away. I mean, I'll be one more reason why you don't want to be family any more. Am I right?'

'You're smart, Randolph, which is not always the same thing.'

'Randolph, what kind of a name is that, do you think, for an actor?'

'There was Randolph Scott,' Barnaby said.

'Who was Randolph Scott?'

'True. But there could still be Randolph Carroway.'

Randolph said, 'I could fit in back. I wouldn't say a thing.'

'It's not going to happen, kid. You're going to school, you're going to learn, because knowing things, believe me, it's part of how an actor prepares, OK?'

'You're bullshitting me and I know it.'

'OK,' Barnaby said. 'And I'm right.'

'I can also buy that,' the boy said.

'Buy it,' Barnaby said. 'And I'll come back. We'll spend time together. You have my word.'

'One day I'm going to find out my real name. You truly think Randolph's OK?'

'I truly think Randolph's fine. Who'd've thought Dustin? But look at Dustin.'

Grimond came rushing through the fence and looked up and down the drive, as if he were late for something. He looked at the car and then at Barnaby and they could have been strangers. He braced himself on long, low front legs, ready to play, and then he ran off towards the house.

'He'll be OK,' Randolph said.

'He'd better be, Randolph. You both had. Because I'll be back, pardner.'

The boy watched Barnaby getting back into the car and he watched them go, with the gun dangling. Barnaby could see him in the rear-view mirror. He could see and he could be seen and both of them knew it and held on to it until they couldn't hold on any more.

Marion said, 'You handled him well.'

'Did I? I lied and I cheated and I got us out of that. That's what men are for, right?'

'Why say that? You did fine. If you ever do what you said you'd do.'

'I was thinking all the time about Chris.'

'I know. Me too.'

'He's going to kill someone one day, that kid. Unless he finds something else he wants to do. Daytime TV maybe.'

'A killer with a following,' Marion said. 'Do you really want me to answer your question?'

'What question is that?'

'That you asked earlier.'

'I was sore,' he said. 'Forget it.'

'Because the answer is, sure. Sure I did. Now and again. You're not *embarrassed* now, are you?'

'Probably. Probably I am, yes. I'm certainly *something*!'

'We don't know each other at all, do we? All those years; four kids. We don't know shit about each other.'

'Yes, we do too,' he said.

'So just don't ask me what with.'

'We know plenty. Good people. Good people, and look what they get, look what happens to them.'

'Look what happens to everybody,' Marion said. 'Did you ever do that?'

'And write comedy?' he said.

'He hurts my dog, I'll kill him.'

'*With?*' Barnaby said. 'Did you say "with"?'

'I mean it. And I don't care how talented the little bastard is.'

'Was I rough with Chris? Is that what you think finally?'

'Rough? No.'

'If I wasn't rough, what was I, with Christopher?'

'You were fine,' she said. 'You were fine. You couldn't have done more than you did.'

'And look what I did,' he said. 'Look at what I did.'

Going Back

'We're not telling them anything about us,' Barnaby said.

'So what's the point of this pilgrimage again?'

'People die,' Barnaby said. 'We'll be sorry if we don't see them before they do, *if* they already haven't. Detour really, not pilgrimage.'

'You really want to see *her*? Miriam? You really do? I'm not sure I even remember her.'

'She was a great cook,' Barnaby said. 'She made great *lutkas*. Don't you remember her *lutkas*? I certainly do. You don't remember her because, at the time, you wished she didn't exist.'

'Casimir has to be eighty. I never wished that.'

'Eight-five possibly. And she's no younger. You wished it because you wanted the guy for yourself.'

'I never *wanted* Casimir. I wanted you.'

'Second best *was* best. You told me you did.'

'He was – Jesus! – forty-five, fifty years old.'

'But he *was* Jesus.'

'Never miss one, do you? An opportunity.'

'Only if it's important. He was my age. *Jesus!* Younger!'

'They're probably both dead,' Marion said.

'Shall I turn around? My letter never came back. You're not *crying*, are you? Let's spill the milk first. They're not dead.'

'You have to be funny. When they write your epitaph, know what it'll be? *That*'s what it'll be: He had to be funny.'

'I'll hire another writer to say different,' Barnie said. 'This is the campus turn-off. Do we do it or don't we?'

'We're going to do it,' Marion said, 'and you know we're going to do it. Your letter never came back. Hence . . . do it.'

'Is it all coming back? And do we want it to? Look at that diner: Frankie's. Is that what it was called in 'sixty-eight, Frankie's? Wasn't it "Frankie and Johnny's" then . . .? I guess they broke up. Everybody does, right?'

'I'm not about to remember *anything*,' Marion said. 'I start remembering things, I'll be a wreck in no time. If not sooner.'

'*She* had to be funny too, sometimes,' Barnaby Pierce said. 'Try getting a chisel round *that*. They've done some building around here. Oh Jesus, look at that, Sweets, will you? "Hanging Gardens Road". Who in hell thought to call it that?'

'Some fancy professor from Babylon, Louisiana. Nostalgic for the hometown ziggurat.'

'I remember why I fell in love with you now. The slight droop of the right eye after you say something a little bit . . . smart.'

'You remember why you fell out of it at all?'

'I didn't. I didn't. Was I the one started talking about divorce? *Conversationally*. Conversationally!'

'You were the one started *thinking* about it. Why lie? You used to call me Sweets all the time.'

'Why lie? Why live?'

'Terrific,' she said. 'Great heart-warming answer.'

'I still do,' he said, 'call you Sweets. Sometimes.'

They drove for a while and then he said, 'Think Caz'll have the smallest idea who we are?'

'Likewise Marion you used to call me. You wrote you said.'

'So I wrote. Marion and Barnaby Pierce. Near as dammit thirty years. We must be crazy. How good a teacher was he really?'

'He was great,' she said. 'He was the only professor ever meant a thing to me. I can't even remember anyone else's *names*.'

'Henderson. Dr Henderson? The one Amy Bradshaw took her shirt off at?'

'You had a heck of a good look.'

'And I'd've had a heck of a good feel given half a chance. Aren't I terrible though? So what can you remember about French and German literature? Name me one book we did with Caz.'

'You bastard,' she said.

'I don't remember that one.'

'*The Magic Mountain*. We studied *The Magic Mountain*. We studied *Madame Bovary*. That's two titles. Can I get off the treadmill now?'

'Transgression and Bourgeois Society. I have the notes someplace. He favoured the one and not the second, do I recall correctly?'

'Don't ask me questions you know the answers to. Montherlant. "The Boys". "*Les Garçons*". One of them was called Souplier.'

'Marion, why are we doing this?'

'What constitutes "this" exactly?'

'Almost thirty years,' Barnaby said, 'and we're fucking strangers.'

'You fuck your stranger and I'll fuck mine,' Marion said.

'Easy pickings,' Barnaby said. 'Easy fucking pickings. Do we swing right here?'

'You swang right years ago,' she said. 'We voted for *Reagan*? Hard right. So go ahead. Do it again.'

'We're here to get his permission is why we're here and you know it. Caz's. We're not going to mention it, but he's going to know and if he says it's OK, then it's OK, is about the size of it. So who was he, your stranger?'

'I used the future tense,' she said. 'As in "I'll fuck mine".'

'He says we should stick together, will that convince you?'

'We're going to be nice to an old man.'

'And an old woman,' Barnaby said, 'don't forget Miriam. Why not let's snow them? Why not let's be happy together? It's a little bit sneaky, isn't it, to turn up and make him into the guy who sits in judgement on a marriage?'

'"*Madame Bovary, c'est moi*",' Marion said. 'There's many a true word, isn't there?'

'But today you have to hunt,' Barnaby said.

'Know what keeps us together? We're both in one of your damn comedy scripts. You don't write them, they write you.'

'Got it,' Barnaby said. 'Right between the eyes. I remember when you actually *laughed* when I crossed them like that.'

'Total recall,' she said. 'What a drag it can sometimes be!'

Casimir always offered a glass of wine to his class. That was why Barnaby had brought up two bottles of Château Cissac from the cellar he had had built (he had brought up one bottle only and then he had thought about it and went back for the second). He looked at the label as they stopped outside 131, Taft Street, and saw 'Cru Bourgeois' and smiled at Marion. She did not smile back.

Casimir came onto the porch as if it were a coincidence. He seemed to be looking for something. He was: it was a book, of course, which he leaned down to pick up, one hand on the swing-seat and a foot swinging up in the air.

Marion said, 'Hi, Casimir.'

He was old, but he was not decrepit. He was wearing grey pants and a collarless striped shirt and a brown knitted vest, which hung open. There were things in the pockets. He looked at her and took enough time recognising them to seem to have recognised them right away and to be playing at not. 'Can it be?' he said. 'I've changed so little and you've changed so much.'

That was when she embraced him and held him and he looked over her shoulder at Barnaby.

Barnaby said, 'Maybe I should leave you two to it.'

'It's taken him this long,' Casimir said. 'And even then he says "maybe". Come in. Nice of you to warn me ahead of time.'

'We thought you'd maybe run away.'

It was still Casimir's house: the books, the records – there were the old LP's in their chapped sleeves, under the compacts, in the canted shelf under the floppy, even yellower French books. The German were above that. The green- and red-wrapped Loebs had the library steps still up to them (oh how Casimir would stop everything to go and find a quote no one in the class could understand!). The books explained why he needed such a big place.

'I told her she should marry you,' Casimir said, 'and yet she comes to see me. *Et dona ferens.*'

'The *dona* are his,' she said. 'How's . . . ah . . . Miriam? Is she . . .?'

'She's . . . out,' Casimir said.

'I hope she left something for supper,' Barnaby said. 'We didn't come here just to see *you*, you know.'

Casimir seemed not so much to *be* older as to *act* older. He mocked his age by exaggerating his submission to it. As he fussed to rearrange the chairs by the fireplace, he was playing the aged professor, but with a measure of exaggeration. His wary nimbleness promised that he lied about his years, or his years about him. 'I never *wanted* you to marry him, Marianne. I only *said* that.'

'So she'd admit she was in love with you, Casimir, right?'

'What was the good?' Marion said. 'When I knew he'd never dump Miriam for *anybody*!'

There was a small foreign car in the street and then it was up behind the Chevvy in the carport and a young woman was getting out with tall brown bags of groceries and coming past the windows, not looking in, and up the porch steps.

Marion had time to say, 'What's this? Professor Emeritus Michaelstadt now has a *housekeeper*? Or is it a housekeeper-*masseuse*? Or *what*?'

The old man looked at her with eyes that were younger, and colder. Marion watched the young woman bend her knees to lower her packages on the hall-stand. She was fair and in her thirties and her eyes were the same colour as Marion's, that pale blue. Her smooth skin aged Marion.

Casimir said, 'I don't believe you've met my wife. Terri, this is . . . Marion and . . .'

Marion was damned if she would help him.

' . . .Barnaby.' He remembered without her. 'Pierce. I told you about Marion, I'm sure. The favourite student I waited and waited for. Until another one came along. Terri with an "i".'

Terri said, 'I hope you're going to stay? We're expecting you to stay.'

'Isn't there still a Holiday Inn? Sure there is. Dinner is imposition enough.'

'Everyone stays,' Terri said. 'He likes them to.'

'You feel so great when they finally, finally go, am I right, Caz?'

'Have I corrected you?'

Marion said, 'I'm sure there's something I can do to help.'

When the women had gone out together, as if they were friends now, Casimir said, 'Are you ashamed of me, Barnaby?'

'I don't know what you're talking about. What did you do?'

'*Actes gratuits*,' Casimir said. 'Do you remember what those were?'

'They were *gratuites*, according to me,' Barnie said, 'until you corrected me in front of the whole class.'

'You're embarrassed,' Casimir said, 'because of Terri. I'm sorry about that.'

Barnaby smiled. After all these years in America, Casimir still *almost* said 'zat'. 'Embarrassed? You flatter me, Caz. I'm through embarrassment. Great-looking woman. Congratulations.'

'Because of Miriam. I saved her life, you probably remember that. I didn't talk about it, I hope, but people did.'

Barnaby noticed that Casimir also still said 'people' *almost* as if it were 'pipple'; affection and condescension were close with Barnaby. He was a tall man. 'I remember that character – it wasn't Olga, was it? – stuck a knife through her hand in some novel or other. To prove she was really free. Or was it someone else who was? Maybe it was Boris.'

'Fifty some years ago, I saved Miriam from – whatever maybe wouldn't've happened to her. Nineteen forty-four. The beautiful Jewess and the smitten interpreter. You should write that sometime.'

'I only do comedy.'

'So laugh at us. What I was smitten with above all was my own vanity, isn't it? Does that mean I owe her for ever? To make a woman who wouldn't otherwise maybe have looked at me feel . . . gratitude, *unworthiness*. Comedy of a kind, Barnaby.'

'But not for the Network,' Barnaby said.

'You make a lot of money?'

'I make some money,' Barnaby said. 'Enough to send the kids through college and leave enough for gas to come see you. Miriam: what . . . happened?'

'When I told her the two big things I liked about Terri? She said just one word. Guess which.'

Marion was coming into the living room, with a swirl of

guacamole and a glass dish of *nachos*. 'That border sure does move steadily north these days. Hispanic Ohio? It'll probably happen.'

'He wants to know what Miriam said to me when I told her how Terri and I . . . One word. Guess which. He can't.'

Marion said, '*Enfin.*'

'Your wife is a genius, Barnaby.'

'That has to be why she's probably leaving me.'

'At last she was free. You *are* shocked, Marianne, aren't you? Respect an old man's hopes. Please don't take this in your stride. Other people's acts can free people too.'

'Know something, Caz? You're the only person ever called me Marianne.'

'I hope so.'

'Where is she now then? Miriam.'

'I didn't kill her, if that's what you're hoping. What do you think of . . .?'

'Terri? I hate her, of course,' Marion said. 'With a big "I".'

'Anything to make her old professor happy,' Casimir said. 'You're meant to. Bosnia, can you tell? She came from originally. A Muslim already! She doesn't know what that does for me.'

'If she doesn't, nobody should,' Barnaby said. 'I'll go see if there's anything I can do. I can still lay a table at least.'

'It's done,' Marion said.

'*Marion*, OK? Can't you recognise tact? You and Caz have so many things to say to each other.'

'And so few we can do,' Casimir said. 'So how are you, Marianne? Grandmother yet?'

'Not that they've told me.' She looked at him with eyes that announced a new subject. 'I'm going to go back and teach,' she said, '*and* study. I'm going to be an analyst. At least I *think* I am.'

'I think therefore I'm not?'

'Bad idea?'

'Never too late to do something useless with your life. Teach what?'

'French was my major. They need somebody in our local high school. You used to say I had a *très bon accent*.'

'You also had those black silk legs. Did a lot for your pronunciation. Did that pattern go all the way up? The faculty frequently speculated.'

Marion said, 'Should we maybe go in and . . .?'

'You disapprove,' he said, 'don't you? Of me and Terri. Me too. Me too.'

'You were always so proud of your marriage.'

'I exchanged pride for . . . what? All right: greed. Know the difference? Greed has the tits.'

'That's terrible. I seriously hate that. What happened to Miriam finally?'

Casimir looked at her and then at a floral pitcher on the end of the mantelpiece. He took it in both hands and looked at it fondly and then opened his hands and let it crash onto the floor. There was time for Terri to put her head round the door before Marion started picking up pieces.

'It's all right, Terri,' Casimir said. 'I'm only teaching.'

Marion was angry and confused: she wanted to cry and she wanted not to cry. 'I *remembered* that pitcher. I remembered it.'

'Did you love it?' Casimir said. 'Did you give a damn about it? Did *I*? Was it valuable? What's valuable? I had it for years. It's broken. Do you miss it or do you want *me* to miss it?'

When Terri came back into the kitchen, Barnaby was taking the corn out of the skillet. 'How long've you been . . . with him?'

'I'm married to him,' she said. 'Three years.'

'Oh, this is quite recent then.'

'For you: not for me.'

'What does it mean to you, may I ask, marrying him?'

'Casals married a girl of twenty when he was eighty. Pablo Casals. The great cellist.'

'I guessed who you meant from just Casals,' Barnie said.

'It means I get his house and his money. We're *eating*! You don't like me for saying that. I don't necessarily like you for thinking it.'

'They had a son,' Barnaby said. 'What about him?'

'He went to Israel.' Casimir was cleaning the *guacamole* dish with his finger as he came into the kitchen ahead of Marion. He sucked it as he indicated to sit in the chairs at the round table in the window. 'Please! He manufactures plastic packaging materials for the grapefruit and pineapple trade. He makes a fortune and never has to read a book. It's what I always dreamed for him to do.'

'Casimir,' Marion said. 'You know what you are?'

'I know what I am,' he said. 'Sit down. Be comfortable. I'm a shit. It was always my secret ambition and now I've realised it. Isn't it most men's? Barnaby, isn't it?'

'It undoubtedly gets a high share,' Barnaby said.

'*Enfin*,' Casimir said.

Marion looked at Barnaby a lot as they ate dinner and watched the shadows grow longer and then fainter and lights prick the new darkness. They talked as they ate and yet there was this silence, and these looks, between Marion and Barnaby. They seemed both to talk and to be silent. It was as if they were overhearing their own voices and resented each other's cheerfulness.

They ate the corn and then there was stuffed cabbage with butter beans and a salad and then there was an apple strüdel, whose excellence came as a surprise. Casimir watched their slightly reluctant pleasure as if it were a small, sweet victory over them, which it was. The front-door bell wheezed as they were finishing their second helpings. It was an academic couple who joined them for coffee and some of that strüdel; the wife had been in school with Marion, Rose Anne Hyman, now Pollock; she was a social anthropologist and was recently back from Chiapas, researching the Zapatistas. It was one of those things that agrarian revolts *never* succeeded, she said. It was pretty well *a priori*: politics belonged to the city and the city always won out. Even when the rural population supplied successful foot soldiers, their leaders would finally sell them out. If they lost, they lost right away; if they won, they lost eventually.

The register of Rose Anne's eloquence suggested that everyone in the room was disagreeing with her, and that she was prevailing against odds, even though hardly anyone else spoke. There might have been other people, invisible to Barnie and Marion, whose doubts were being allayed, or refuted. Rose Anne's husband was a mathematician who did a lot of marathons and also triathlons.

It was an evening full of talk, much of it informative and lively, that might – *mas o menos* – have been frozen in the Sixties and kept for just such an occasion. It was adult and progressive and very *bright*, but it seemed to be a substitute for some other conversation which someone – was it Casimir, or the Pierces themselves? – either wanted, or decidedly did *not* want to have.

Rose Anne and her husband asked if the Pierces were staying over, because they would love to see them again and have them enjoy some of the material from Chiapas (she had slides, she had documentation, she had fascinating tapes), but Marion said that they had promised to get to Chicago the next night, so . . .

The guest room was a room they had been in before, when it had not been so pretty. The quilt was the same though, wasn't it? From the Ozarks, where Cas had taught before he came to Ohio.

'Funny meal,' Marion said.

'Funny evening. Funny day.'

'That ghastly stuffing – pork! – and then that great strüdel.'

'*Uneven* meal,' Barnie said. 'Your friend Rose Anne has turned out pretty formidable.'

'I don't know about the pretty part. Or the friend.'

'We're back in this room,' Barnie said. 'I hadn't figured on that.'

'He was pretty nice to us, wasn't he?'

'But you don't like him as much as you remembered, do you?'

'He's much the same. And maybe we're much different.'

'Casimir with a child bride. Not quite what the script called for.'

'You're a little bit pleased. As if he'd done something to me and not to you.'

'And hasn't he? He hasn't done anything to me.'

'Except maybe liberated you a little bit. Your imagination at least.'

'I'm a little disgusted, just like you.'

'Is that what I am?'

They got into the bed, which seemed narrower than when

Casimir first loaned them its use. Back in the Sixties, he used to go away for weekends sometimes, with Miriam; favoured students were invited to house-sit for him.

'Imagine,' she said, 'I left my virginity in this very room.'

'I don't remember getting this far.'

'You maybe didn't; it did.'

'We shouldn't have done this, should we? Come here.'

'In the first place or . . .?'

'You know what I'm saying.'

'The things you shouldn't do, aren't those sometimes the ones you should?'

'I bet you he's fucking her tonight. I bet you he's making a point of it. Because we're here.'

'I hope he is,' she said.

'Against us,' Barnie said.

'Good night, Barnaby.'

He woke in the night and she was breathing steadily, against him, he thought. He lay there listening to the calm rhythm of his sleeping wife and he was touched and infuriated by the untroubled independence of her life from his. Was he so thirsty that he had to get up, or did he get up because thirst gave him an excuse she could not deny? He went out onto the landing and along the gallery above the hall to where the stairs went down. The house was one of the oldest on the campus and, in the bluish moonlight, it seemed as dated as the kind of black-and-white pictures in which people lived unthreatened lives in an unthreatening America where the Hayes Code applied as much to people in real life as it did to what they did in the movies. Was that why he had voted for Ronald Reagan? Because he wanted life back in black and white?

He went downstairs as if there was something in the house that he wanted to grab back, his serious youthful self maybe, slung like an old coat on the back of a chair, a coat that could still slip easily back over his shoulders and still had all kinds of things in the pockets that seemed to have been lost for ever. He went into the kitchen and there was the table in the window where the grown-ups had talked about Mexico and politics and it was as if they were still there, himself included, and they had no idea that their talk was talk-talk and they did not really care whether the Zapatistas got licked or got lucky. No, they wanted them licked; they were good people who wanted the good causes to go down, because that way no one could be blamed for not doing enough to support them.

Barnie went to the big Mountain Stream water-dispenser and drew a paper cup of water and stood, barefoot, looking at the bruise-dark shadows of the maple trees and the frosty whiteness of the moonlit sky and sipped the water he did not want all that much. Was there anything he did want very much? It made him sick to think of Marion leaving him, or being about to leave him. But then he thought of Terri, those bouncy tits, that stupid pouty mouth, those eyes that said 'yes' because – maybe – they had seen things, back in Bosnia, that made yes or no in Ohio not too important. The terrible thing was, you envied people the terrible things that had happened to them more than you were grateful to have been spared them. You tried to be glad to be who you were, but were you?

He took another cup of water, in case Marion was awake and wanted one when he went back upstairs. But he didn't go back upstairs: he went into the living room, imagining that there was something there that he wanted to take. OK, to steal actually. He had no idea what and he had no intention of really taking it. He wanted to have had the chance, only he didn't know what of.

There was a ladder-backed chair at the desk under the front window and someone in a high-collared robe was sitting in it, with her back to Barnie as he came into the room. The collar was up around her ears, as if she were pretending that the June night was colder than it was.

'Terri?'

The woman did not turn. She leaned her head against the top rung of the laddered chair and braced her neck and the way she did it denied, with a sort of humour, that she was Terri in any way whatsoever. 'Hullo, Barnaby,' Miriam said.

Barnaby said, 'OK. Now I get it.'

'What do you get, Barnaby?'

'The strüdel. Now I get why it was so good. What the hell is going on around here?'

'He's a funny man,' she said. 'Not a bad one. But . . .'

'Funny,' Barnaby said. 'Not the word I might have chosen.'

'He was good to me. Why shouldn't he do what he wanted to do?'

'Do you want a glass of water?'

'No. I don't want a thing. Not a thing.'

'Do you . . . do you still *live here*?'

'Are you shocked?'

'Shocked? No.'

'Disgusted. *Disturbed?*'

'How come you didn't . . . have dinner with us?'

'I'm here; I'm not here. I don't need to explain: you know why not. I'm old. I'm tired. I'm bored with Mexico and stuff. When he and . . . she, when they first . . . got together, I went away. I went to Israel as a matter of fact. Which I had waited all my life to do, I thought. Let me tell you something, Barnaby: what people waited all their lives to do, they should maybe never rush into. I went and I thought it was exactly what I wanted. It wasn't; so I came back. I'm a citizen. He found it . . . surprising.'

'I bet he did.'

'She didn't. She was nice to me. She is nice, Terri, which is not at all her name of course. She said I should stay; I stayed. It's a big house. I wouldn't be in the way. I'm not in the way. I never see them. I'm not lonely because all the time, I have this little purpose in life, never to see them, never to talk to them, never to cross them.'

'So when did you make the strüdel?'

'In the night. I do a lot at night. I listen to the radio and then, in the day, I sleep very often. I take walks. I'm not a ghost. I have my life all to myself.'

'You literally never see him?'

'Why would I see him?'

'Doesn't he check to see how you are?'

'You think he should? Why should he? I think it's very kind of Casimir finally, to let me bury myself in his house, don't you?'

He went back upstairs with the glass of water, but Marion was still asleep. In the morning, Casimir made scrambled eggs and bacon and fresh coffee. Terri said to leave the sheets on the bed; she would take care of it, no problem whatever. She had all day.

Barnaby enjoyed not telling Marion about his meeting with Miriam. He enjoyed it all the way to Chicago. He thought that he just might enjoy it for the rest of their time together, however long that turned out to be.

I Could Have Died

'How sure are we this is such a great idea?' Marion said. 'And what's his new one's name?'

'Anthea, isn't it? Anthea. What's wrong with it?'

'We've kinda wished ourselves on them.'

'Unless it's Anita. It was their idea. I only said we might be coming through Chi and maybe we could take them to a meal . . . And Stan immediately said come stay the night.'

'You put the bait on the hook, but it's the fish's problem if it swallows it, right?'

'I'll call them and say we suddenly doubt their sincerity, is that the best plan?'

'I'm only wondering, is it tactful to drop in on someone you haven't seen in twenty-something years on the assumption . . .'

'Assump me no assumptions. We've talked. We've written. We've *almost* met. Stanley asked us a coupla times before. If not eight. I like Stan. I want to see him. Fact that Karin is no longer part of his scene doesn't really change that. He and I worked together on two whole series *and* a pile of pilots. It definitely is Anthea.'

'Pretend I didn't speak.'

'And go on pretending you're Marion Pierce?'

'Do I talk a lot? At least I don't joke a lot.'

'That's true. Increasingly. I'll tell you something funny about jokes. You only ever remember so many. They don't keep; like soufflés. You remember *some*, but never many, and rarely the best ones. Like I can still remember the first drug-related joke I ever heard. Nineteen fifty-six, seven maybe, this had to be. Which makes me like thirteen years old. Today they're fucking at that age. No, they're *bored* with it already. They're looking for something else. Do I joke a lot?'

'I don't mind seeing Stanley one bit,' Marion said.

'OK,' Barnaby said, 'you don't want to hear the joke.'

'Anthea. What do we know about her? Is she in television too?'

'Stan isn't in television. He's been clean for, Jesus, fifteen years now. He wouldn't live in Evanston, believe me, if he was still writing comedy. Not that Stan wasn't funny. He was too funny for the networks; there was always something angry finally in what he did, and they hate anger because it's always against something, and TV is never against anything, is it?, except a smaller share.'

'So what's the joke?'

'The joke is, Stan got eighty-five thousand times as rich being something he didn't want to be as he ever would have being what he wanted to be, which was basically a nightclub act for the kind of nightclub doesn't exist any more. Second City. How can Chicago have changed this much? I mean, how come they managed to move everything back from the shoreline like it was no more difficult than letting out a pair of pants?'

'They filled in Lake Michigan with money, didn't they? The drug-related joke.'

'I don't recognise where I am any more and I was *born* in this city. I was born here. No, I was born *there*! The Grant Hospital. That's where I was born, Sweets.'

'What do we do? Remove our hats?'

'The Grant Hospital. These two guys are walking down a hill, right, two pot-heads as they used to be called, and someone comes running, lickety-split fast as he can go, down the hill and he can't stop so he calls out "Excuse me" and dives right between them, still at full speed, and runs on down and disappears. After a coupla minutes, one of the pot-heads turns to the other one and says, "Know something? I thought he'd *never go*!" I laughed at the time, but I had no real idea what the joke was.'

'And what is it?'

'You're joking. You are joking, aren't you? You did get it, didn't you?'

'I remember it now,' she said. 'You told it before. I guess it was funny back then.'

'Evanston still has to be straight ahead, right?'

'You're the one was born here.'

'There was also the one about the Statue of Liberty and the same two guys crossing to Staten Island and the one says to the other, "Dig the crazy table-lighter!" Imagine: because who has a table-lighter today? The terms of reference change, the jokes change.'

'Terms of reference,' Marion said. 'They're bastards for change, those things.'

'You don't like me any more,' he said, 'do you?'

They went by the renovated hulk of the Drake Hotel. It was where it always was, he guessed, but it still seemed as though it had lumbered deeper inland and taken up a new pitch. He remembered a breakfast meeting in a high suite, which smelt of the perfumed night before, with a movie producer called Walter Griefer. Barnie and Stan had decided to convince the man that they were totally familiar with Los Angeles, where the picture was set, even though, at the time, they had neither of them been there. Agreeing beforehand on the pretence, and trying to live it through, had tanked them up with the adrenalin they needed for the meeting. It would also leave them with a little victory, no matter what. How old were they? Twenty-seven? *Old!*

After Walt Griefer said he would get back to them, they walked to Stan's bachelor apartment, right across from Wrigley Field, and Karin Costello was there taking a shower. She leaned out to ask how it had gone and they both said, 'Great! Great disaster', absolutely together, and then they looked at each other and realised: it really *had* been a disaster, even though they had promised each other, all the way back to the apartment, that Griefer really *might* get back to them.

They laughed like one person. They positively yelped and held on to each other. Maybe some kind of jealousy was why Karin stepped clean out of the shower, shining and naked, looping a quick turban around her head. She wanted to be laughing too and if she couldn't laugh, she wanted to stop them. Barnie saw the sleek badge of black hair and the free swing of her breasts while she reached, in not too much of a hurry, for her robe. Oh that totally normal, good palsy smile she gave them both meanwhile! Whenever Barnie happened to be alone with her from that moment onwards, nine times out of ten, he'd wonder how much of what he saw had been meant for him. He was Stan's friend and he didn't come on to his friends' girls, but he couldn't believe she hadn't meant at least some of it for him. After that, he always felt he and Karin had unfinished business; it made him angry somehow with her. Even when he was best man, speaking at the wedding, and she was pregnant, and he was flattering her and smiling, and she was smiling back, he knew that he was really sore with her. He always guessed – unless it was hoped – that she knew how he damn well felt. After the marriage, and Janet was born, when he and Stan would be working together and she would come in and say hullo after she got home from her job researching for *The Kup Show*, she would kiss Stan and only touch Barnaby on the top of his head, their minimal thing together. Maybe Karin had something to do with why he and Stan finally split and Barnaby went solo with *Oh, Partner!* and Stanley decided to go get rich.

'What's she doing now?' Marion said.

'Karin? She has to be fifty something,' Barnaby said.

'Then what can she *possibly* be doing?' Marion said.

Even now, when Karin wasn't going to be there, her absence was going to be there. He wondered what this Anthea, who was supposed to be a tax lawyer and had helped Stan organise himself as a food and wine importer, what she was going to be like; meaning, how she would look at him. He would not be surprised to be a little angry with her, a little cruel even, because she had deprived him of seeing Karin and, like all second wives, had to expect a little loyal resentment, *and* presumption, from friends of the first one.

Barnie said, 'I never wrote back, know that? The last time Karin sent us a card. She wrote a message and I never wrote back, did you?'

'I sent a card, she sent a card back,' Marion said. 'She went to

61

Europe, didn't she? Bologna? You never liked her too well, did you?'

'Karin? She gave Stan a pretty bad time, towards the end. Which always starts a little sooner than anyone can guess, doesn't it? I liked her. Why would they call their daughter Janet? You have one little girl, you can call her anything in the world you want to. You call her Janet. She has to be thirty years old. Janet has to be thirty years old.'

'I wish I did,' Marion said.

'I hope she's happy. *And* rich, of course. Rich is happy, isn't it?'

'I like you all right,' Marion said.

When they hit Evanston, the traffic thinned and Barnaby was glad to pick up a little speed in the shaded streets. The E-type Jaguar was always a great car with a tendency to get hot when you had to do a lot of stopping and starting. Big houses began, with servants' quarters. Pruned shadows from the regular trees freckled fresh white paint. Mercs and BMWs were stubbed up against the domestics in crowded driveways.

'Chicago's full of ghosts, is the trouble,' Barnaby said. 'Like I miss the buildings I never saw more even than the people I knew. My grandfather. You know what's hard to believe? Herm lived with us, for years when I was a small kid, and yet, when I try to remember him, he never seems to be there, except on the week-end. Sunday mornings, I used to get into bed with him. He had these striped pyjamas on even though he'd already walked clear to the corner, in his outdoor coat I guess, to get the paper. We'd read the funnies together. Rimless hexagonal glasses. It musta been the war still. He wanted to teach me German. And I didn't want him to. I didn't want him to *badly*; it was like he was trying to do something disgusting to me. He never did anything, never had a job; he just seemed to be waiting for *her* to tell him he could come home. What did he do all day? He went for walks. He walked and walked and then he came home and read the paper. It was years, maybe three, he was with us, and the apartment wasn't any too big, and Dad never complained, never said anything sarcastic, was always polite and yet ... that's all: and yet! You liked him, didn't you, my father?'

'I liked your dad fine,' Marion Pierce said. 'What happened finally to him, your grandfather?'

'My grandmother never liked him but I doubt she ever had anyone else, even when they were apart. Maybe I'm being naive but I don't think sex interested Annie a lot.'

'It wasn't so well marketed in those days,' Marion said.

'Alternatively, who knows? Maybe she had a lot of men in St Louis. One day she wrote a letter to Herman and he packed his things, which there weren't too many of, 1945 maybe this was, and he went back and opened a deli with her in KC and they did pretty famously. She had this favourite nephew, Shelley, who was a Dakota pilot and the Germans killed him, after he'd crashed and surrendered, shot him and his whole crew, except for one guy who lived and some Dutch family sheltered him. I met him one time. It was right in after that she wrote to Herm that they should try again. Soon as she crooked the finger, he was on his way, only I don't remember him singing about it. My father never even *indicated* he was pleased that Herman had gone and I think he maybe even missed him in some way, the aggravation he handled so damn nicely. In some way I guess we miss everything that ever happened to us, don't we? Not to mention the things that didn't.'

'I liked your father,' Marion said. 'I remember him at the funeral. That's when I particularly remember him.'

'Do you have that map?'

Fountain Drive turned out to be a No Exit sidestreet leading off from a big circle right by the lake. It stopped short where three fancy houses turned their backs on each other round a concrete clover where there really was a fountain that rose and checked and rose and checked. Barnaby stopped the Jaguar a yard from the gates of the Tarlo residence, which were solid, heavy wood. He didn't turn the engine off yet. There was a locked gate to the side for pedestrians. A steel grille gave them a squared sight of the garden a cat couldn't squeeze into. There was a camera on a gantry on top of the gatepost.

'Import enough Greek yoghurt,' Barnaby said, 'and you too can install peace of mind. Had we maybe better go back and get some flowers? Suddenly I don't feel like the complete works of Charles Dickens are going to be quite enough in the way of a present. *And* we didn't bring them either.'

'You're funny, Barnaby.'

'You used to laugh when I was funny. Now you only tell me I'm funny.'

'We brought them the Gould. You want to get flowers too?'

'They've probably got the Gould. Why would they have everything in the whole fucking world and not have the Gould?'

They were sitting there, glaring, as if one of them was right and the other was wrong, when neither had said anything the other one disagreed with, when the wooden gates sighed and sagged open in the centre. They eased back on metal arcs to reveal the driveway down to the house, and the garden.

'They've certainly got flowers,' Marion said.

'Wholesale,' Barnaby said. 'Know something about the way those gates open? It's like the opposite of a welcome. It's like the withdrawal of something, don't you think that, the way they open? Are we supposed to drive on in?'

'*Walk down the avenue?* Since when are they the Vanderbilts?'

'You could write comedy,' Barnaby said. 'Maybe that's what we could still do together.'

'Has to be something!' she said.

Weedless gravel crumbled under their tyres. Barnaby put the E-type behind the Range Rover in front of the long garage where the tilted, half-closed door made a white peaked cap over the three shaded, serious cars inside. He still liked the ratchety noise the hand-brake made, a little bit *broad* somehow.

'Cut and run? What do you say, kid? I scent monogrammed towels.'

'Easy on the overt sarcasm, Barnaby. They probably run to concealed microphones too.'

The grey house was long and low, with a concrete upper storey that receded towards the lake they could not see from where they were. There were no windows looking in their direction. The mansion didn't look big enough for the kind of money Stanley Tarlo had to have these days. There had to be things they had yet to see.

The front door opened and there was Stan, balder and still smiling, without the glasses, but wearing *espadrilles* (he now imported those too) and tie-up cotton pants and a collarless, striped shirt.

'You're twenty years late,' he said. 'What happened?'

'Traffic,' Barnaby said.

The two men leaned against each and patted each other's backs. They would have done it for longer but each of them knew that Stan had to embrace Marion, although he and she had never been that close, so Barnaby broke away and hoped that Marion would at least go through the motions of being moved, which she pretty well did, although she did it looking over Stan Tarlo's striped shoulder at Barnaby with a look that seemed to be saying that she was doing this for him and never for herself, which was true enough, but not easy to forgive, like a lot of things that were true.

Wide windows faced south, onto the lake. The expected surprise was that the room they served was concourse-sized and encaustic-tiled; its generosity was concealed, from the drive, by the fact that it was cantilevered way out over the water. A sailboat leaned in and disappeared under Barnaby and Marion's feet. The next time they saw it was in the windows facing west. A girl in a ribbed white jersey and white pants waved to them, as if she had easily achieved something difficult, and as if she could assume that they and she belonged to the same rich club. Come winter, she would ten to one see them in Aspen, unless it was Klosters.

'Great house, Stanley,' Barnaby said. 'Terrific house. What are those over there?'

'What are what? The books? All kinds.'

'You mean you can still *read*?'

'OK, Barnaby. Straight into the act, right? So go straight and fuck yourself, will you? Has he changed? He hasn't changed. Here's Anthea.'

She was slim and tall, maybe in her late thirties; unless she was in her forties already, only you'd never guess it. She wore linen pants and a sleeveless linen jerkin which showed how long and smooth her arms were and how uncreased her elbows. The white, white smile was tinged with some kind of seriousness, as if she had happily broken off in the middle of doing something intelligent. There was a gloss on her high cheekbones and the brown, highlighted hair was curly and abundant. It had been carefully done to look careless. She had her Mexican silver-ringed hands hanging down and then she turned the palms outwards, as if to indicate 'Finally!', and closed confident, shy eyes for a second and they were shining more brightly when she opened them. She might have been moved. 'At last,' she said, and held out her hand. 'I'm Anthea.'

Marion said, 'How's Janet?'

'Janet is great,' Stanley Tarlo said. 'She has two kids, only Anthea doesn't know this, of course, because who wants to have a nuptial agreement with a grandfather? Janet is living in Rome and she's married to a professor of anthropology who also has a *daily* column – paragraph anyway – in *Corriere della Sera*, I think the paper is called.'

'Sounds like a bastard to me,' Barnaby said. 'Italian? Good for Janet.'

'That's what she would have me believe.'

'I bet you guys would like to see your room and maybe freshen up a little.'

Marion said, 'Should we maybe get the bag in?'

'Unless there are things you need,' Stan said.

Barnaby said, 'I was hoping you'd be fat. Possibly with respiratory difficulties which we could do our best not to notice. Whereas there isn't a damn thing about you I can honestly sympathise with, is there? You look like you can play three sets of singles and still breathe calmly through your nose. Have you no consideration? You sell more rich food than you eat, Stanley. Deny it.'

'I want to live for ever, don't I?'

'I had a house like this, I'd feel the same way.'

The two men stopped at the bottom of the wide straight steps which the women had already started to climb and they were smiling at each other as if this was the first real opportunity they had had.

'Marion looks good.'

'Didn't she before?'

'How are the kids?'

'They're OK. They're fine. We're on our way to see Stace in Minneapolis and, well, I told you, Benjie's getting married. Zara's at Santa Barbara. Doing *Greek*. You know what happened to Christopher.'

'We spoke at the time.'

'But we try to keep smiling or, in my case, try to keep other people smiling. I wish I'd gone into selling Greek yoghurt with you. That's an art. Anthea's beautiful. What was that gag you told me about how to recognise yoghurt is really and truly Greek?'

'You remember damn well and I'm not repeating it. Do you want to see the pool? We had them put in an all-weather pool.'

'And it has sailboats in it, I see.'

'OK, OK. Through here. Do you ever see any of our old shows on the museum channel? I stumbled on a coupla episodes of *It's a Crime* a little while ago. Do we still collect on those at all?'

'Do you need the money? No, but you think I might. And I might very well as a matter of fact.' Barnaby reached into his pants pocket and rattled the change that was in there. 'Not easy to jangle a dime and two quarters. Which channel was this again?'

'Harv was to die. I was truly surprised.'

'It's pretty surprising.'

'This is the pool,' Stan said. 'As if it mattered.'

'What else does? I suppose it ends somewhere down there, does it? Over the horizon, but before the state line.'

'Marion seems . . .'

'She's good at it,' Barnaby said.

'You two've been together for so long . . .'

'Don't kick shit, Stan, OK, when you say that? I know it's a tough line, so tell you what: let's just drop it. Sweets wants to have a life of her own, she believes. And she seems to know where she's going to get one, which I never have. It's not a tragedy. It's not quite a comedy. My agent would not be surprised to discover that we're having difficulty placing it.'

'Still Jackie?'

'Jackie retired, went to Florida. He still loses a lot of balls.'

'I never knew he had a lot.'

'I now write with someone called Teddy Fidgeon. I don't believe it either. You're rich, Stanley. You're rich and happy and your water is at twenty-nine degrees and you very evidently did the right thing. And you seriously expect to keep your old friends?'

'You don't want to talk about it?'

'What've you got?'

'You and Marion.'

'What's to talk about? What happened to Karin?'

'What happened to Karin! She's living with another woman. In Baltimore.'

'Which came first? I don't believe it.'

'Sure you do.'

'Karin? Are you responsible for this?'

'My lawyer says not. My lawyer says I *say* not. Am I? Are you?'

'Me?'

'You fucked her, didn't you?'

'*What?*'

'Come on, Barnaby. She told me about it.'

'How was I? Did she say?'

'She said you were great. She said you were everything I wasn't.'

'That's horrible. I always wanted . . . You know there isn't a word of truth in it, don't you?'

'Do I?'

'Do you *care?*'

'I don't know. Officially, not. Officially, of course not. But I don't know.'

'I never *kissed* Karin. Once.'

'She didn't accuse you of kissing her.'

'It's a total lie. It's completely untrue. There is absolutely not one iota of truth in it. Remember flabbergasted? We had that Englishman said that? Stanley, it's not true. God help me, I wish it was. Looking back, I wish it was, very much. Despite your displeasure. I feel like . . . I feel like Alger Hiss.'

'Alger Hiss was guilty. They've proved that pretty well.'

'Who feels like Alger Hiss? That isn't why you parted, is it? You and Karin. I *know* why you and Alger parted. It isn't, is it?'

'She was throwing a lot of stuff at me one time and that was one of the things. She also fucked Buddy Schultz.'

'I know,' Barnaby said. 'I don't know "also", because "also" happens not to be true, but I knew about Buddy because . . . well, I knew. You must've hated me?'

'No.'

'But I'm close, aren't I?'

'I didn't hate you. I just saw you differently.'

'I'll just bet you did. It's not true. It was, I'd tell you. I'd admit it. Why wouldn't I? Today?'

'What's so special about today?'

'After this much time. It's also my birthday.'

'It's not.'

'No, it's not. We brought you a present. It's in the bag.'

'You didn't need to do that.'

'I know, but we steeled ourselves. I never fucked Karin; I wish I had. I really wish I had. I almost called her when you guys split up. I dreamed about her for years. I fucked a woman called Paula, but I didn't start it. And that's not why Marion and I . . . I don't know why.'

'Sounds like that's why.'

'Do you believe me, Stanley?'

'What does it matter?'

'What does matter? Do you have a list? I never fucked Karin. I never touched Karin. She used to touch me, on the top of the head. You can't fuck people like that. Clinical tests prove it. I love you, Stanley. I loved you.'

'Above all, don't sob. This is a no-sob zone.'

'Fuck you, OK?'

'So you didn't fuck Karin. What difference does it make?'

'Is that why we haven't seen each other?'

'You don't come to Chicago. Not that you tell me.'

'You go places. You never come to Boston? You come, and you don't tell me. Better than . . . Right! I never fucked Karin once. You were my friend. How could she say that?'

'She probably wished you had.'

'You're my oldest friend and here you are trying to destroy me. I come to your house and you have this stock of smart weapons, primed to attack my psyche and render inoperative whatever is left of my vital centres. Why? Why, Stanley, why, why, why?'

'How about we cut the last "why"? Might help.'

'She's living with a woman. Does *she* know what I did to her, and you? What's her name? Does she hate me too? Is she going to come after me possibly one day? When I think of the blacklists you can be on without even trying! I didn't do those things. I never did those things. Never. Imagine. Is it OK if I drown myself in your beautiful pool? It's not too warm to drown in, is it?'

'What was the old song? "When I grow too old to drown . . ."'

'" . . . you'll have me to dismember"?'

'Print it,' Stan said. 'And that's a wrap. We'd better go see what those two women are doing.'

'In *Baltimore*,' Barnaby said.

The octagonal dining room was two steps up and projected over the lake at the east end of the house. Anthea said she thought Stanley was terrible to have had her serve caviar, but he had told her he wasn't having people come all the way from New England and then have to eat something that was good for them. After that, they had a selection of northern Thai dishes cooked by the two beautiful girls from Chiang-Mai they were so lucky to have working for them. When they had finished, Anthea said, 'I wish you could have tasted their *migrob*, which is truly spectacular.'

'I guess we just came on a bad night,' Barnaby said.

'I told you he was a funny guy, didn't I?'

'More than once,' Anthea said. 'We have some people coming in for coffee. Lee Conrads and his wife.'

'Lee produces a lot of stuff out of Chicago these days.'

'I just about heard of Lee Conrads,' Barnaby said.

'He particularly wanted to meet you, so that's what's going to happen.'

'She's so bright, his wife,' Anthea said.

'Put the Gould on, Anth, what do you say? I'm longing to hear it.'

'That's for another time. You don't have to do that. I'd sooner you did your Eddie Cantor.'

'Your what?'

'Oh my God,' Barnaby said. 'Have I said the wrong thing? Does she not know about you and Eddie Cantor?'

'Who's Eddie Cantor?' Anthea said.

'You were right,' Barnaby said. 'She is younger than she looks. She's actually twelve years old. Anthea, you never heard of Eddie Cantor? America, 'tisn't of thee!'

'Was he maybe a singer?'

'Maybe Jack Benny was a comedian.'

'I'm sorry,' Anthea said. 'Eddie Cantor. I guess I heard of him.'

'Your husband made him famous.'

'Excuse me?'

'Your husband made him famous. Eddie was – famous like that – until Stanley . . . You never did it for her?'

'She never appeared to want it,' Stanley said.

The two women looked at each other like mothers whose kids like to play together and what real necessity was there for them to be there too? It gave them something in common, however.

'Did you know about this?' Anthea said.

'It's pretty good as a matter of fact. In fact, it's brilliant.'

'What does it consist of exactly?'

'He also does Ray Bolger. Ray Bolger, who was in *The Wizard of Oz*? Old rubber knees? He does him too.'

'I did that for her one time, didn't I, Anth?'

'Lee Conrads,' Barnaby said. 'Now I wish I'd brought my wrinkle-free pants.'

'I'm not doing it for him,' Stan Tarlo said. 'Eddie Cantor. So don't ask me, all right? Those are some people I'm seriously not doing it for.'

'Is that a chink in your armour possibly? Through which I can just see that you might be persuaded to do it for us?'

'I wish you would,' Anthea said. 'If it's this brilliant, I want to see it. It's like he's been hiding something.'

'It's such a long time since I did it. I don't think I even know the words any more.'

'"If you knew Susie . . ."? The hell you don't know them.'

'I roll my eyes I might lose my contacts.'

'Take them out. Fly blind. You won't lose them and you know you won't.'

'The Conrads get here when?'

'They couldn't make it before nine-thirty. At the earliest. You've got time.'

'I have to go change my shoes.'

'I'm so glad you came,' Anthea said. 'This is a side of Stanley I don't get to see.'

When Stanley came back downstairs, he had found the words and the music. 'I'm not at all sure this is something I can still do.'

'As your agent, Stanley, I'm here to tell that I share your doubts. Luckily, it's a very thin house with radically low expectations. Break a leg, OK?'

They waited while the two Thai girls cleared the Carrara marble table and shut the door behind them and then Stanley said, 'Well, as Gary Gilmore would say if he could be with us here tonight, "Let's do it."'

Barnaby clapped and so did Marion, but she looked at him when she did so. Stanley rolled his eyes and said, 'If you knew Susie, like I know Susie,' and Anthea said, 'Eddie *Cantor*, of *course*.'

Right by the hi-fi, there was a section of imported walnut parquet floor suitable for dancing. Stanley said, 'What do you know, folks? We can do the whole show right here in the barn!'

Barnaby remembered Stanley as good, but he was better than that: he was *young*. He sang and he danced and he was really, really funny. Anthea couldn't believe it; she clapped and then she sat there with her hands together, as if in happy prayer, and shook her head and really liked Marion suddenly, as if they had discovered something they *truly* had in common.

Stanley said, 'One more time and that's it.'

Barnaby said, 'Who asked for one more time?'

'And that's it,' Stanley said.

Anthea said, 'What do you do, Barnaby?'

'I do the collected, unabridged works of Karl Marx, in a funny accent. I can drop the accent though. I drop the collected, unabridged works of Karl Marx, that can make a dent, even in stone. One more time, Stanley, and this time . . .'

' . . . *do it right!*' They said it together, like they always used to, and the two women might as well not have been there, except that it was private to them and just a little bit *against* the women.

Stanley rolled his eyes and he sang, 'If you knew Susie, like I know Susie / Oh, oh, oh what a girl! / She's so classy / Oh, oh, oh what a chassis! (Or something like that)' and for a follow-up, when they insisted, 'Jeepers, creepers, where'd you get those peepers? / Jeepers, creepers, where'd you get those *eyes?*' Then he launched into his dance again, in his shoes with the long laces with metal ends that clicked and flew, and when he'd tapped himself breathless, he stopped and bowed and the three of them clapped and whooped. That was when he toppled right over backwards and lay flat on his back on the imported walnut. The telephone was ringing and Anthea started over to it and called over her shoulder, 'Get up, Stanley. This is no time to lie in. People are on their way.'

Marion said, 'Stanley, are you all right?'

Barnaby frowned a little and then he bent down and said, 'There's a Mr Bolger outside, Stan, do I tell him to come in?' And then he looked at Marion and said, 'He went down with a bit of a bang. I don't like it. Stanley?'

Anthea was calling that it was Mrs Biebel from Ipswich for Barnaby and then she heard their silence and she came back with a little diagonal run towards them. 'Stanley? You're not dead *again*, are you? He does this. This is something he does.'

'I don't think so,' Marion said. 'Maybe if we had some water.' She was loosening Stanley's collar and then she was pushing at his chest and she was frightened, Barnaby could see, because she was looking angry with him, and he was frightened too. He saw Anthea was holding the telephone out to him.

'It's nothing,' he said. 'It's not important. I'm sorry: I left the number, I never thought she'd call.' He turned away and said, 'I'm sorry, Mrs Biebel, I truly can't talk to you now. I don't care to discuss *anything* right now. Please don't call again.'

'Stanley? Stanley!' Anthea looked round and she took some flowers from a vase on the piano and threw them on the floor and then she threw the water into Stanley Tarlo's face and he didn't blink and he didn't move and she said, 'We've got to get a doctor.'

'Get an ambulance,' Marion said. 'Forget a doctor. Call the paramedics.' She was on her knees beating on Stan's chest. 'Do you have a number? Barnie, get the number and get them here. Fast.'

Anthea said, 'If he's kidding us, I'll kill him.'

Marion said, 'Nobody's killing . . . *kidding* anybody.'

'I hate the way he's on his back like that,' Anthea said.

Marion said, 'It's all I know to do.'

'And his mouth,' Anthea said. 'The way his mouth is.'

The paramedics were there inside eight minutes and they did all the things they knew to do, but one of them told Barnaby that Stanley's heart went, in all probability, before he even hit the floor. They rolled him out to the ambulance, which was already the right way round, and Anthea climbed in back.

Marion said, 'Anthea, they say . . .'

Anthea said, 'They can say what they like, I'm going with him. Now let's go, can we? Let's go.'

Barnaby said, 'Wait a minute. We'll drive you. We can follow the ambulance.'

'He's my husband,' Anthea said. 'You fucks.'

The ambulance moved away through the wooden gates and they heard it whooping down Fountain Drive to the big circle and then fade.

Marion said, 'You know he's dead, don't you?'

'This hasn't happened,' Barnaby Pierce said. 'I know it hasn't. Am I responsible? I am. He should never, never have done Eddie Cantor.'

'He wanted to do it. He was dying to do it.'

'That could be better phrased. Now what?'

'Fucks,' Marion said. 'She doesn't want us here. We're just about the last people she wants to see when she gets back here. She's going to hate us, Barnaby, for the rest of her life.'

'She's entitled to. Did he have a history? He must've had a history he didn't tell us about. She could've stopped him. Maybe they'll . . . maybe it's not as bad as it looked.'

'He's dead. I know. I did a course and I know.'

'All right. You always know.'

'I hate you, Barnaby, if you really want to know.'

'Save it,' he said. 'Maybe we should go to the hospital.'

Barnaby drove the Jaguar down to the gates and they opened automatically and there was a Lincoln town car facing them ten yards away and the driver spread his hands as if they were old friends. It was the Lee Conradses, come for coffee.

Barnaby got out and walked to the driver's window and it went down and he said, 'Did you pass an ambulance on the way here?'

'Heard one,' Lee Conrads said. He was a black man, in a grey silk suit, with a pale wife. 'We heard one. Didn't see it.'

'It's Stanley. He was . . . he passed out. I'm afraid it doesn't look too good.'

'Stanley?'

'He was . . . doing something and he . . . keeled over.'

'Where's Anthea?'

'This is my wife,' Lee Conrads said. 'This is Googie.'

'Barnaby Pierce. Hullo. She went in the ambulance. I think they went to North Western. And that's my wife, Marion.'

Lee Conrads waved to Marion. 'You have an E-type Jaguar.'

'Yes, we do.'

'A car I always wanted to have. Heart?'

'I guess so. I don't know what you want to do.'

'We may as well go home, Lee.'

'We may as well go on home,' Lee Conrads said. 'In view of this. I'll call the hospital. I was looking forward to meeting you. How long are you in town?'

'I guess we'll leave pretty well right away,' Barnaby said. 'We have a long way to go.'

'You never know how long it's going to be, do you?' Lee Conrads said, and he was already looking over his shoulder because he had to back up before he could turn. 'I liked the work you did on *Kowalski and Crunch*. I liked the premiss too.'

'It was a good premiss.'

'Next time you're in Chicago, give me a call.'

'This way, we can catch the fight,' Googie Conrads said.

'What?'

'The fight you wanted to see. We can still catch it.'

'What do you want to do?' Barnaby said. 'Wait here? Go to the hospital? What?'

'Want to do,' Marion said. 'What do I want to do?'

'What are we going to do now, Marion?'

'Why do I have to decide these things? You tell me.'

'She doesn't know us and now she doesn't like us and the last thing she's going to want is have us in her house when she gets home. Am I right so far?

'She isn't even going to want to play the Gould,' Barnaby said. 'Ever. Is she?'

'We should go to the hospital maybe. For Stan's sake.'

They drove to North Western and sat in the lobby for a while and then they were told that Stanley Tarlo had not been admitted, because the girl was sorry to say he had been dead on arrival.

'We can't stay for the funeral,' Barnaby said, 'even if we want to. So we may as well go. You wish we were out of here, don't you?'

'In a way,' she said.

'In what way do you *not* wish it?' he said.

'In the way that I wish I didn't wish it. Are you sure you don't want to go find a hotel and . . .?'

'I only ever wanted to come to Chi to see Stan.'

'If you hadn't,' she said, 'he'd still be alive, wouldn't he?'

'I never fucked Karin Costello,' Barnaby said. 'Before or after they were married. I never came within a mile of it.'

'He sure did a great Eddie Cantor,' Marion said.

'Think of that Gould,' Barnaby said, 'nobody's ever going to play now probably. Isn't that a shame?'

On the Road

'Would you say you'd been close to her?'

'Stace's my daughter.'

'So's Zara. We're talking about Stace.'

'It depends what you mean by "close" exactly.'

'No, it doesn't,' he said. 'You and Zara are close.'

'*Were*,' Marion said. 'When she was small. Before she went to study so far away. Since when, you know as well as I do.'

'So what do I know? Why did she? Why did Stace?'

'They possibly needed to have their own lives. They needed to be *less* close maybe. People can't stay in Ipswich for ever. What those girls want to do doesn't necessarily have too much to do with whether or not we were . . . close. Unless it does.'

'So what're we talking about? You and Zara or Stace and me?'

'You had your relationships with the girls. I had mine.'

'What are you so sore about?' Barnaby said. 'I recognise that you're sore. I wish I knew what about.'

'Don't call me sore.'

'Look at your face. Just lower the sun visor, Sweets, and look at your face for two seconds in the mirror.'

'Now you're getting at me.'

'Sweets is getting at you?'

'I don't have to do things you tell me to. Or see the things you do. I know what I look like. Maybe they thought I stifled them. Maybe I did. I wanted to be doing what they needed, and who ever gets away with that?'

'Imagine you'd gotten a job, when Stace was, oh, three, four years old, would that have helped?'

'Helped what?'

'Her. You. You. Looking back, isn't that what you wish you'd done? And today you'd be somebody *established* somehow, you imagine at least, in an identity that was really and truly yours?'

'You ask me about Stace and this is where we wind up.'

'I was furnishing the silence, you might say.'

'I would never say anything like that, remotely.'

'No? You can be fancier than you admit. OK, I was wondering if the life that you now think you want to lead, and hence – no, don't deny it – you think you already should be leading . . .'

'You go teach writing to college students one day a week and this is what you turn into.'

'Be warned, Marion. The closet pedagogue is at his most elaborate when unqualified and untenured. I was honestly speculating . . .'

'I don't think so.'

'Yes, I was too.'

'What's this got to do with how I get along with Stace?'

'You know damned well. Number one, if you'd had this career you're planning – '

'You should hear the hate in your voice, Barnaby, the scorn anyway and then you'd know why I want it, why I need it, so badly. What you call a career as if it couldn't possibly really be one.'

'I don't think that does you too much credit. You underestimate yourself if you think that my tones of voice – rightly or wrongly interpreted – require you to be or do anything.'

'Unless it's maybe absent myself.'

'That's up to you and felicity.'

'Sometimes we could be on different planets.'

'Hamlet. In another context. Forget it. Trust a trashy hack to lard his unprofessional conversation with fancy references which have absolutely no resale value whatever.'

'Cue for denial, that what that is? What happened to "number one" and its consequences?'

'If you'd become somebody else, so would Stace. It wouldn't have been the same girl who admired you for your tenured career as a professor of French, or whatever, as admires you now, and wants to see you now, because you wasted your best years being a great mother. Ditto Zara incidentally.'

'Who worships the Great Mother any more?'

'Stace would now be a girl who was not *Stace* Stace in anything but name name. Smile, baby, just once, before we get to the twin cities, could you possibly?'

'She might be something better. Ditto Zara is not a name she would appreciate.'

'Or worse. Much worse. Why not admit it?'

'I don't know what she would have been and I don't know what I would have been. I don't even know what *you* would have been.'

'Another kind of a nobody. How many kinds do we have?'

'You don't think you're nobody.'

'Not after those Norwegian residuals on *Sergeant Bimbo*. They build a man's ego right up to the sky.'

'I like *Sergeant Bimbo*. Mark me down if you want to.'

'If you want to know something about *me*: at this minute, I don't know – I genuinely do not know – whether the way I feel is the reason that I can consider being, OK, divorced from you without dreading it, in the smallest or – *or* – whether it's the reason why I still feel like I love you, quite a lot, and don't want anything more than to have all this, whatever this is, blow over, be a passing phase, turn out to be the result of a misunderstanding. Same cause, different effects; same man, different emotions. Same everything, different everything.'

'Now you're boiling over on me,' Marion said. 'All I get a sense of is a lot of steam billowing around. Have you ever considered that the whole of life is possibly the result of a misunderstanding?'

'It goes back to Chris, I guess, finally, doesn't it?'

'What's that?'

'This. That. And the other.'

'Does it? I don't know what goes back to what. Or what Chris goes back to. Went back to.'

'Alternatively Hal,' Barnaby said.

She looked out of the window at the gusts of wet peeling back at them from the tyres of the metal truck in front. The traffic was thickening as the highway bent in towards Minneapolis. Barnie's posture said that he wanted them still to have a lot of miles to go, but a reef of buildings was growing mushily out of a sunless sky as the wipers slicked grease on the windshield. They were nearly there.

'Is maybe when it all started.'

'It started before Hal,' she said. '*All*, by the way, is a lot. And why did Hal start? A question I sincerely don't want to get into right now. And not because I have anything to hide.'

'There we are,' he said. 'There we have it. There is an "it". So what is it?'

'It started when it started, is when it started. Whatever it is. It started, if it matters, as if it could *not* have started, when marriage wasn't what I thought it was. Not you, it. Not you, me, you might say, and might not be wrong either. I mean that, Barnie. I do.'

'You should never have married me is what you're saying,' he said. 'Except you don't have the courage to say it.'

'I never thought saying things was too courageous,' Marion said. 'I think *not* saying things is what takes courage sometimes.'

'It gives you very tight lips though.'

'My problem is not your problem. My problem is not you. My problem is me. My problem is the history of men and women until now. Big one, right? What makes me think I can lick it? Nothing whatsoever. It's just sometimes you have to go to bat knowing that.'

He drove for a while, and then he said, 'You could just as well say that there isn't *anything* that doesn't require courage sometimes. Including cowardice. Particularly that even.'

'One day,' Marion said, 'you'll maybe reflect on why it is that you save so much of your cleverness for saying those kinds of shitty things only to *me*.'

'And writing shitty comedy. For money. I don't need to reflect. I know.'

'And then you can go on – but only if you seriously want to – to ask yourself why all your real feelings are so angry and why you save them for when we're alone. Whereas . . .'

'Aw-aw.'

'. . . when there are people around, not including the children however, you are Mr Considerate Sweetie-Pie, as seen on TV.'

'I'm only nice when I'm faking it is what you're saying. Which is truly cute of you. Not kind. Cute. And shitty.'

'Look at your own goddam face, *old boy*. Pull over, if you want to be a responsible citizen; then take a long hard look at your own face in the mirror. And ask yourself where it came from.'

'*Goddam* face,' he said 'is what you said. Don't start toning down. You risk becoming unrecognisable. Whatever my face is, it's what you've made it.'

'And mine?' she said. 'Who's liable for mine?'

'If it's me who's liable for what you look like, I don't think I have to lie awake worrying, but go ahead – consult your lawyer. Ask Jonas. We're getting into the city. Lake Minnetonka? St Anthony Avenue? Which the hell arrow do we follow to where? Let's concentrate on practicalities here for a minute. Have you got Stace's instructions?'

'Fuck practicalities,' Marion said. 'Practicalities are what stop people from getting to what's important.'

'That's almost certainly why they're so important to people.'

'You never made up your mind, Barnaby, did you, what you wanted to be? In the sense of whether you'd be someone who did things, and felt things, or someone who kinda played with what it would be to do things or feel things. I hope you didn't do that for me, knowing only too well you probably did. And the kids.'

'What is this? A pat-ball session suddenly? Or are you about to come to the net and finish things? You're a woman with fast feet and a killer overhead, Sweets, whatever else you are! And that's rare.'

'Remember when we played that Russian guy and his son down on the Keys that time? After he'd offered to give you lessons?'

'Sasha. And Todd. You blitzed them off the court.'

'We did,' she said. 'We both blitzed them off the court. A Ruskie called Todd!'

'We were some team in there. We could really be happy, don't you think so sometimes, baby? We have been, haven't we?'

'Sometimes I think absolutely everything,' she said. 'You'd be surprised. I am.'

'You're either kinda pitiless,' he said, 'or you very much wish you could be. Which?'

'Suppose I only very much wish I knew.'

'What Hal goes back to is when I started to . . . Why talk about it now? When it's too late. Or is that the time to?'

'You started being secretly divorced,' she said. 'Making preparations. And stopped telling me the truth, not least about that.'

'OK, what I started doing was, I started to work in anger. Secret anger. Open comedy. Nothing quite centred. Am I making any sense?'

'Plenty,' she said. 'And I'm really sorry about it. I'm sorry I did that to you. Always assuming I did. Because what happened right before I contributed to ruining your life?'

'As soon as we seem to get close, we start kicking new holes in the bottom of our whole lives. You and I. Why?'

'It's the only pleasure we have left possibly.'

'That's not true either. We have our daughters. We have a son. Why should pain be our only pleasure? Or is it compensation?'

'The girls are all over. Ben's getting married. He's going to be in California. Or if elsewhere, God knows where. How much pleasure is that liable to yield, if we're honest? I don't say they shouldn't be . . . everything you want them to be. But – between ourselves – are they?'

'Between ourselves threatens to be quite a big distance these days, doesn't it? Between ourselves, damn it all to hell, Sweets, OK? However many blessings we still have to count.'

'The dead man in the cargo,' she said, 'and he has to be our son.'

'I always wondered why people thought Ibsen was all that great,' Barnie said. 'Do you think he is?'

'He's great because he was a man could imagine what it is that makes men so hateful.'

'To women.'

'Right.'

'Because not to each other. Not deeply to each other. Can you think of an instance? Men and men can always . . . make a deal. Men and women . . . And I suppose Strindberg is so great because he knows what makes women so hateful to men. Does that complete our session on the Scandinavians here today?'

'You sure know how to do it.'

'Do I?'

'Close a wound and leave something inside.'

'I was probably right not to be a surgeon.'

'You are a fucking surgeon,' she said.

'When did you first say "fucking" all the time?'

'How can you first do something all the time?'

'When did women then? Things aren't done for centuries and then they're done and now they'll probably never not be done. Divorce. People didn't used to divorce.'

'There was always divorce.'

'Not *therapeutic* divorce.'

'Only it was mostly a one-way street. Even when it was a cave. Men dumped women; women couldn't dump men.'

'No? Remember when we were in France that time? That great restaurant we went to in the place where the queen used to throw men she didn't want over the cliff? We stood up on the edge of that damned cliff . . .'

'Les Baux,' she said. 'In Provence.'

'Was where it was, and I looked at you and, believe me, I could see you doing it all right. Queen Marion. I took one look at you and I moved away from the edge and you laughed.'

'Because you looked so *accusing*, is why.'

'Because someone else was there. That Englishman. She wasn't married to them, was she, when she threw them over? The Courts of Love. He knew all about it. *All* about it.'

'He sounded like some kind of a missionary, the way he kept pausing in case he was going too fast for us.'

'You coulda pushed *him*,' Barnaby said, 'and made us both happy, but did you?'

'Suppose I had,' she said. 'Because can you imagine?'

'I haven't tried in years,' he said, 'have I?'

'I hate it when you pretend to be bitter.'

'While all along my true nature is that of a kid who only wants to go and throw horseshoes and maybe get a soda? Not to mention getting laid, which we never do these days. But let's not talk about that. Let's add that to a steadily increasing roster of forbidden topics.'

'OK,' she said. 'You want to get to Stace's house in a lousy mood. I know exactly why.'

'Exactitude is some specialty of yours, isn't it? You are accurate to a millionth of a second in your own estimation at least. Why?'

'I don't have to tell you, if you don't want to know.'

'Ha,' he said, 'as if those weren't the *precise* conditions under which you always do have to.'

'You want to be really nice and loving to her, against me. You want it to show that you're pretending to be a good father and a nice husband so she won't ever guess that anything is seriously wrong between us, and then, and then, when it turns out something is, it will all have to be my fault, because you'll've totally proved that you are the innocent one who really and truly wants everything to work, only I don't, which will leave me totally isolated and the reason why everyone has to have a brutal time of it, when the time comes. Set up the villain of the piece. You always preach structure, don't you? That's the structure.'

'And I've got it all worked out, have I, to that degree? How about considering the possibility, since you're so *fucking smart*, since you're so fucking smart, that this little scenario is *your* baby not mine and that what you've just accused me of is what is in your head? I don't *particularly* want to arrive at Stacey's, when I haven't seen her in going on for eleven months now, and start right in being so honest and truthful and without pretence that she has to have all our problems sicked right over her in the first ten seconds we see her. You're quite a manipulator, Marion, so now you can manipulate that into evidence of my, my *duplicity* and my, my inability to be anything but superficial and dishonest in my emotions. *That*'s the fucking structure.'

'You could always cry a little bit,' she said, 'which is what you usually do. Sincerely but also, of course, *angrily*, because, of course, you are both much, much more sensitive than I ever give you credit for *and* because you hate anyone – i.e. me – to think that a woman – i.e. me, again – can so frustrate you with her injustices that you can only cry instead of smacking her in the puss as she deserves, but would put you in an invidious light.'

'You're almost the writing partner I'm looking for sometimes,' Barnaby said. 'You're perceptive, you're articulate, but you could do with someone to put a little icing on your arsenic. You may notice that I am not crying. What's his name again, because I can never remember?'

'Excuse me?'

'Stace's man. Why do I always think it's Chesterfield, when I know it isn't?'

'Davenport,' she said.

'Is why. Is there someone else whose name I should know, or not know? In your life, possibly, I mean?'

'Save it, Barnaby. I wish there was. You wish there was. Only there isn't. I said I wanted to be free and that, strange as it may seem, is all there is to it.'

'You haven't said that one thing you won't miss is a man. Shouldn't you now say that, in a constructive spirit and without the smallest malicious intent? A fucking man.'

'You take a right where it says you can and then you go over the river and then we're getting down to specific streets.'

'You think I should have done something different, is what you meant, I presume, about Chris. What would that have been exactly? Since exactly is so very much your thing.'

'That's cruel. That's deliberately cruel, because I had no such thought.'

'Do you seriously not somehow think that I was the reason he had the accident?'

'Do you want me to?'

'That's cruel, Marion. If you want to know what cruel is. When did it start exactly, this desire of yours to be cruel?'

'You could be right,' she said. 'Because maybe it was then.

Only it wasn't you particularly I wanted to be cruel to, as you put it.'

'You just homed in on the likeliest target? You're one smart weapon, Marion. Or can be.'

'Maybe I said those things because I sensed accusation in your attitude, and I thought if I . . . said things, I could provoke you into coming out with something. But you were cruel enough, possibly, to frustrate me.'

'I was too concerned, believe me, to defend myself. Is this doing any kind of good to anybody?'

'I don't imagine so, do you? Pull up. We're way past doing good to people, aren't we? Barnie, pull up here.'

'What's the matter?'

'I think that has to be Stace's building. It does. It is.'

'So why pull up here?'

'You won't tell her anything, will you?'

'About . . . .?'

'What we talked about.'

'Talked *around*, you mean.'

'I love Stace. And I think she probably needs us. She needs us to need her, even if . . . she wants to think we don't. And we do. So.'

'Got it.'

'You would never tell her that she was no compensation, would you, for Christopher?'

'People never compensate for people.'

'I know that. I'm talking about you and what you might say I said.'

'Do you think you said something terrible? Something I could use? I won't use it. I'm not even so sure that it was you who said it. I thought it was me. Which leaves us with a deal, as they say in the business.'

'I hate the way they say that.'

'Thirty years of comedy,' he said. 'It's enough to make you cry sometimes.'

Breaking News

Stacey had one hand on top of the sharp red door to the apartment when her parents stepped out of the slow elevator. The apartment house was a converted granary. The new floors were hardwood with rugs on them. There were big windows high over the river.

'This is great,' Marion said. 'This is amazing up here, isn't it, Barnaby?'

'Now I know,' Barnie said. 'Why Minneapolis. Now I know.'

'You know that much.' Stacey squeezed a small space between thumb and forefinger.

'We only just got here,' Barnie said, 'and already we don't know everything?'

'How's the job?' Marion said.

'I didn't get fired, if that's what you mean.'

'Why would I possibly mean that?'

'Thursday afternoon, I'm not in the office. I took the day off. I figured you'd want to check that my clothes were correctly folded.'

'She hasn't changed,' Barnaby said.

'She thinks I haven't,' Marion said.

'Some things, they changed, a crack would open down through the centre of the world. Small but perceptible.'

'I don't think so necessarily.'

Stace was no different, was she? She was still tall; she was still blonde; she still had that bounce in her walk as if she had just come from playing something. Why did Barnaby think that it was some kind of a disguise, the fact that she looked just like he expected her to look? Wasn't there something a little bit wilful in that, if not downright deceptive? He watched her go to the refrigerator and bring out cold glasses and a bottle of Chandon and he thought how great-looking she was and how thoughtful it was of her not to be different, in any recognisable way, when he knew – didn't he? – that she was.

Marion stood in the window, unsurprised by the great view. It might as well not have been the first time she had seen the sheen of the river and the steel and concrete and business of the twin cities it divided. She felt a small anger – no, something previous to anger, something tight and incipiently bitter – as she watched Stace bring the cool glasses to the table and look at them both with a look that seemed to say, 'You're my parents, you're together and you're going to stay together, aren't you?' Stace's competent independence, the I-don't-often-do-this wince as she twisted the clever opener on the champagne cork, her air of totally open welcome, Marion experienced all of them as intimidation.

'So,' Barnaby said, 'the office. How is it?'

'Am I going up or down? Up, I think. Like the market. When the market goes up, we're the smartest people in the world. Today it is, so today we are. Give us your money and we promise to double it. My bonus could run to eighty grand this year. I'm rich.'

'And happy?'

'Aren't the two things synonymous? Don't I look it?'

'I never saw you look better.'

'Maybe I never will,' Stacey said. 'Maybe this is the top.' They touched glasses and sipped, looking tall through the big steel-framed windows. Outside was a long ledge, dressed as a terrace, with plastic-tubbed evergreens and a white tubular metal fence. An EMERGENCY USE ONLY ladder went up from it to the roof.

'What kind of emergency are they expecting?'

'What kind have you got, Mother?' Stacey came and stood beside her. 'Does that kind of bring you conveniently to it?'

'To what?'

'Come on. What did you come all the way out here for?'

'We wanted to visit with you. And we're on our way . . .'

'Do you know what business I'm in?'

89

'Financial Services, *aren't* you? You've changed your job?'

'Straws in the wind. Is the business I'm in. I'm hired to pick them out of the air and draw conclusions from them. You two come out of the elevator, looking eminently polite with each other, and you ring about as true as a Lincoln Rockwell . . .'

'Lincoln Rockwells are picking up in price, did you see that?'

'Whatever picks up in price, I see that,' Stace said. 'So what's happening?'

'Nothing yet,' Marion and Barnaby both said.

'Evidence of collusion,' Stacey said.

'Top and carbon,' Barnaby said. 'Remember those non-recurring days? Only who's the top and who's the carbon?'

'And who gives a damn?'

'Your mother is top.'

'You're finally getting a divorce, is that the situation? It's decided?'

'No,' Barnaby said.

'Yes,' Marion said.

'And now we *know* who's top. She's top.'

'I'm happy it's out of the closet,' Stace said. 'Unfolded and out of the closet. Let's drink some more of this stuff. In the newly cleared air. When was it decided?'

'When your mother said "yes" and I said "no". Anybody hear me say that? It is possibly the situation, but it is not finally decided. Not by me.'

'You never did want to make final decisions about anything. The things you do, you're not sure you want to; the things you didn't, you think maybe you should have. I know you, Daddy. I lived with you, remember?'

'Highlights I remember,' Barnaby said. 'We were afraid . . .'

'I'm trying to dispense with those, the fears. I'm trying to prove to you that, contrary – I hope – to appearances, I have changed radically and have become, OK, sane. I've become sane. I can confront what I know without getting into panicky denial. Is this maturity, resignation or evidence that . . . what do you think? Impressive maturity in my view.'

'Shouldn't you think of your mother sometimes?'

'Leave me right out of this,' Marion said. 'This cutesy stuff. This is strictly between you two. As usual.'

'Think of *your* mother,' Stace said. 'Think of Alice. With her hat in the air. If she doesn't have one, she'll buy one. Yes, *sir*!'

'Grandma absolutely doesn't come into this. This is something that . . .'

'You stayed together for us, are you about to tell me? For us, and against Alice, right, mother?'

'Wrong.'

'I heard the split second in there when you were tossing the mental coin. That was when the truth was bought and sold, right?'

'The truth is, we love you,' Barnaby said, 'always have, always will. Nothing's going to change in that department. Not even the Supreme Court is going to throw that one out, is it?'

'Is that me? Am I the Supreme Court now?'

'Has something changed? Have I been misaddressing my mail? No wonder I never get a stay of execution.'

'Comedy,' Marion said. 'Thirty years I've been laughing my head off? No wonder I can't find the damn thing.'

'Your mother also does comedy, you see? But in the modern style. Brutal.'

'OK,' Stace said. 'So get the divorce. As far as I am concerned the court has heard enough.'

'Don't you think it's a little bit . . . well, unfeeling to be taking it this well? To be pushing us over the edge quite this cheerfully? Haven't you got even a residual feeling that we really ought to give it another try? Fuck it, Stay, to tell you the truth. Can't you be a little bit older than your parents at a time like this? Tell us what we damn well ought to do.'

'He doesn't know what he thinks,' Marion said. 'He never does. He waits for other people to tell him.'

'How can I know what the script is like until I get the notes? Or hear they just hired two other guys to give it a polish.'

'You should've had a partner,' Marion said. 'He'd had a partner, he wouldn't ever have needed a wife; because all he ever wanted me for was to tell him how great the script was, how funny it was, how much they'd like it, maybe, if they had any sense.'

'That'd be the day.'

'And then back he'd go into self-doubt mode and there'd be another draft, which I might not have time for; so could I please look at it right away?'

'Mother, spare me these intimate details, OK? I've avoided the primal scene all my life. Don't dunk me in it now.'

'Davenport is evidently interested in sports.' Barnaby had squatted down, knees wide, on a low chair and was looking at the stack of magazines on the cut-off-at-the-knees laundry table between the long rumpled blue couch and the windows.

'As far as I'm concerned,' Stace said, 'all I want is that you should both take the opportunity to live a little. Now that . . .'

'It's too late? Were you going to say? Or merely intimate lightly? Because it almost certainly is.'

'That's crap, Barnaby.'

'Crap Barnaby, that's me! On the air from dawn to dusk, with brief periods of rewriting in between, if hired. Never-on-spec Barnaby they call him. I thought Davenport played the viola. Since when did *viola-players* also *jump*?'

'OK,' Stace said. 'My turn. Time I told *you* a few things. Like number one . . .'

'Of how long a programme is this?'

'Barnaby, could she conceivably be permitted to fly solo for a coupla seconds maybe?'

'Barnaby. You get called by your own name sometimes and you know exactly what it means. Asshole, as the moderns say, only too often. If indeed they ever say anything else . . .'

'Fuck,' Stace said. 'How about if you two go and get divorced, like now, and then come back separately – or indeed together but in a different posture *vis-à-vis* each other – and then I try to tell you what, in an ideal world, might be the good news?'

'You're pregnant,' Marion said.

'Nice of you to tell her, doctor.'

'Will you quit . . . *auditioning* for one minute. Because you should be ashamed of yourself with your own daughter.'

'Wait a minute,' Barnaby said. 'Or possibly longer. Wait a lifetime, now I come to think about it. Wait a fucking lifetime before you start wishing this kind of shit onto me.'

'I'm pregnant,' Stace said. 'I'm pregnant. And you're my mom and my dad and fuck you, incidentally, for making this incidentally.'

'You don't look it,' Marion said. 'When did this happen? Last night? This morning? When?'

'You're right, Dad. She's always secretly envied you your career. She's secretly into comedy.'

'Secret comedy is when people don't laugh; and the secret is, it's not comedy.'

'Now you know what he's like,' Marion said. 'Your daughter wants to tell us that she's pregnant and what do you do?'

'OK,' Barnie said, 'I defend myself. I say that I'm innocent on all counts. Does that prove I'm guilty necessarily?'

'I'm ten weeks,' Stace said. 'You two!'

'And is . . . is Davenport, is he as happy as you are?'

'Which brings us, very swiftly – and just as well since we have a reservation to honour – to item two on the agenda.'

'He's ambivalent,' Barnaby said. 'Young men always are.'

'Extrapolation from a very small sample is very much your father's style.'

'At least I'm still your father,' Barnaby said. 'So far.'

'I have no indications about Davenport's feelings.'

Marion said, 'Clarification possibly? Or do I guess what I guess.'

'He's vanished from our screens. Davenport, to answer an earlier inquiry, and we appreciate your patience, is not into sports. Whatsoever. I don't think you should mourn exactly either. I certainly don't.'

'Are we supposed to like the idea of you raising a kid all by yourself? Is that how modern we have to be about this?'

'I don't like the idea any more than you do. And luckily, I'm

93

not going to have to do it. Which brings us, if the chair allows, to item three. I have someone I want you to meet. Which is how come we have this dinner reservation. Which is how come let's go, can we possibly do that?'

It was getting dark, and potentially stormy, when they reached the Black Angus Grill. They were led to their table by a lady in a long, pleated black skirt with butterfly-winged glasses on a beaded loop. She knew her way literally backwards, it seemed, through the candlelit room.

'You're right,' Stace said, while they unsheathed *grissini* and waited for whoever was going to fill the fourth place. 'Davenport has been superseded, and nobody is sorry, unless perhaps it's Davenport. He couldn't read the writing on the wall, even though it was in big, big letters. And now I'm glad.'

'So who's the new one?'

'He's in TV as a presenter. And a very, very good one too, very popular too, in town, as you will see when the heads swing round as he comes in. And . . . cue! Because here he is.'

The hostess was being particularly happy to greet a tall (*very* tall), handsome (*very* handsome), black (pretty black) man in a dark silk suit. While he was coming towards them, with one finger in the air at Stace, like a pupil sure of the answers, other diners were leaning towards each other, and sometimes one of them was mouthing a name, because if one of them did not recognise him, the other one surely did.

'The lucky man,' Stace said.

'I'm late,' Clifford said. 'Wrong from the start.' He glanced at Barnaby as if it was a quotation he should recognise. 'Director had just one more little thing that wouldn't take a minute. And nor it did. It took ten.'

'Marion. Barnaby. Clifford. In that order.'

'I'm exactly what you expected, right?' Clifford said.

'Clifford Wordsworth?' Barnaby said. 'I saw you play a few times. A few more than that, if we're counting. This character could score under pressure like nobody's business.'

'You're a hockey player?' Marion's question might have been

designed to give the men a chance to smile together, but it was not; to prove it, she frowned. 'Or what are you?'

'Hockey players are very rarely six feet seven,' Clifford said. 'You didn't tell them, did you?'

'I wanted them to have a surprise,' Stace said.

'And see how they handled it, right? They handled it pretty well. Imagine having to come all the way to Minneapolis to find out that your beautiful daughter is dating a *basketball player*!'

'She wanted to see us take it on the chin.'

'So! We've seen that. Now we need to see some menus. Raymond!'

'Right away, sir!'

'World-famous in Minneapolis,' Clifford said. 'Why not? I love this town. Until we hear from the networks, after which . . .'

'Mother, Clifford is not the father of . . .' Stace patted her stomach. 'If that's any kind of a – what? *Concern*.'

'Oh,' Marion said.

'Davenport left me a little something, but I'm not going to remember him by it.'

'Davenport may have views on that one,' Clifford said. 'So what are we going to eat? The grilled jumbo shrimp is unashamedly high on cholesterol and the steaks do nothing to help, but they do do it beautifully.'

Barnaby's glance at Marion said that Clifford was doing well, but that he *was* doing it, wasn't he? And she agreed with him, in an only slightly disagreeable way. It made her feel closer to her husband than she had decided she intended to feel. Everyone was being very *easy* around the table, which showed how difficult things threatened to be. The unarrived storm had a thumb on the evening's scales.

'We never met Davenport either,' Marion said.

'Meaning you haven't met Cliff? Mother, this is Cliff. Equally, Cliff, this is my mother. I was under the impression that we already did that, but . . .'

'Your mother is saying something else,' Clifford Wordsworth said, 'and very understandably. She wants to know whether the father of your child was white or whether they should brace themselves to hear the rest of the local news.'

'That's not fair,' Marion said.

'I played pro basketball six seasons, Mrs Pierce. What isn't fair is what you get away with when people aren't looking.'

'He's putting you on, Mother, because Davenport was, as Clifford knows full well, whiter than white.'

'I'm just relieved,' Clifford said, 'personally, that she doesn't have a history of black guys. Who wants to be part of a recurring pattern? I'd sooner constitute a one-off source of amazement, but not – I hope – alarm.'

Platter-sized plates came with big portions of tastily charred food on them. They went and chose their salads as if that was the evening's serious business. They ate some and nodded to each other. Then Marion said, 'Is Davenport . . .?'

'Let me guess,' Stace said. 'Reconciled?'

'That's a beauty,' Barnie said. 'Reconciled is a beauty.'

'He didn't need to be. Whatever you do, Mother, don't picture Davenport as the bright shining son-in-law that never was.'

'I just don't want you to have any problems.'

'There were, if truth be told, some quite conspicuously despicable things about Dav.'

'I liked him,' Clifford said. 'He was my best friend as a matter of fact. He introduced us.'

'They always do,' Barnaby said. 'We don't expect explanations of *anything*. When did we ever expect them?'

'How about that burn on the dining-room table back at 5764? That was the subject of a prolonged inquest. And I don't remember the expression *sine die* being assigned to that one. I didn't do it, even though I *still* say I didn't do it.'

'Let's not, shall we?' Marion said. 'Tonight at least.'

A trio had taken the covers off the drums and the double bass on the dais behind an oval of polished parquet. They seemed to be playing for the one straight couple that came promptly to the floor, but the piano player looked over to Clifford, who stood up, to do him a favour, and waited for Stace to go on ahead of him.

He was not in the least bowed by celebrity; if anything, he rose way above it. They watched Stace turn and take him in her arms.

'What do you know?' Barnaby said.

'More than I thought I ever would,' Marion said. 'I don't know how much that's saying.'

'Can I tell them? I know I can't.'

'What?'

'About your fantasy. Clifford. As if you didn't remember.'

'You do it and . . . I'll – '

'What? *Stay with me?*'

'You can't help it, can you?'

'I could, would I still be doing it?'

'Making it something . . . unreal. That's sort of . . . a caprice. A whim of mine.'

'Whereas in truth, it's what exactly?'

When Clifford got back, he said, 'Do you like to dance, Marion?'

'You should be advised,' Stace said, 'Mother always shakes her head to indicate "yes".'

Marion shook her head at Stace and then she said, 'My big chance. I don't usually take those, but . . .' She went to dance with Clifford, but she didn't take an offered hand to get her there.

Stace sat down and slid her chair in closer to her father. 'I'm really glad you guys are doing this.'

'Does it really bother you that much?' Barnie said.

'How about you?'

'I'll tell you, *everything* bothers me. I may not be an artist – OK, I'm *not* an artist – but I'm enough of one to say that the only thing that *doesn't* bother me is working. And that's probably why I bother to work, wouldn't you say so? What bothers me, I mean, isn't what's going to happen but the simple fact that anything is. She's not happy, your mother, and she wants that to be something she can take care of by herself with her own prescription. I hope it is; I doubt it is. Half the time (no, a third, maybe), I wish she was gone already; the other half or whatever I wish she'd never raised the subject.'

'Which might have left you free to.'

97

'I'll tell you something, Stay, which you already know. Possibly. If you don't, stop your ears. I'd sooner cheat than switch games, or partners. I didn't say I was, or am, or mean to, but . . . that's men, in case it's a species still interests you.'

'They really seem to like each other,' Stacey said. 'Mother and Clifford. Look at them.'

'That's what makes them maybe. Us looking at them. Good for both of them. Pretending to like each other is more of an art than liking each other and the trick is to keep pretending it when no one else is looking.'

'Why didn't you ever write anything else?' Stace said. 'Aside from comedy. I thought we'd have dessert at home. We have this great *pâtisserie* in the mall around the corner.'

'I'll get the check,' Barnaby said. 'What's his name? Raymond? Raymond, can I have a check here, please?'

Stacey said, 'So getting a divorce was all her idea?'

'It – remember when we had the moth in Christopher's room? It fluttered around the house, I guess, and then it, well, it laid eggs and . . . that was it. You get rid of things for a while; then they come back. Meaning almost certainly they never went away. And never will.'

'Look at that! Mother is seducing Clifford away from me even as we watch helplessly.'

'I always watch that way,' Barnaby said.

'I remember Christopher,' Stace said. 'I don't think I remember the moth.'

'Don't bother checking,' Barnaby said, 'not with your mother anyway.'

'So finally you're giving Benjie the Jaguar,' Stace said.

They took the two cars back to the apartment and Stace brought coffee in cups that had been made at a pottery near Lucca in northern Italy. Clifford had recently brought them home after a charity tour; he had them wrapped for serious travel and then he sat with them in his lap all the way across the Atlantic, whatever the guys had to say about it, which was plenty. 'When it comes to love,' he said, 'I have no sense of humour whatsoever.'

'Never trust people who do in my experience,' Barnaby said. 'Almost as bad as a sense of proportion.'

Stace told them that the *tarte tatin* came all the way from the Pâtisserie Belge and the *crème fraîche* from À Coté, the *fromagerie* which was, logically enough, next door to it.

'Maybe you should come teach French in Minneapolis,' Barnaby said.

'When they know so much already? You want me to be wasted? It's so pretty up here at night.'

'Top of the world, Ma! That's what I think too.'

'You should've seen her as a little girl . . .'

'Mother, you know what Daddy always says: no flashbacks.'

'I'll bet she climbed a lot of trees,' Clifford said.

'We had this neighbour. Paula.'

'I think I possibly know.'

'What you may possibly not know is, she came up to me one time, when we were waiting for the fire engine to come and get you out of the top of the sycamore tree, I think it was, and she said, "Marion, don't you ever *wonder* sometimes about Stacey?"'

'Wonder? Wonder what?'

'Like whether we shouldn't have called her Rick or Rock or something like that with trousers on it.'

'She was some sexy fatso, Paula, at one stage, wasn't she, Dad?'

Barnaby said, 'Paula?'

'Great tart,' Marion said.

'I'll tell you what it is I wanted to ask you. I hope this is the right moment. But . . . OK if it's a boy . . . which we don't know yet, obviously . . . would you either of you have any objection if we called it Christopher?'

Marion said, 'Yes.'

Barnaby said, 'Marion . . .'

'I thought . . .'

'Yes? Well, think again,' Marion said. 'Would you?'

'Mother, it's seven years.'

'Yes, it is. Over. And shall I tell you how many days over? I can. A hundred and three. And the hours? I can do those too.'

'He was my brother as well as your son. Because you seem to be accusing me somehow . . .'

Marion checked which plates were empty and stacked one on top of another and then she was on her way to the sink with them.

'You can always tell when Mother is seriously pissed. She starts doing favours. I'd stay out later than I should: all my washing got done. Even things that were clean. Make it a whole weekend and you just might have a complete paint job and *certainly* drawers turned out, shelves tidied, drapes laundered.'

'And did they need it usually!'

Stace looked at each of the men and put the rest of the things on the tray and picked it up. 'Maybe it'll be a girl,' she said.

Barnaby and Clifford were glad to be up there and looking out through the undraped windows at the lights and the river and the nervous night. It was nice to have a beautiful reason to be silent.

'Time was,' Barnaby said, 'I'd offer you a cigar. Do you still train?'

'I do a little coaching. I try to show them how a little bit. I wouldn't call it training.'

'But I might,' Barnie said.

'Are you having a problem handling this? Come on, please. Don't look puzzled. Because of me and your daughter. *That* problem.'

'Stace's been a big girl for well over a week now. She always does what she wants.'

'And do you always want her to do it?'

'I'm a little in awe of you, if that puts any kind of a new shine on things. That's some shadow you throw.'

'If the light's low enough a tall guy sometimes can.'

'No, no. What was the toughest team you ever faced?'

'Aside from you and your wife?'

'That's very . . . polite. I guess that's what it is. Because we're not too much of a team. I'm sorry if we've – what? – embarrassed you by coming here. Have we?'

'You don't embarrass me. I expected you to be white.'

'You're pretty . . . experienced, when it comes to . . . the way you say things. I'll tell you what I meant by that, since . . . I meant we maybe embarrassed you because you haven't entirely decided whether you're serious or not. About Stace. I wouldn't want to put you in a false position. I'm floundering here.'

'I'm letting you,' Clifford Wordsworth said. 'The way a man flounders tells us a lot about him. What false position?'

'You know damn well,' Barnie said. 'You're a big star. You may play Mr Modesty, but you're a big star. And big stars are used – I imagine, and not *only* imagine, because I've known a few – to getting all the girls they want, and quite a few who want them and . . . like that.'

'Stacey isn't girls. She's strictly in the singular. And I'm not . . .'

'Floundering a little bit?'

Clifford said, 'OK. OK. I hate to explain myself. It makes me wonder what I'm supposed to be hiding. Especially when there isn't anything. My guess is, you're a little concerned what my folks are going to be like. And whether everyone is going to be happy at *our* wedding like you think they will be at . . . Benjamin's is his name?'

'We call him Benjie. I wasn't wondering anything like that.'

'That's funny,' Clifford said. 'I didn't have you down for a man with no imagination whatsoever.'

'I can be deceptive,' Barnaby said.

The women finished the dishes, which did not need all the rinsing they received, and then Stace said, 'Still sore?'

'You asked me something and I answered. No one's sore.'

'Meaning I now don't get my rug shaken in the bedroom?'

'He seems to be a very nice man.'

'Do you want to see it, the bedroom?'

There was a very big, low bed, with – look at that! – an Ozark quilt on it. A bunny, with one floppy ear, lolled against a row of cushions with all kinds of stripes on them. A long green silk robe was hanging on the bathroom door, tassels fanned on the tiles.

Marion said, 'He's been here a while then?'

'Six weeks nearly.'

'And he doesn't mind about the baby?'

'He loves me. I didn't entirely believe it either, but it's true. If anything is. Which has yet to be established, of course. When Davenport got nasty, I thought maybe I'd do what he said and get rid of it. But then, at the same time almost, I asked myself what I wanted to do, and that was when I thought I wouldn't. I realised that I wanted to have it, and not him, and also that I damned well would.'

'But are you sure . . . are you sure that you want it because you want *it* and not . . . because he didn't?'

'You're afraid people're going to think it's Clifford's.'

'Never occurred to me.'

'So what should I do in your opinion?'

'You know the best advice a mother can give: not what I did.'

'And what did you?'

'Are those weavings from Guatemala?'

'Peru.'

'I thought so.'

'Mother?'

'All right,' Marion said. 'I got rid of it, and then I married him. He thought he had to. I thought he wanted to. And that was thirty-two years of my life.'

'That's neat, but it's not . . . true. When did it happen? At college?'

'Why else didn't I graduate?'

'I thought it was true love.'

'Me too,' Marion said. 'And possibly your father also. So don't ask for my advice. Don't ask for anybody's.'

'I won't,' Stace said. 'Can I bring him to the wedding?'

'Why wouldn't you?'

'The MacWilliams. And what they might say. Or look like.'

'I wouldn't know. Benjie says they're nice people.'

'Everyone in the world is nice once in a while. Hitler just loved kids. So how come the massacres? I don't want to embarrass you and Dad.'

'Stace, whatever you do, don't base your life on doing what you think your parents wouldn't like. You'd be truly horrified if you ever found out just how broad-minded they can be.'

'To the point of being *glad* to have a black son-in-law?'

'Are we talking about Clifford here? Are you going to marry him? Or just . . .?'

'I guess I'll toy with him for a while. I might, well. I love him. What other ingredients are required before you marry someone?'

'I never clipped the recipe,' Marion said.

They were sitting on the bed now. Stace leaned back on the cushions with her head by Eric, the bunny, and put her hands behind her head and looked at her mother. 'Did you ever fuck anybody else?'

Marion breathed out and closed her eyes. Stace was still looking at her when she opened them. 'The Sixties came a little bit too late for me,' she said. 'I mean, we were *in* them, but we weren't part of them. I'll never quite get used to talking that way. No, *thinking* that way.'

'Just to have something of your own maybe. I always suspected you did. At the time when Dad had those two series running pretty well back-to-back and he was getting a little bit *presiden-tial*, let's say, from time to time. Late Seventies, early Eighties.'

'Ask him what he was doing in those days, why don't you? You might get more interesting answers.'

'Me and Zara always suspected you did. Christopher did too.'

'You talked like that about your *mother*?'

'What are you going to do, divorce me? Hal Pfeiffer?'

'What about him?'

'My precise question.'

'We're planning to maybe go see him. Them. The Pfeiffers. First time since we were all in Chicago together before . . . well, before pretty well everything. Before you got to talk about me with Christopher, that's for sure.'

'Listen, if I *do* marry him,' Stace said, 'will you come to the wedding?'

'Try and stop me. If invited.'

'And wear a hat?'

'What's so enviable about today,' Marion said, 'is that people don't feel they *have* to marry people.'

'You dread it that much?'

'Do you need me to?'

'One thing holds me back. I'm not afraid to have children with him. I mean, after . . .' Stace patted her flat belly. 'I'm going to kinda owe him, but – between you and me, all right? – I only want to have his daughter. I don't really want his son. And these are things – aren't they? – you don't control. Which leaves me where? And, if it matters, why?'

Marion was not going to say one word.

'I think I'm thinking about *him*. The son we might have. But am I? And aren't sons what men want? So why am I deciding to deny him something already? Do you always want to hurt people a little bit? Is that the ultimate sign of not wanting to give yourself to them entirely? In which case, is everybody like that?'

Her mother's silence said that everybody was not, and that she was certainly not going to say so.

Stace said, 'Does Daddy know?'

'What's that?'

'You may not have anything to hide, Mother, which I do not concede for one moment, but either way, you sure hide it good. Just an ittybitty bulge under the rug, though, do I see somewhere along the line?'

'None worth talking about,' Marion said.

'And then would you talk about it?'

'You know what maybe my problem is?' Marion said. 'I've been unhappy, I've certainly been that, but never because of anything *I* did. Maybe that's what got me into this phase of my life. I want to make *myself* unhappy.'

'Everything comes back to Christopher,' Stacey said.

'Maybe he's the reason,' Marion said.

'For?'

'You. Not wanting . . .'

'Who knows?'

'Whoever he is, he sure ain't tellin',' Marion said.

'Are you guys going to mind a double bed? Because in the spare room, that's all we have.'

'Your father and I've only ever slept in a double bed since can't remember when.'

'I thought you might be into gestural separation . . .'

'I wouldn't recognise it if I saw it. Gestural separation?'

'That's OK then,' Stacey said.

The spare room was the far side of the living room. It had a window onto the end of the long ledge that ran along outside the living-room windows, right by the ladder to the roof. There were slim white shutters that unfolded inside the room. Marion and Barnaby recognised the foxed quilt they had given Stace when she went away to college. There were books from those days in the shelves. A darkening baseball bat was hanging on the wall: Christopher's. It was a child's room in which the parents were now the children. The bed was narrower than they were used to. They had not recently touched each other too often at night and they were irritably shy, both of them, at the enforced proximity.

Barnaby said, 'I like him. How about you?'

'I'm disgusted.'

'Really?'

'Jealous of my own daughter. That's not disgusting, what is?'

'Why do you suppose she's doing this?'

'Don't know; don't care.'

'You know; you care. Good night.'

What was Barnaby listening for? He lay there and he was listening and he did not believe that he wanted to hear what he could not, in any case, ever hear from way down the hall. He had never heard, never wanted to hear, any of his children making love. He almost believed that they never did it in his house, even when the boys brought girls home, or Stace a man. He was listening to the distant gush of the traffic. There was nothing in the foreground but the steady – why did he think of it as *critical*? – breathing of Marion as she hurried, so it seemed, into the separate peace of her dreams. It was as if he was waiting for an excuse to move. The sound of weight coming down onto the ladder from the roof seemed to provide it. He was listening with a purpose now. He heard the mutter of voices outside the shutters. Something blocked the faint lines of light and then jostled them before they were clear again.

Barnaby gloried in Marion's sleep as he slipped out from under the covers: it felt like a brave escape. She rustled behind him and maybe she was reaching for him, now he was gone. Cheating her this way pleased him more than pleasure might have. He went to the window and confirmed that they were out there. He did not open the shutters. Did he fear the burglars might attack him or was he afraid of scaring them away? They had moved towards the living room; he could hear the groan of worked metal. They had to be busy on the locks. Barnaby realised, in a parenthesis of excited calm, just how unhappy he had been lately. He had thought he was pretending he was unhappy, but he realised he really had been, because now he was not. He was scared, but not unhappy.

He felt for, and found, the baseball bat on the wall and unlooped it from its hooks and went into the hall. Tall striped pyjamas were coming towards him from the other bedroom. Clifford was like a ghost with no head in the darkness. Then he got to the living-room door and light filled him out. The profile was professionally steady. Clifford had not acknowledged Barnaby; perhaps he had not noticed him; he was a man who didn't need allies. He went into the room, quick and unhurried. There was the wild twitch of a flashlight as the two guys realised Clifford was there and the fight began uncertainly; the two of them could not decide whether to run or to fight. Indecision split them and Clifford was proving to the one who had chosen to fight that he had chosen badly. The other one was stuttering around on squeaky feet, wondering what he could hit Clifford with or whether to go for a private getaway.

Barnaby stepped into the room, twisted on the light, which was dimmed at first, and saw that one of the men was white. The other one – a long-armed pretzel twisted under Clifford's cool attention – was black. Barnaby was relieved that nobody had a gun and at the same time, he felt a rush of violence in himself that made him want to sap the white guy before he turned round. He wagged the bat and shouted, 'On the fucking floor. Flat. Now.' He was using this big borrowed voice. 'The both of you. On the fucking floor. Face down, you bastards.'

The white man frowned and then he did as he was told. The black man was unable to obey because of Clifford. Clifford blinked and let go of the black man who stumbled towards Barnaby, checking out the arm which Clifford had been twisting. He might have been going for a weapon but Barnaby again wagged the baseball bat. 'One move,' Barnaby said. The black man dived for the Mexican rug alongside the couch. 'And I bust your fucking black ass. We're talking splatter here.' Barnaby had not needed to make the speech, but he had never written one like it and when would he have the chance to use it again? He was breathing as if he wasn't used to this much exercise.

'OK now,' Clifford said. 'Game over.'

'Think so?'

'Know so.'

'This is a game? I don't think it's a game. Fuck you, if this is a game.'

'We came to the wrong house,' the white man said, flat-faced, with his mouth tight against the blue and green of the rug.

'Nobody moves; nobody gets hurt.' Clifford was feeling them for guns, but he didn't find any. 'What brings you girls up here at this time of night?'

The black guy maybe sensed a more social atmosphere. He lifted his head and blinked to one side, as if he had taken a punch. 'I thought I knew that voice. Clifford Wordsworth? I watch your show, man. Never miss. I also saw you play. A dozen times.'

'Me too,' the white man said, without moving. 'I also hear you on the radio.'

'Suddenly I have my fan club meeting convened right here in my own home.'

'Hey, man, give us a break, what do you say? Nothing got broke. Nothing got busted. Two seconds and we're out of here.'

'There's my locks,' Clifford said.

'Which I can take care of. I'm a registered locksmith.'

'*Registered?*'

'You won't ever see us again,' the white man said.

'We weren't *meant* to see you this time, were we?'

'Promise. Hey, you two guys aren't gay by any chance?'

'You're all out of luck,' Clifford said. He looked at Barnaby – was it the first time? – and the expressions of the two of them were there to prove just how wrong the burglars had to be. Something that was not said in their looks said 'Imagine!', for just a second, if that long.

Stace said, 'What's happening?'

'We have company,' Clifford said. 'Suppose you call the cops and see if they care to come by for them.'

Barnaby looked at his daughter as if she had arrived to take him away from a party. He did not want her to recognise him. He also hitched his pyjama pants, which he had not thought about before.

The black man said, 'We tried; we failed. Story of my life. Clifford Wordsworth! Of all the places we had to choose!'

'And he has to have this pet gorilla,' the white man said.

'Would you believe it, Clifford,' the black man said, 'Penrod here did the tarot cards before we came out tonight and they said to go for it? What's *bad* luck going to look like?'

'He calls me Penrod,' the white man said.

'Penrod seems a long time ago,' Barnaby said. He sighed. He was not going to get to hit anybody with Christopher's baseball bat. Pretty soon, they could hear the police cars way down in front of the building.

'When you don't particularly want them,' the white man said, 'do they get here!'

'We're fans. You wouldn't say we were violent, would you, Clifford, about us? We love you.'

The cops took the men away, but they seemed sulky about the ease of the operation. They looked to admire Clifford less than the two burglars. Stace was wearing a semi-see-through cotton nightdress and she went 'Oh' in the middle of all the men and had to go away and came back, after the cops had gone, wearing panties and a floral wrapper and Donald Duck slippers.

'Thank you, Barnaby,' Clifford said.

'Didn't do much.'

'But you did it right on time. I had them off balance, but . . .'

'Weren't you scared, Daddy?'

'I don't know what I was. I don't even know *who* I was.'

'That said, "Bust your black ass."'

'*Fucking* black ass, is what I heard,' Stace said.

'You heard that?' Clifford said.

'Woke me up,' Stace said. 'It was on Long Wave and FM. I bet you they heard it right across town. Do you guys want something to drink maybe? I mean, what would be appropriate? Hot chocolate?'

'I didn't hear one thing I said,' Barnaby said. 'I'm not even sure it was me saying it.'

'These things come out sometimes for the damnedest reasons.' Clifford was smiling at Stace. He touched her shoulder and then he went to the window. 'Registered locksmith! Maybe we were less than men, calling the cops. What do you think, Barnaby? Character'd be more use to us up here than in the can.'

'Mother slept right through?'

'Far as we know.'

'She doesn't want to be here, does she? She wants to be miles away.'

Clifford said, 'Half a glass of milk is what I could drink. Confirm your worst suspicions does it, Barnaby, about the man your daughter's shacking up with?'

Barnaby sat on the couch with the baseball bat across his knees. 'Am I on the defensive here suddenly?'

'What's sudden about it, Daddy?'

'If you want to know what was shitty, that was bringing up Christopher the way you did. Earlier, with your mother.'

'You call that shitty?'

'I call it a little shitty, yes, I do.'

'What did I tell you?' Clifford said. 'I said that was how it would look.'

'He was my brother,' Stace said. 'And I'm allowed to remember him; I'm allowed to talk about him. What's shitty about any of that?'

'Timing,' Barnaby said.

'Does it occur to you how – OK – convenient it is, sometimes, the way you guys – '

'Your mother and I?'

'Make Christopher's death the thing that dominates everything else, even though, and particularly of course, when you don't talk about it and don't let anybody else talk about it?'

'That's what you call *convenient*?'

'Let's not now, huh, all of us, shall we?' Clifford said. 'This is kind of ... time out time, and ... it's privileged and also dangerous.'

'Because you don't know anything about us.' Barnaby ignored Clifford. That was how he paid attention to him. 'Or how we feel.'

'What you feel deepest you deny fastest. That much – '

'That's not – ' Barnaby cut in and stopped. Did the two of them have to laugh that loud? 'Can't it be enough for the young to have all the fun and all – all – '

'We're so so spoiled, right? Or is it soiled? All all what were you about to say?'

' – the opportunities and the freedom.' He turned the baseball bat over as if there might be something to read on the other side. 'I was *acting*,' he said. 'When I said what I said. I was acting; maybe I was even acting black.'

'Forget it,' Clifford said. 'You throw shadows too, don't forget. You came in here swinging and I appreciate that. You were hero enough. Just be glad nobody got hurt.'

'I'm trying,' Barnaby said. 'It was a relief and it was also frustrating. This is funny, but I somehow envied those guys; they really had nothing whatever to be said for them. No excuses. It must be kind of a liberation to be that *decided* about what you are.'

'What was frustrating exactly, Daddy?'

'Not being able to show Clifford I was the same age as he is, probably. We should never have come see you. If we fight, it's shameful; if we don't, it's ...'

'Anticlimactic.'

'Unsatisfactory. Because finally this is about all the things that aren't personal and we want them to be. It's about you guys have your lives in front of you and we have death, Marion and I. We think it's all about grabbing at second chances and never having been what we pretended we were. Is it? Isn't it more about she sees age in my face and . . . and I see age in her ass and we both remember when we didn't do that. She thinks she can get away from it by getting away from me. We'll see; she'll see. "Mirror, mirror on the wall / If you weren't there, we'd have a ball!" We like to think. But not too deeply. People fall out of love with other people less easily than they assume; what they do just as often is fall out of love with themselves. And that's what . . . your mother and I, maybe.' He looked up with shiny brightness. 'We're out of time, folks, is what we really are.'

Stace sat on the wide arm of a chair with her chin on her knees. Then she said, 'We did kinda . . . foresee this, some of it. And foresight is a kind of . . .'

'This? What's this?' Clifford said. 'I never even knew your folks.'

'Still and all,' Stace said. 'If you're honest about it. He came to your help and you still make out he's a little bit of a racist.'

'This was between us, Stacey. You're pushing me into a corner here. But it's a corner you were in before I was. So . . .'

'Fuck off, cunt, right? No, no, is *exactly* what you meant. Don't worry about it. I probably need that. I probably even rely on that. Give me those extra inches that hate adds to love.'

'Bullshit. Your dad was a *mensch* in there. Nothing but. And I never said different.'

'Then why point it out? It's all part of the process.'

'She uses you against me,' Clifford said, 'and me against you.'

Barnaby said, 'Please. This is just what we didn't come here to have happen.'

'I called the cops and I shouldn't have. I called the cops the way Mother used to sweep up when I was out of the house and she was sore with me. To avoid knowing something. We should've been big and we were small.'

'We don't have to press charges,' Clifford said.

'What could they've taken that really mattered a damn to us?'

'I did bring those damn cups all the way from Italy,' Clifford said.

Stace tried to stay angry, but neither of the men was fooled. Her anger was part of what made them laugh, that was all. She was laughing too, so who still wasn't? The room still harboured anger somewhere.

'You want the bad news, Barnaby?' Clifford said. 'I love this woman.'

'The cunt,' Stace said. 'He loves the cunt. And the cunt loves him.'

'Maybe the police shoulda taken *me* away,' Barnaby said. 'Because who needs to feel quite this superfluous?'

There wasn't anything more to say then. They sat there, the three of them, happy and unhappy to be together. Then one of them looked up and so did the others and Marion was in the doorway, hugging herself with her head through that old poncho of Stace's, and no make-up on her face and none of them knew just how long she had been there, or outside in the hall, and how much she had heard and how much of it was news to her. And she wasn't ever going to tell them, was she?

In the Rockies

'Finally, what did you think?'

'Finality . . .' Barnaby said, 'is something I was never into. Like God. By which I mean, He was into it, if correctly reported, but I was never into Him.'

'Fastidious,' Marion said.

'Leave my mother out of this. Not that she would appreciate it. This country, how many people are supposed to believe in God? Ninety something per cent and what evidence is there? I mean to say, are people better, are they *nicer*, because they believe or is belief just an excuse for not thinking, like TV?'

'Polls would show, if polls were asked, that TV comedy probably makes some people think more than any other form of available philosophy.'

'And I can tell you why, and what. If you want to hear it.'

'Why, and what?'

'What first. It makes them think that they too are, or could or should be, in TV comedies. There ought to be a word *chould*, don't you think so? It's one we could use; meaning could *and* should. It makes them think they're cute and folksy and innately, if incoherently, wise although they didn't get to study too hard in school. It makes them feel like failure is just their particular form of success and being unknown happens to be the form which their particular fame takes. TV is Prozac for the eyes. You don't need a glass of water even and down it goes.'

'Leaving why.'

'Why is duller but also easier: because TV is the only form of adult education, apart from going through the divorce courts, of which the majority of our fellow Americans have any experience. And it costs less than litigation. It's less fun, but . . .'

'You can never resist, can you?'

'Not unless force is used. By which I mean . . .'

'I can get it without the explanations sometimes,' Marion said. 'I have good days.'

'Spoil my fun,' he said. 'See if I care.'

'I always can,' she said. 'Whatever you can hide, it's rarely your feelings.'

'Or my money, do I?'

'Would I know?'

'You see every penny there is to see. I do have a pension, but you know about that. And you have the maximum share.'

'You want me to despise you, don't you? Talking like that.'

'I also want you to ache with remorse, but how often can we always procure the effects we desire? If we could, all of us would be writing comedy. So . . . the mountains should've been spires enough, I sometimes think, but there weren't enough of them in New England, I guess, and by the time the pioneers got out here, it was too late to revise the Constitution or pull down the churches and stuff. You ask me, freedom of worship implies that the Founding Fathers didn't have the smallest belief in what they guaranteed. They were selling brushes they were never going to use personally.'

'You escape me.'

'But I always leave a trail, don't I? I mean to be caught if you just harness the dogs and . . . I hope they're looking after Grimond. Nessie and Cal.'

'Of course they're looking after him. They deeply resent us leaving him with them and they feel totally put upon, so of course they're looking after him. They'll nurse him through anything just so next time we go there he will look at them and not us with those big eyes that say "love you".'

'Oh, are we going back?'

'They'll keep him alive until we do. Or I do. She's my sister. *They* believe, you see; there's a couple that believes.'

'They sure do; they believe enough for the entire population of a small town, and still have something left over. I guess they are ninety something per cent of the population, those two. Except that they aren't. *E pluribus unum*, that's the final evidence that there's never going to be any such thing as unity, isn't it? I mean, nobody says they're united unless they're not. One flesh, that's what marriage was supposed to make people. Imagine.'

'I did,' she said. 'I really did.'

'But somebody opened your eyes, didn't he?'

'What did you think about him?' she said.

Barnaby was busy taking a bend. Four big rigs were tailgating each other up ahead, like a trail of dogs sniffing at each other's rear ends. The drivers probably used the pass all the time and they closed right up tight on each other. Barnaby was proving how carefully he was keeping back from the blurts of black exhaust that came bowling down the road towards them. Finally, he said, 'Him?'

'You know. Clifford.'

'You slept right through our big number. We had this bonding experience with the two no-hopers.'

'He's a black guy,' Marion said.

'You're not colour-blind any more than the rest of us. Despite what the legislation says. He's a black guy who doesn't break into his apartment and threaten to kill people.'

'He's a *famous* black guy, right?'

'Right. One of the greats. Moved like a dream. Still does, probably. Those guys, they retire and they're still ... what twenty-eight, nine? He's smart.'

'You liked him.'

'What's not to like?'

'He seems to be marrying your daughter.'

'True.'

'Think it can work?'

'I don't think anything can work, do I? I overtake one of them, we're trapped in the middle for who-knows-how-long, is my problem.'

'Are we in a hurry?'

'To get to Seattle? We should probably tick separate boxes on that one.'

'Don't do this again, Barnaby, will you please?'

'The first time is again?'

'The first time is not the first time, and you know it.'

'You called the guy,' Barnaby said.

'And you told me to.'

'I always put the stones in my shoes before I tie the laces. Did you ever read that story *The Long March*?'

'Styron.'

'Best thing he ever wrote.'

'And the shortest.'

'That's what was best about it. He didn't have time to tell us what it meant or how long he'd been pondering the deep problem of why liberals want the good opinions of Fascists, why they want them so much. They wanted to make a movie out of it is why I got to read it; someone sent it to me, Mike Rantzen, he sent it to me. He has a genius for casting. He tried to do something with Sly as a college professor. My mother called taking a crap "grunting" when I was a kid. Did your mother do that?'

'Since when do girls grunt?'

'Right. The guy marched all day, didn't he, with this nail in his shoe just so as not to look chicken in front of people he hated and despised in the normal way of things?'

'And you've marched for thirty-plus years with a wife in yours, is that how I'm to interpret this?'

'Bingo,' he said. 'If you want ... bingo! You sure do draw wide inferences.'

'And a lot of water,' she said. 'Am I putting on as much weight as I think I am?'

'Probably. I didn't know I was supposed to look any more.'

'Bullshit, Barnaby.'

'You see? Your vanity isn't totally dispersed, by any means whatsoever. I haven't destroyed as much as the official history says.'

'Clifford,' she said, 'is what we were talking about.'

'And other male subjects. Caucasian in one case. When did people first start calling white folks Caucasians? Can you put a date to that? We first started saying "fuck" all over the place like it was the most natural thing in the world when? 'Sixty-four, 'sixty-five? And women started saying it, back when? Who do we thank? Do we thank Kate Millett? Do we thank Erica? I remember a movie – do you remember that movie – where the *climax*, the climactic revelation was that this Great Man, when he was dying (after a road accident, wasn't it?) managed to scrawl this one word on the mirror in the men's room, at a filling station, I believe, and they never told you what it was, but the fact that he *wrote* it proved that he was absolutely *not* the great man we had been led to believe.'

'He didn't write it,' she said. 'He *said* it. He said it because he was dying in this accident, which he I think caused himself, and it was *reported* as being one of those words that delinquent bastards wrote on the walls of, OK, men's rooms.'

'You are sometimes a miraculous woman. Sometimes.'

'*The Shrike*,' she said, 'was the title of the picture. Don't ask me who was in it.'

'But who *was* in it? José Ferrer? Could that have been a picture with José Ferrer?'

'I don't recall. I recall being bored, but I don't know who with. Save it, Barnaby. Save the obvious for once.'

'Why not? If it's obvious it's bound to sell someplace. I think it was José Ferrer. What it illustrates finally is that the Bible was right. In some respects. Do you think he's actually going to marry her?'

'One minute we're pulling down the churches, the next . . . In what way was it right?'

'Drawing veils. Between the generations. That gap was a great idea. There's no way, I *believe*, that our – let's say – grandparents woulda thought they should be concerned about who their children . . . OK, I'm talking crap, aren't I?'

'I think so.'

'You *look* so. I'm talking crap, but not total crap, because what you're asking is – and maybe what *I'm* asking is the same – what I feel about Stace making her life, or her bed, with a black man in it. The question is pretty well taboo, which means it must get asked quite a lot, if not incessantly, but we must never admit it because that would put us out in back with the bigots.'

'Gets pretty crowded out there.'

'What's wrong with Stace getting involved with a black man? Nothing. How do I feel about it? How do you feel about it?'

'I'm afraid he'll hurt her.'

'Isn't that part of what . . .? Because I could imagine her hurting him.'

'What you can't imagine is her loving him, is it? Even the possibility that she might is . . . alarming, isn't it?'

'All right,' he said. 'Yes.'

'And can I tell you why?'

'Can you not?'

'Because you think it has to mean that there was something *you* didn't do right. You think it has to be evidence of something being wrong that she would choose to do something so . . . peculiar.'

'And you don't have those feelings?'

'How else do I know you do, except that, yes, I do, of course I do, in part.'

'The part you don't admit being?'

'I'm not her father.'

'So you know what I didn't do.'

'I absolutely do not. You were a good father to her and you have no reason whatever to have those feelings. You don't believe I mean it because it suits you to think that I could never think anything good about you.'

'Chould,' he said. 'Thank you. I appreciate it. Maybe the truth simply is that along with ninety something per cent of God-fearing Americans I fear black people at the same time as knowing that I should be ashamed of myself.'

'Watch those percentages when you start adding riders like that. They're not ashamed of thesselves, most of 'em, not one bit, no sirree and stuff. You even thought one time you should try *writing* with a black guy.'

'Only because I had this black character wished on me.'

'Have you noticed how it's only in TV and movies that people regularly have black bosses? To trust Hollywood, this country's security is almost wholly in the control of black admirals, and all of them totally without the smallest stain on their characters. They teach us how to behave, don't they, in the movies at least?'

'Marion . . .'

'I should not notice this?'

'You should not *say* you do. I just might be able to prove that you were an unfit mother. *Grand*mother. You're handing out hostages to fortune here. I liked Clifford and . . .'

' "And" sound likes "*but*" when you say that.'

'What's the difference? In this sense, *because* I liked him – and this is, I admit it, horrible on the face of it – I wonder just how smart he's being hiding things from me. I mean, and now you'll think I'm being terrible about our daughter, I sort of wonder whether Stace can really want someone as nice as Clifford is as good at being. How about *your* Clifford? What kind of a Clifford was he?'

'My Clifford?'

'That you fantasised about,' he said. 'Was he anything like Stace's guy?'

'That was a . . . joke.'

'No, it wasn't. What kind of a joke is it to imagine having sex with a black guy called Clifford? I know better jokes that I automatically cut out of first drafts. "Spell chrysanthemum", for instance.'

'Spell chrysanthemum,' she said.

'Come on, Sweets, you remember. It got told around a few years ago, about the white man and the black man die and go to heaven and St Peter meets them at reception and says there's no discrimination any more of any kind to get through the pearly gates but there is a simple spelling test, if they wouldn't mind taking it before their welcome drink in the land of eternal bliss. The white man died first, so he gets asked first, and the test is, "Can you spell cat?" '

119

'And he says c,a,t, and goes right on in and then it's the black man's turn and St Peter says, "For your test, Winston, kindly . . ."'

'" . . . spell chrysanthemum."'

'Timing,' Barnaby said.

'*Timing?*'

'Is the crucial thing in comedy. And you're a master of it.'

'I remembered the story.'

'Which is the only possible excuse for your conduct.'

'So what's that got to do with Clifford?'

'What that's got to do with Clifford – Stace's Clifford – is two things in fact: one, that we want him to be able to spell chrysanthemum and, two, that we will never really believe that he can.'

'How *do* you spell chrysanthemum?' she said.

'C,h,r,y, et cetera. *Don't* you?'

'So what's the catch?'

'The catch is, and so is the joke, which is what makes it contemptible, that the assumption is that black folks cain't remember, if they ever knew, that there are silent letters in English spelling. St Peter knows as well as we do that the black guy is going to start in c,r,y . . . and that's the way heaven can stay white without anyone having to post a sign.'

'Did people laugh at that joke?'

'In private, yes, they did. Because they were laughing at their own prejudices, and being reassured that we all shared them, all at the same time. It was like the Kinsey Report, which told people that most everybody did what most everybody imagined only they did. Masturbation . . .'

'Princeton plain-stitch . . .'

'You think you're right about that? You probably are. I guess Rex Tischman was right: people must've stopped doing those things the minute they heard my footstep on the locker-room threshold. By the time I was in there, they had their towels on and they were using their hands exclusively to put new laces in their sneakers, god-dammit when you think about it.'

'Don't ever think I didn't love you, Barnaby, because I did. And do actually.'

'Sometimes.'

'We have the stars,' she said.

'When they come out,' he said. 'When they come out we do. No sense in lighting us both cigarettes though, is there, when neither of us smokes any more? Paul Henreid. The winner, for once. That's another one we used to have to cut, "Do you smoke after sex?"'

'The answer being?'

'The girl's answer being – you know perfectly well – "I don't know, I never looked."'

'There was another one I liked,' she said.

'Implying you liked that one?'

'It was OK, and that was the one about the cop and the girl has all her clothes ripped off in the street accident.'

'You didn't like that one. If it's the one I'm thinking about.'

'Which is?'

'Tell me yours,' he said. 'And I'll tell you if it's the same one.'

'There can't be *many jokes* that're about a girl in a street accident and she gets all her clothes ripped off.'

'How many good tunes are there?'

'This cop comes along and sees that she's completely naked in the middle of the street . . .'

' . . . so he takes off his cap . . .'

'Right! And puts it . . .'

' . . . where it seems to be most needed and at the same time he calls the ambulance . . .'

' . . . and when the ambulance arrives, the paramedic takes one look at the girl and where the cap is and he says . . .'

' "We'd better get the cop out first." '

They had said it together and, the way they looked, it could have been something that had made them really unhappy.

'I remember when I thought *Thurber* was funny,' he said.

'And I remember when you thought so.'

' "Maybe this will refresh your memory." That was funny. The kangaroo, wasn't it?'

'It was funny when you *saw* it,' she said. 'You used to *tell* it.'

'James Thurber,' he said.

'"What a dumb moll I picked!"' Marion said.

They stopped for the night at the *Where Eagles Dare* resort-motel. It was on the west side of the mountains and they sat on the deck outside their log cabin to watch the sunset.

'If only I was a hero,' Barnaby said, 'I'd ride right into that. Randolph Scott, he'd be straight-backed and remorseless and know *exactly* where he was going, even if he didn't, and be glad to be going there. Me . . . I need a drink and I can't even say what drink I want. Can you?'

'I guess a white wine, if there's a white wine.'

'That's a good idea.' Barnaby went into the cabin and found a Chardonnay in the minibar and two goblets, either of which could have swallowed the entire half-bottle. 'Where the hell did Randolph and people go and how did they work it so easily, without one of them that I remember ever looking back? Do you remember one that looked back?'

'They didn't have children, did they?'

'Women had children in those days. The only children heroes had were there to be massacred by the bad guys to give them an excuse for shooting them down later in the show. The great thing about Westerns, I guess, is that they were full of mayhem but there was never any such thing as *accidental* death, which somehow . . .'

'I never liked them,' Marion said. 'Westerns. I never did. You'd suggest going . . .'

'You never showed it.'

'I'd wince inwardly though.'

'That usually shows,' Barnaby said.

'Are you really going to do something for Randolph?'

'Am I going . . .? Oh, Randolph. Sure I am. If I can. I have to, if I can, because I said I would and because I don't want to.'

'You ride off, you know what you should do.'

'By which you mean that when *you* ride off, you're going to leave me instructions. Which will be what?'

'Write something on spec. I don't say something great; I don't say something serious. But something that you do for yourself.'

'I'm not that kind of writer; I don't write for *fun*. I never wanted to do that.'

'Memoirs, for instance.'

'And have them buried with me? Who wants to read the memoirs of a hack?'

'You've met a lot of people. If you just wrote about your partners. Stanley.'

'Did we do the wrong thing there? We did, didn't we, walking away the way we did. Riding away. What made us think there was something *noble* in those guys riding into the sunset? They were actually being . . .'

'Irresponsible.'

'Is what they were being? It's a little late now, isn't it, to do anything about Anthea? She's probably remarried by now. Relocated anyway. Good-looking woman.'

'Look her up on the way back.'

'I'm giving Benjamin the car. I don't have a way back via Chi. You're not coming with me, is what you're saying.'

'We have a house to sell.'

'I should maybe call Mrs Biebel. What time's it in the East?'

'Later,' she said. 'What? Nine o'clock.'

'Good. I don't want to call her,' he said, 'is the truth. I don't want to sell the house.'

'Go back and live in it,' she said. 'I won't make any problems for you.'

'Leave that to your lawyer,' he said. 'Because he surely will.'

'You still don't fully trust me, do you?'

'Myself,' he said. 'It wouldn't be the house if you weren't in it.'

'You told the simple truth about the Network, about the hassles you've been through, about the people you worked with, that would be a wonderful book to write, and read. Some of your stories . . . like that guy you told how you knew *exactly* what he should do with his script. Roll it up real tight and . . .'

'Timothy Beer. I wasn't the first guy thought of that line.'

'You were one of the first to actually *use* it in combat.'

'You're leaving something in the oven for me, Marion, aren't you, is what you're doing? You want to get out of the house without feeling that I don't have my next meal. I have my next meal. I have not had an *illustrious* career – I am not going to receive any Lifetime Achievement Award, not even from the Hacks' Circle – but, *but* I do have financial arrangements in place which will allow me eat regular, if lonely, meals. Timothy Beer! Called me "buddy".'

'You want this to happen,' she said. 'You're getting useder and useder to it as we go along and every time you tongue the place, it tastes that little bit sweeter to you.'

'I don't think so.'

'Well, you are.'

'He was thinking of going bowling, Randolph, wasn't he? He was thinking "There's always bowling I can go and do."'

'He was thinking about Cary Grant,' Marion said. 'And how he maybe wasn't him but he could still make a living if he took it real slow.'

'I'm not going to find anyone else like you,' he said. 'I'm not going to find anyone else.'

'Barnaby,' she said, 'I don't blame you. For *anything*.'

'Thank you,' he said. 'And I should damn well think not.'

The log cabins were ranged on the hillside overlooking the main building where the public rooms were. There was a large car park. At the entrance was a totem pole with a notice-board mounted on it. The side they could see carried a big sign: BAR-B-Q TONITE.

They finished their wine and stood at the rail looking at the embers of the sunset and then they went inside the cabin, which was high-ceilinged and had firewood stacked alongside and under the mesh-fronted fireplace. It was not cold yet, but Barnie lit the gas and leaned kindling together and watched the splinters darken and catch while Marion had a bath. He wasn't going to turn on the TV, but he did anyway, and there was an episode of *Sergeant Bimbo* on some channel with a high number. He watched with pity and admiration and once or twice he laughed genuinely aloud, which brought tears to his eyes because he wondered how he could have been that smart and that stupid and because he wondered if he still was. Comedy was like sex: you forgot how easily you used to do it, even when you didn't feel like it, and then, later, like now, you wondered if you could still do it, and how many more times you would. He had his hand down there, checking quietly, but he moved it and used it to kill the TV when Marion came out of the bathroom in the robe the motel supplied. At two hundred a night, why wouldn't it?

She went and crouched by the fire and he watched it flickering in her eyes until she had to look at him. 'I'm glad we stopped,' she said.

'Nice quiet place,' he said. 'What do you say we eat something?'

'Want to have a bath first?'

'Think I need one?'

'I'm not your mother,' Marion said.

'You should put something warm on,' he said, 'if we're going down to eat. After a bath . . . You always have them hotter than I could ever stand. I can't believe you get into some of the baths you get into.'

'I have unusual tastes.'

'You have unusual nerve-ends is what you have. Do you really – have unusual tastes?'

'Maybe you were one of them.'

'Rex Tischman,' he said. 'He was probably bisexual is what he was telling me, right? He didn't *have* to tell me that I was one of those people who was not attractive to either sex – '

'Barnaby, for Christ sakes.'

'The point was that he wanted to tell me that *he was*, one of those. Meaning . . .'

'Got it,' she said. 'Can you smell the barbecue? I can smell the barbecue.'

'He was rich, he was attractive to both sexes, and he killed himself in Venice, I think it was. It could've been Ravenna. One of those places with an "n" in it.'

'Ferrara. Do noses get bigger before dinner conceivably?'

'Ferrara.'

'Was where Rex killed himself. He took a whole stash of pills and then he put a plastic bag over his head I was told.'

'I could have sworn it had an "n" in it.'

'Not Ferrara,' Marion said. 'And Ferrara is where.'

'I'll take a quick shower,' he said, 'if you can wait. I don't smell anything. I smell *you*. And it isn't my nose that gets bigger when I do. What is that you have on you?'

'The usual,' she said.

'It smells better than usual,' he said. 'You look great. You look seriously great.'

'Then take a bath,' she said, 'and we can go eat.'

The steps down to the restaurant were fenced with split billets of lumber and there were lanterns on short stanchions spiked in among the mountain greenery. It was a nice, quiet place and it seemed optimistic of the management to have laid so many tables in the cathedral-ceilinged restaurant with its wagon-wheel chandeliers and their many electric candles. At the far end, up a single step, there were four refectory tables, all fully laid, with rolls and wax candles and napkins enough for an army. Marion and Barnaby were shown to a particular corner selected from her plan by the hostess in the black velvet skirt and puff-sleeved jacket and the old-timer's string tie. Her name-tag said that she was called Rosine. The Pierces sat there, with a few other couples around them, like survivors from a bigger company.

The long barbecue flashed and sizzled in the centre of the room. Rosy-faced chefs, like white-coated devils, were busy with long forks teasing steaks and chicken and lobster-was-that? on griddles, in back and in front of them. The charcoal heat generated just enough breeze to make the flames uneasy on the candles.

'Pretty,' Marion said.

'Very much my view,' he said.

'Are you folks planning to partake of our barbecue this evening?'

'Seems like we'd be fools not to,' Barnaby said. 'My wife smelt it all the way up in our cabin. Looks delicious.'

'Then I don't need to do a thing right now except wish you a bone appeteet.'

They were back from their final visit to the heat when Rosine said yep to a message on her mobile and went right away to the big double doors to the restaurant (they were made of bobbly glass arranged in the form of two Indians, facing each other, with colourful feathers on their heads) and bent to the floor to peg them wide open. The chefs were busy putting new slabs of meat on the raked griddles, plenty of it, while Rosine and a trio of clean waiters in narrow pants with crimson cummerbunds and fringed waistcoats went and lit the candles on the refectory tables.

'Seems as how the stage got in,' Barnaby said.

About three hundred men, wearing blue forage caps and a variety of acceptable, mostly blue, suits came into the room in platoons of ten or eleven, and they were rubbing their hands together when they saw the barbecue and the little bursts of noise they made, the laughter and encouraging slaps they exchanged, like souvenirs, promised that they had travelled quite a ways and that they were all set for a great evening.

'I'll tell you what,' Barnaby said. 'They've come up from the West, because I'll bet you there is another message on the other side of that Bar-B-Q sign, saying "Welcome to the American Legion" or words to that effect and if we'd seen it, we'd'a never stopped here, because these people are going to make a night of it. Quiet place? Forget it.'

'You want to leave? We could always have a sudden message.'

'I don't like to fake things,' he said, 'do you?'

'I don't *like* to, but needs must sometimes.'

'All those men,' he said. 'Not a woman among them and you know what, they all hate faggots. Ask any single one of them what they think about faggots and you know what they'll say, and yet look at them.'

'Two, three hundred guys,' she said.

'And Rex Tischman wouldn't want a single one of them.'

'The waiters are cute though.'

'The waiters are very cute. We probably won't hear too much from where we are. I wondered why they put us up there almost on the snow-line. I thought maybe they knew I was a writer, but maybe it was tact. We can maybe get some rest before they get to the choral stuff.'

'Don't worry about it, Barnie. We have a big bed; we have a log fire; we have a lock on the door. That was our idea of heaven once.'

The Legionnaires were silent, for a moment, and stood and bowed their heads when the Reverend Gosling said grace, but the noise was already beginning to get happy by the time Marion and Barnaby left the restaurant and went out and shuddered at the stars. She put her arm through his and hid against him as they walked up between the brighter lanterns to the cabin. There were several rows of cars in the lot now and a big bus which must have brought most of the legionnaires up from wherever they came from.

'Think they'll have a stripper later?'

'It's possible. Those things always begin with a prayer and end with get-'em-off.'

'Like the Bible and Revelations. Imagine doing that.'

'Did you ever?'

'I don't have the architecture,' she said, 'do I? To imagine doing anything but embarrassing myself, and other people. I never had the kind of front men lean forward for, did I? Like they'd dropped something and just had to check out where in *hell* it went.'

'When you were pregnant you did.'

'You make my point. Have you been deprived?'

'You're beautiful, Marion; don't . . . will you, please?'

'Think of all the women in the world,' she said.

'That's what you were,' he said.

'Bullshit, Barnaby. Bullshit. Crap. That's crap.'

'I think you should go join the Legion, Marion. You have the full range of vocabulary. From B to C.'

'What was Paula?' she said. 'If that's what I was.'

'An aberration. A break for freedom by a man who never really wanted it. A slice of turkey while no one was looking. What was Hal? What was Hal, if we're going to talk about those things?'

'A long, long time ago. And then some.'

'And tomorrow . . . he's going to be tomorrow now, isn't he?'

She found a way to make the cabin seem larger than it had before. She went for a couple of walks in it, to the closet, to the bathroom, and she didn't sigh or look at him. He sat on the bed and he was her spectator and she was as natural as she ever was when she knew he was longing for her to say something and, quite naturally, she did not. She had the knack, and she used it finally, of not acknowledging him for however long it was and then she looked across and he might have just come into the room and taken her by surprise. She lifted her brows, just once, fast and then she was totally still and looking right at him.

'That worked,' he said. 'It always works.'

'I don't know what you're talking about.'

'I'm talking about what we don't talk about. It's sort of now or never, isn't it?'

'Let me recommend never,' she said.

'What kind of a woman is it,' he said, 'is angry because you want to tell her what you admire about her?'

'It's not admiration. You don't talk the way you talk to me if you want to convey a compliment.'

'You are too a teacher, whatever I say. Yes, miss; you surely are. How are your ears, are they growing, because listen to those patriots down there, will you? I don't ever want to know what it is they're baying for, but they're baying for something.'

'Get 'em off,' she said. 'I guess there are girls really get off on that hunger coming at them, that rage, that desire.'

'Maybe it's the baked Alaska they're bringing in, Rosine is bringing in, that brings out the beast in them.'

'Did you double lock that door?'

'I put the deadlock on, I put the whatsit across; we're safe against anything but Arnie. Imagine a country that worships Arnie. That seriously *exports* him.'

'He laughs at himself, *almost*, is what they like. He's camp if you ask me, is what they like.'

'And imagine going and telling them down there that that's what they like. A brute who's camp. The dragon that says "shucks" and still burns down the building and everybody in it. Camp! I never thought of that before.'

She was looking at him again with that flat meaningless look that meant something she was never going to tell him exactly what it was. There were more noises from way down below them, as if the sound were flowing and then trickling up the hillside. It arrived weak but it arrived.

'Tell you something, Marion: get 'em off, what do you say?'

'No, you don't.'

'Don't what?'

'At this point in my life. Why pretend?'

'Does this look like pretence? Is this what you call pretence?'

'Why?' she said. 'What for?'

'Old times,' he said. 'For old times.'

'Do I like those?'

'Because we're strangers in the night. Because we've been together since whenever and done all the things we've done – '

'And the ones we haven't.'

'And those, and we still don't fully know, don't fully trust *anything* about each other, don't trust anything to last, to still be true, to ever have been true possibly, and we're alone in a log cabin with a fire that isn't going to go out for an hour or two and a pack of wild frontiersmen whooping in blue suits and silly hats not two hundred yards from where we are and what the hell?'

'Coincidence,' she said. 'Right?'

'Coincidence,' he said.

'That tomorrow we go to Seattle.'

'You talk about my tongue being on the place. You put it on the fucking place and you know you do and you seriously like to do it, whenever you feel like it. Look what you just killed; you just killed that, Marion. You don't have to be Arnie to be a killer, and like yourself for it, do you?'

'Asymptotic, isn't that a word you used once, and explained to me?'

'Is it?'

'Meaning a line that converges on another line and almost, almost but never quite touches it?'

'I used it only the once? I'm surprised it wasn't every day.'

'I used to lie there and ache for you to reach out and you

didn't. It lasted longer sometimes, the pain, than any kind of pleasure you could think of.'

'You did that? I did that. I did that a hundred times. What you *never* did was you never lay alone in bed and listened to The Moon is Blue and knew that I was with somebody else. That's one of the sweet pleasures that life has denied you. It's a pip, believe me.'

'Blue Moon.'

'The Moon is Blue is another tune entirely, which was in vogue at the time I'm talking about.'

'We don't have to go to Seattle,' she said. 'We can drive right on down to LA and tell him we had to sidestep the North-West. He won't care.'

'He'll care; you'll care. Anyway, we promised.'

'Promises!' she said.

'You know what's terrible, don't you, for me at least? Not that we're selling the house, that we're selling our memories, not taking them anywhere, not keeping them with us, just . . . And they won't even notice, the next people, they won't see our ghosts, they won't recognise where the bumps and scratches came from or what they signify.'

'And you blame me,' she said.

'Murder,' he said, 'is what today? A misdemeanour.'

'Do you have any idea how frightening *you* can be? Because you can.'

'I knew a guy once, I guess it was about the time I first met you, who'd been in the Service and he and I went and had some beers one night in a place downtown, off campus, and he suddenly said to me, "Hey, Barnie, how about tomorrow you and me go and get ourselves tattoos?" This guy wanted me to make a date to go with him and get ourselves tattooed. Imagine if I had this big tattoo on my biceps or someplace to this day. I didn't dare say no so I said yes, and that meant I had to avoid this character, who dropped out luckily, end of the semester, because it was crazy to think of being tattooed with some ex-marine and yet . . .'

'You didn't ever see him again?'

'He caught up with me, but like days later, which was past my tattoo-by date and he didn't care anyway, but you know what I did, I wrote a coupla essays for him, to improve his chances of a favourable assessment. I just this second remembered that.'

'And he still dropped out.'

'He still dropped out; he wasn't chased out. I feared this guy, not physically, not morally, so how? I feared his challenge is what I feared. The look he'd give me when I went back on what I'd said.'

'That's how come you married me, is it?'

'That's how come I married you, Marion. In a pig's eye it is.'

She turned in the bed and looked at him and he looked at the fire and then he pulled the covers right back and her nightgown was rumpled between her thighs and high on her hip on one side and they were looking at each other and not smiling and he was thinking how sweet it was to want to hurt someone so badly that it made you patient and tender and you didn't care how long anything was going to take or what it meant in any way whatsoever.

Hal

The receptionist at the *Herald-Examiner* asked if Mr Pfeiffer was expecting them and Barnaby said, 'Just about.' She hesitated a moment, fearing he was trouble from the expression he used, but then she buzzed and said who was here and listened and asked why didn't they go up to the sixth and someone would meet them.

'What do they do on the floors below the sixth,' Barnaby said, while they were riding up, 'do you suppose? You go to newspapers, you go to Networks and places and you never see anyone on a floor lower than the sixth. It feels like you could rent those floors very cheaply, because there's never anybody on them.'

'Accounts and stuff.' Marion watched the numbers on the electronic board melt into each other until they came to 6.

'Mr and Mrs Pierce? I'm Lynn. I'm Mr Pfeiffer's assistant.'

The editorial floor was open-plan. They walked past the low ramparts dividing one personalised section from another. The busy journalists gave perfect impersonations of busy journalists: they talked on the telephone and swung slightly from side to side and reached for pencils; they checked their screens and sipped coffee and looked into the cup to see how much was left in it; they peeled back pages in files while they were still on the telephone, like detectives who knew exactly who was guilty, even if they could never bring a case; one of them even tapped top teeth with a pencil and seemed to find inspiration from glancing at the Pierces as they went along to the glassed door of the editor's office. Barnaby wondered what kind of a show Hal Pfeiffer had decided to put on; what kind of naturalness and business he would elect to be caught in the middle of.

He had a black beard. Barnaby was surprised; he was surprised as if Hal had grown it while they were on the way up, entirely to be surprising. He looked shorter than Barnaby remembered too; he was plumpish and bald, and shiny, on the top, with black wings on each side of the shine. The moustache was part of the beard, but Barnaby saw it as something else again, because Hal was already growing it when they knew each other in Chicago. It was the beard, spiny and shiny and shot with a flash of grey, that seemed to make him overdressed. Barnaby looked at Marion, but Marion had no eyes for him, at that moment.

Hal was sitting at a double desk which was loaded with papers and realistic evidence of long tenure: a bust of Napoleon, alabaster maybe, and another of someone who, knowing Hal, had to be Mencken, and a third, of Hal himself, in plaster, with a plaster pencil behind a too big ear. There was a pink piggy bank with 'Leave Your Buck Here' written on it: one of those presents, you could be pretty sure, from the staff on some anniversary or other, the kind of thing you were doomed to keep for the rest of your life, even if you wished someone would steal it or knock it clumsily, and finally, to the floor: upset and relief would be indistinguishable.

Hal said, 'Yes, can I help you?'

He went on making marks on the text in front of him and once he smiled, showing pipe-smoker's teeth that always were somehow *wider* and straighter than you seemed to remember or quite want them to be. Lynn looked at the Pierces and then she left them to it.

Hal threw down the pencil and there were the teeth again, but for them this time. He came round the desk, one hand flat on the corner, like he was going to vault over something, which turned out to be a chasm of years. He came to Barnaby first and somehow they were embracing each other before they had looked each other completely in the eye. The hug was easier to do than it might have been just to hold each other's looks.

'I'll be damned,' Hal said, and Barnaby knew, or guessed he knew, that Hal was looking over his shoulder at Marion and what was really going on was between the two of them.

'You will be if I'm on the jury,' he said, and that was enough for Hal to let go of him and move on towards Marion.

'I'm the wife of the foregoing,' she said.

Hal did not hug her. He took her hand and didn't shake it or, as Barnaby almost hoped (because it would be so phoney), kiss it. He didn't kiss anything. He stood there with Marion's hand in his and it might have been the whole of her that he was weighing.

Why did Barnaby think of the silent blurring numbers in the elevator? Why could he see the numbers going on and on, running into each other, higher and higher?

He turned and looked through the unfrosted panels of Hal's office at the journalists and they were all doing what was expected of them as if an expert First Assistant had drilled them to it: some looked happy, some looked old, some were on their way out, others were coming in.

'You must've treated her right, Barnaby, because she looks great. She looks wonderful. You too.'

'Things change,' Barnaby said, and Hal patted his arm with the palm of his hand, just above the elbow, giving him marks for that one.

'He still has hair,' Hal said, 'the bastard.'

'Only on my head,' Barnaby said. 'As opposed to my face.'

'Right. So: now that you've seen me in my editorial glory, and I've proved to you that I am the first man in the village, what do you say we get out of here before some world-shattering local news threatens to keep me here all night? It only takes one more local businessman to fly himself into a mountain and we're here all night figuring out a new way to tell the people what an indispensable member of the community the sonofabitch was.'

'Only sonsofbitches are,' Marion said, 'indispensable. Or think they are.'

'They can do without me,' Hal said, 'but they must never, never know they can. I'd better tell them I'm taking off.'

He went out of his office and along past the windows to the next cubicle and they could see him, through the other glass, talking to a young man in gartered sleeves (another realistic touch) who was already on the telephone but waved with a suavely shaky hand that said everything would be fine, and sure, go right ahead. Hal stopped in the young man's office doorway and had something else he needed to remind him about, but the young man's new wave said he had already thought of it and pretty well taken care of it. All this time, Barnaby seemed to see two things, one close, one distant, at the same time: Hal and Marion.

'Hasn't changed that I can see,' he said.

'He has the gift of eternal middle age,' Marion said. 'Hal: he would, wouldn't he?'

'OK, so!' Hal was back with them, exclusively. 'The things we devote our lives to. Would that they were worthy of us! Or, on second thoughts, pray God they're not, because what would that make us worth? *Me* worth. Because you guys . . . back East . . .'

'Still full of shit,' Barnaby said.

'You look *great*,' Hal said, and it wasn't to Barnaby at all.

They rode down in the elevator and Barnaby was alone with the two of them. He was almost grateful to feel that same loneliness he had known in Chicago when she told him that what she had denied was true. They had left Christopher and little Stace in the apartment with Barnaby's mother, Alice, who was visiting, and they went to the Art Institute. They were standing in front of that little Van Gogh of the orchard with the ripe green sky above it and she looked at the picture and said, 'He loves me. It's nothing to do with you.'

He said, 'And how about you?'

She said, 'All right, I love him.'

'All right, did you say?'

There was a polished floor in the gallery that seemed to bulge slightly upwards, it was so springy and so tightly chamfered; he thought of that word – chamfered, rightly or wrongly – at the same moment as he wanted to throw up. The air-conditioned room had no air in it at that moment and he felt his brain dying in his head. Marion was breathing through wide nostrils and it seemed that her nose had a new arch to it, no, a kind of haughty curve, like a horse's and she rolled her eyes towards him and instead of, as he perhaps hoped, a vestige of pity or at least

136

anxiety, there was nothing in them but rage. She was furious with him or with something that she feared he would do. He didn't throw up; he wanted to believe that he had been dignified, even defiant, that he had failed to break down the way she expected, but he knew then, and feared later, that he had kept himself together only because that was the very least she expected of him. He formed the phrase 'What about the kids?' but her glare had him swallow that too and say nothing until they had finished with Van Gogh. All he said was, 'When did you ever see a green sky?' And she said, 'Is that the point?' and he said, 'Do pictures have points?' And then he had to say, 'Does anything?'

For some reason, they were in the old Chicago Wheat Exchange, which had been restored inside the Art Institute, when he said, 'That's how you feel about him, you'd better go to bed with him.'

And she said, as if he deserved it, and maybe he did, 'I already did.' He could have killed her then, under the names of the old councillors and annual presidents in the handsome, shining chamber, but what he did was, he said, 'I still love you, unfortunately.' The strange thing was, he felt privileged, as if she had done him some kind of a cruel favour. He was never more sure that she was his wife.

Hal's Honda was parked in his reserved space outside the newspaper building. 'We're over there,' Barnaby said. He had put the E-type on a meter across the street. A couple of kids were bending down to look warily inside. 'Looks like they're afraid they might see a dead mobster slumped at the wheel.'

'I thought we'd go to the house. Erica wants to see you.'

Barnaby thought that Hal had some difficulty in saying the line, despite having evidently decided on it well in advance. He said, 'And we want to see her.'

'So listen, you have the address, but why don't you follow me would be the simplest thing to do? It's a little bit complicated unless, of course, you can do it blindfold like I can.'

Hal was in the car and backing when Barnaby said, 'Tell you what, Marion, you go with him, why don't you?'

'Barnaby, please could we try to get through this without . . .'

'Is that such a selfish suggestion?'

Hal was out and level with them and he rolled down his window and said, 'Tell you what, Marion, suppose you ride with me for a change?'

Hal had to go round the block before he could come level with Barnaby in the Jaguar and did a little double jab forwards, to indicate the way he was going to take. For a moment, they were in a buddy picture together. Howard Hawks: why not? Marion sat there next to Hal and smiled at Barnaby as if she were doing something irrational and not exactly what she wanted. How much trouble people could take over how they looked when they were not being in the least honest about it! The two of them, he did not know which, had given him back his desire and he felt the same old bitter gratitude as he pulled out and made the Jaguar snarl on its way.

'This is comfortable. The car. It's real comfortable.'

'It's a cheap Japanese car, Marion. Real comfortable!'

'That Jaguar,' she said, 'try sitting in it for hours and hours. It's fine to drive, but those seats were made for Englishmen. They like to suffer. Me, I don't, not for that long.'

'I don't think you ever did too much suffering,' Hal Pfeiffer said, 'did you, without . . .?'

'Yelling?'

'Doing something about it.'

'The wrong thing, you're thinking.'

'All I think about these days is deadlines. So . . .'

'You still do that! Say "so" followed by dot dot dot.'

'So?'

'So I'm going to have a new life,' she said.

'We lost him,' Hal said.

Barnaby was following the Honda, but not too closely. There was something experimental in the distance he allowed Hal and Marion to get ahead of him. He was playing with pain and liberty, tasting their juices on his tongue, not sure which was which or whether they could be separated. He let the Honda get away for more reasons than reason could supply. He gave them the licence to be without him and he gave himself a sort of angry nobility with nothing more to show for it than the way his elbow jutted from the low window of the Jaguar. He drove with the unhurried power of someone who had a lot more he could do, if he wanted to do it. As it was, he had time to brake with noisy courtesy at a changing light and let two girls cross the street knowing that he could just as easily have gone on through. They were in their twenties and the look they gave him, together and yet somehow one and then the other, with a quick duck of the knees to see into the low car, said that they thought he was probably eligible and, if a little old, cute enough. They went on talking together and he knew it was about him. It was nice to be someone that they had no idea who he was and yet they knew he was somebody.

By the time he had changed down, with slow urgency, and ridden on past them again (oh no, they weren't about to look this time, but their not looking still acknowledged him), he had lost the Honda and didn't know where the hell he was or where he had put Hal Pfeiffer's address, and Erica's.

Hal said, 'He'll find it.'

'Or not. And if not, what?'

'He'll call the paper. My Lynn will tell him. He'll find us. You always like to think he has less resources than he does.'

'Because I know I do.'

'Never mind why. Don't you?'

'Not any more,' she said. 'I've moved up a grade. Now I like to think he has more.'

'That's exactly the selfsame thing,' he said. 'Isn't it?'

'You're the editor,' she said. 'Your Lynn?'

'A manner of speaking. A *dated* manner of speaking.'

'Meaning?'

'Nothing. Like . . . OK, I won't say it.'

'Exactly the selfsame thing.' Marion twisted in her seat. 'As you would say.'

'If he lost us before, he won't be there now,' Hal said. 'Unless he has a truly extraordinary second sense. I am not having any kind of a relationship with Lynn except I pay her. As if I owed you any kind of an account! So . . .'

'I don't even have a toothbrush,' she said. 'Or a change of clothes.'

'Marion,' Hal Pfeiffer said, 'you have not seen the last of him. I guarantee. Unless you want to have.'

'Do I call Lynn?'

'Do you want to?'

'I was showing knowledge,' she said, 'you know?'

'I know.' He drove for a while, and then he looked over at her and said, 'So it's really going to happen is it, this time?'

'It was never going to happen before,' she said. 'And I never remotely indicated it was.'

'Exactly,' he said, 'as before. So . . . why?'

'Things come to an end; naturally or no, they come to an end. Benjie's getting married. Stace ditto, or so we are led to believe, hope or maybe fear. She's with a black man now. Clifford Wordsworth?'

'*The* Clifford Wordsworth?'

'There are others?'

'Not for me,' Hal said. 'He's one of the all-time greats.'

'Me, I thought he played hockey,' Marion said. 'So . . .'

'I remember Stacey when you had to get back and read her bedtime stories.'

'Me too. But that was never one of them.'

'You're not happy about it?'

'I'm not about it at all, I don't think. Exactly the selfsame thing are you about to say?'

'Am I?'

'So . . . I'm allowed to think of me, which I do with some reluctance more times than you, or certainly Barnaby, might imagine. I wonder where the years went and I want to believe that they can be recycled and lie somewhere up ahead of me. So . . .'

'He has someone else?'

'He does?'

'It was a question. You look like I know something.'

'I thought maybe you spotted something I missed. You live with someone long enough and . . . what do you see?'

'That's all it's about, "long enough"? I don't believe that.'

'I'll tell you, it doesn't matter any more what it's really or supposedly or presumably all about. It may be all about nothing but what can't be changed now. You ever see a painter stand in front of something he did once it's in the gallery? I had a girlfriend had a show and I went to it with her and all she wanted to do was paint things in and paint things out. You never criticise things really thoroughly, do you, until it's too late to change them?'

'Try running a newspaper,' he said, 'if you want that experience every single day. My people, they're never so intelligent, never so goddam *trenchant* as when it's too late to do a damn thing about it, whatever it is. So . . . we break up like we finally knew how not to do anything like that ever ever again, and the day after, in they all come and – whaddaya know? – we do it again.'

'He had someone else,' she said. 'A long time ago.'

'And you saved it up until you were ready.'

'You used to like me,' Marion said. 'It isn't really that way, I don't believe. If I even think about it, it's only because it's convenient, not because it's the true trigger.'

'The true trigger! Isn't that what the Lone Ranger's horse was called? Trigger?'

'You're the reader,' she said. 'I still have your *Deer Park*.'

'Dear God,' he said. 'You and Norman must be the only people still have copies of that one.'

'Do you want it back?'

'Give me my twenty-four years,' he said, 'and you can keep Mr Mailer. How about *To the Finland Station*?'

'Excuse me?'

'That I lent you around the same time.'

'Either you didn't or I gave it back. I guess you find it kind of . . . amusing, do you?'

'Plus or minus one Edmund Wilson, you have to take these things in your stride. I told you: he isn't going to show up behind us now no matter how often you do that sudden . . . *Amusing*? . . . twist.'

'Is ironic any better? You always did say we were a golden instance of a mismatch made in heaven, Barnie and me. And I.'

'Did I really?'

'You don't remember?'

'I remember saying it once. While you were getting dressed, with your back to me. You always got dressed with your back to me, like there was something I still shouldn't get to see. Even after we'd just fucked, you did that.'

'OK,' she said. 'So . . .?'

'I wanted to believe it. I needed to believe it. I needed to have you say you did, but you didn't.'

'You live a long way out of the city,' she said.

'Have I misled you into thinking otherwise?'

'I said the wrong thing,' she said, 'evidently, but I don't know which one it was. Which one was it?'

'You denied it. So vigorously you almost fell over twisting round with your panty hose halfway up those legs.'

'One thing at a time, my mother used to say, but I don't seem to have had enough time for that. Even now . . .'

'You're going to do what as well as what?'

'Teach, French, and study psychoanalysis.'

'Physician, analyse thyself.'

'Is probably part of the lure, and the threat.'

'Threat is a lure.'

'You taught me that,' she said, 'among other things.'

'One of which, the *principal* one of which was, go back to your husband while he still wants you.'

'He was almost as sorry to lose you as he was me.'

'A tangle of pronouns, that's life: me, you and him. But first and foremost you and him. I said it one time, Marion, because I needed to see what happened.'

'And what did? Aside from my nearly falling over myself.'

'That's the problem when there are two of you.'

'I told him we shouldn't come.'

'I don't think you ever thought you should. I even remember one time when you should have called out "Yes", if you'd been the Molly Bloom I guess I wanted you to be and instead, what did I hear you say? NO!'

'Oh no,' she said, 'if you really have to be accurate.'

142

'Meaning you remember too?'

'Is that tricky of me are you about to intimate?'

'You're getting ready to be sore with me,' he said. 'Why would that be?'

'Of course I remember. I remember because I was so . . . shocked. I was shocked.'

'I thought I'd hurt you.'

'I was shocked at how great it was. How much I was going to have to . . .'

'Lie to him?'

'I guess.'

'Meaning not that at all. What?'

'Is this hurting you, talking about this?'

'*No*,' he said. 'Hurting me? Absolutely not.'

'I was *terrified*, in a way I never wanted to forget, at how far away from home I was at that moment. How I didn't care about Chris or the baby or still less Barnaby. That was what that no meant, among other things doubtless, among which were do it some more and don't stop and I don't know what else.'

'You cried.'

'Yes, I did.'

'And wouldn't explain why. You looked angry more than anything else.'

'I didn't want it to have happened.'

'And have you come all this way to tell me . . .?'

'Not that. I'd forgotten about that.'

'Except that you didn't.'

'Correct.'

'Nolan,' he said. 'I got to call you that a few times, didn't I? I had this idea it was something he never got to do.'

'He has since,' she said.

'I don't like to hear about what happened since.'

'There are things I don't,' she said.

'That was terrible,' Hal Pfeiffer said. 'Christopher, that was just the most terrible thing.'

'So how are yours?' she said.

'Patsy is in Toronto. Still. Billy is post-graduate in journalism, which shows how much good I've been to him. I won't give him a job although I'd love to until he's worked someplace else, so we're not going to see too much of him for a while. They're fine. So . . . everything is, isn't it?'

'And Erica?'

'Is at the house.'

'You had other . . . relationships, didn't you, after you and I . . .?'

'I scored a few times. Nothing . . . serious.'

'Scored,' she said. 'Is that what you did with me? Is that what the recording angel put down at your dictation? You live in another *state* is where you live. How is Barnaby ever going to get to find us?'

'Scoring is scoring; loving is loving.'

'And we know where the twain can always get to meet: in the male mind. I was that summer's ripe tomato and don't tell me I wasn't.'

'I loved you, whether you like it or not.'

'Maybe I needed you to say it a few more times.'

'I said it plenty.'

'About me and Barnie being a mismatch.'

'I wasn't interested in you and Barnie. Fuck you and Barnie.'

'You weren't that *interested* in me. I think you were pretty happy to take me away from him. I think I was the dupe in the sandwich, that's what *I* think, sometimes at least; I think you both, in your different ways, had a pretty good time with me.'

'I had a lot of respect for you, Marion Nolan. You told him that was what I called you, didn't you?'

'Unless you did,' she said.

He was not the kind of man to blush, but there was a sudden new bloom to the face, as if the beard itself had taken on a new shade of black, from the roots up. 'I wish you were wrong, but you know something, I remember now, that last time I talked with him, I told him that I had gotten a job out here, and for what salary, which in those days he couldn't believe he would ever equal, let alone double or treble or whatever he's done subsequently, I did too call you that, and knew I did, to hurt him.

That was the deepest hurt I could think of to wound him with, having a name for you he never did, until he did. If you'd said *yes* with the same passion as you said no that time, maybe I woulda told him about that instead, but I don't think so.'

'*To the Finland Station*,' she said. 'I don't remember you lent me that. We must be nearly there though: Finland.'

'You're clever, Marion.'

'And that's not the only thing you don't like about me are you implying, none too subtly?'

'You're reminding me of every single damn thing I've spent all these years keeping locked out of my mind. I just hope you're not doing it for fun. Is that why you're doing it? Because please don't, even if you already have.'

'I wanted to see you. You asked us. We came. I should have stayed in the car with Barnaby. I should've driven out with him. I wanted to.'

'And that's why you're here.'

'It was his idea.'

'You and me, were we his idea too? *Tomato!*'

'I don't know,' she said.

'Thanks,' he said. 'Thanks a whole, whole lot. I was something you were using against him, wasn't I? Which is – and don't shake your head, if you want to be an analyst you know this already – just like using me *for* him.'

'This is what I came out here for,' she said. 'It has to be, doesn't it? I loved you and I told you so.'

'And why hullo was the same as goodbye.'

'Which you know already.'

'Me and the Beatles! But did I then? Which you taught me is the truth of it. I didn't know it at the time or . . .'

'We were both married and we both knew we were both married and if I'd . . . You would not necessarily have liked it. You would not necessarily have liked it *one bit*.'

'One bit of me would've liked it.'

'You and Barnaby were friends. I sometimes forget that. But when you say things like that . . .'

'Buy one, get a second one free.'

'To think I dragged him up here to see you! I must've been out of my mind.'

'OK, so . . . if we're going to get nasty – '

'It makes you seem a lot more alive suddenly, so presumably we are.'

'If we are, do you think I don't know, even if you do not, that *why* you dragged him up here, as you put it, is because you wanted to rub his nose in it just one more time before you headed on to Splitsville?'

'Splitsville. Is that where you live? I thought it was one last chance to mend some fences is how stupid I am.'

'Who's going to be the handyman? Not I. I hammer anything, there goes my thumb. Like when I fall in love, I get dumped on my butt. Bruises, bruises, but do I complain?'

'I always thought you were so strong. So did Barnaby.'

'I heard a story . . . that I'm not going to tell you on second thoughts. That I'm definitely not going to.'

'You and jokes,' she said. 'I remember you used to be so funny Barnaby didn't know whether to hate you or ask you to come write with him.'

'How about both? Because he tried both, until hate prevailed.'

'I don't actually think it ever did. You'd be surprised how much he envied you.'

'Strong?'

'Mature.'

'There's no machinery for appeal against that one, is there? He meant bald.'

'He meant bald,' she said.

'Damn you, Marion, because you haven't changed too much, have you?'

'That's just . . . no, that would be . . .'

'Because I hope I haven't? You're right. Do you know what I do, in the scoring department, these days? I go down to Portland and there's a number I have down there I call and I go see the woman whose number it is, maybe once or twice a year. She thinks I'm CIA, because I told her so. That's what I do.'

They seemed to be on a part of the suburban road system that he didn't know so well suddenly because he was seriously concentrating on where he was going with both eyes and both hands. It was one of those areas where all the buildings seemed to have been thought of at the same moment and put up in the same twenty minutes: banks, pizza joints, supermarkets, houses, post office, schools, Mormon church (ALL WELCOME), the hospital, the veterans' administration, everything.

She said, 'Erica. How is she?'

'What did you say?'

'Should I not have? I wondered how she was.'

'Erica.'

'Yes.'

He had stopped the car by the entrance to a huge mall with all kinds of familiar stores under a single steep, high roof. He said, 'How about you get out of the goddam car, right now?'

She said, 'Do you need something?'

'I need you out of this goddam car like instantly, so . . .'

'Did I do something wrong?'

'You think it out. Out. Go get your goddam divorce and how about you don't ever come back and tell me? Erica is Erica. She has been for years. You know it; I know it. And that's quite enough of that, and this, and anything else that you have in your admirably and only slightly despicably open mind. I find, to my own mild surprise, that I can't stand another minute of this *shit*.'

'Where am I? I have no idea where I am. I don't know where Barnie is.'

'You'll work it out.' Hal Pfeiffer was leaning across her and she could smell used smoke on his sweater and noticed that his back was quite humped, almost deformed, and he had the door open and gave it a tiny push with the tips of his fingers and he was getting himself up from over her, taking trouble not to touch her and his face was turned her way and only inches from hers and she saw the snarl of his teeth and the luminous flare in one of his eyes as it caught some of the lowering sun and then he was right back in the driver's seat. 'Please let's not prolong this, shall we?'

'No? You're loving it,' she said. 'You bastard.'

'Barnie,' he said, 'is that a damn silly name or not?'

147

'Why did you ask us to come?'

'For the sweet pleasure of doing what I'm doing now possibly, though I didn't think of it at the time. I told myself that we were going to celebrate twenty-five years of middle-class humbug and hypocrisy. It's a tribute to us all, wouldn't you say so, in a time of *immense* social change, upheaval even, when all the old sexual and moral shibboleths – boy, I like to work that one in sometimes – all of them were being questioned, if not openly derided, and we went on suffering from the same old back pains no one else had to live with for a *second*? I mean, it takes some doing, in the decades between, to go on living an old-fashioned life, full of *angst*, knees and bumpsadaisy, though not too much of it in my case. It's like the silver jubilee, isn't it, of our . . .? We should be riding through town drawn by white horses, not that white horses draw too well, but . . .'

The door was still open, but he did not seem inclined to push her out of it and she did not quite have the nerve, or the desire, to close it. The air felt good, and a little dangerous. She huddled her shoulders together and then she looked at him, as if it had needed courage.

'You still have it, don't you, the look? You still have the look.'

'The look. Do I?'

'And you know you do.'

'Then it's all I do still have.'

'And need. Why did you come?'

'Easy, and you know it: I wanted to see you.'

'Do you still screw him?' he said.

'He's still my husband.'

'You did it last night, didn't you?'

'How in hell did you know that?'

'I can still smell him on you.'

'That's not true. That is not true, and you know it.'

'I sniffed; I knew. Probably something about the way he was looking when he walked into the office, the way he stood there. The way *you* looked too, and look. So . . .' Hal Pfeiffer sniffed himself and looked over at her and they were so, so nearly laughing together that she could almost hear the sound of it.

'While you were doing it, did it occur to you that he was doing it to screw me, and that you were doing it for the selfsame reason?'

'We had three hundred members of the American legion sharing the motel with us. They were blowing trumpets and singing songs and, as it finally turned out, one or two of them, no one yet knows how many, were doing things they voted against, to a man, to one of the waiters who was unwise enough to go to one of the cabins with some late, late refreshments. We had the police at the door at like eight-fifteen in the morning wanting to know if we had heard anything. Anything! Nothing they wanted to hear about however.'

'They did what exactly?'

'Oh my God, I've given you a story. There's a light in your eye. That one.'

'I doubt it was in my jurisdiction, was it?'

'I don't know. The *Where Eagles Dare* motel?'

'No,' he said.

'They'd come up from this side of the mountains, Barnie said. Barnaby isn't a silly name. Nor is Barnie. What's so silly about Barnie?'

'He knows,' Hal said. 'He said to me one time he hated it.'

'That's no excuse,' she said.

'So maybe they were from this state? What happened exactly?'

'We didn't get into exactitude. They found this waiter in a coma and it wasn't because he'd been overtipped, OK? Tipped over though. Is all I know. Young kid, half Chinese if it was one of the ones I think it was, or possibly Japanese.'

'He wasn't dead though? What did they do to him, did the cops tell you? Tipped over is good.'

'They did things, but I don't know what. You can guess.'

'Not in print. Want to know the last time Erica and I . . .?'

'Not in the smallest.'

'Right after you wrote that letter saying you wouldn't be writing any more letters. Then. That was a nice thing you did.'

'Barnie – Barnaby – opened one of yours and I thought . . . By mistake.'

'You sure did. You thought we shouldn't give him any more cause to do what?'

'Either something had to happen or . . .'

'Why? Why was that, Marion? Complete your sentence for me, please.'

'I thought, at that point, that I was going to stay married to Barnaby and that, OK, we should be serious about it.'

'*OK?* Fuck you. Fuck you, good and loyal wife.'

'It was that or . . . That was right after Christopher happened and, it's easy for you to get mad, but I needed him and he needed me and I'm sorry.'

'Do I need this? Do I need this?'

'I thought we could all be friends again. I hoped that was something that we maybe all needed now.'

'You thought he needed *me* is the truth of it. You thought, wait a minute, why not let's dig up Pfeiffer, dust him down a little bit, and maybe the two of them . . . didn't you, *dear?* Could do what? Go *fishing?*'

'You really hate me. The thought never entered my mind.'

'There are other points of entry,' Hal Pfeiffer said.

She wanted him to do something to her right then. She ached for him to do something she could despise.

'I was healed,' he said. 'I was healed, I thought. Not well, not happy, but healed I really did think I was that. I figured you and he, for whatever reasons, OK Christopher included, and why not, were together and, believe it or no, I very very nearly wished you all the happiness in the world, because I guess that, like money, somebody has to have it and why not you? And then you tell me, like it was something I wanted to hear, that you've decided to – what was the phrase, not too original? – live separate lives. It came down like an axe right on my head.'

'Leaving no scar whatsoever that I can see.'

'"Kindly nod" – remember that one, the Chinese executioner?'

'I saw you in that office, Mr Editor, and you were no kind of a tragic figure. You love it there; you revel in it.'

'It's the only revel in town. Know the best part? An editor never has to go home unless he wants to, and I never want to, but

I do, I do. When she's asleep. I thought you loved him. You told me you did. I thought I loved him. I saw him one last time, you know.'

'Yes, I do.'

'Did you know I kissed him? He didn't kiss me, but I kissed him.'

'You were the winner,' she said.

'The what?'

'In his eyes.'

'My God, did we take it all seriously or what? We suffered; *I* suffered anyway.'

'How come you grew a beard?'

'I got in a fight in a bar and someone cut me with a broken glass. Years ago now.'

'You wouldn't have been happy with me, Halifer.'

'Who cares?' he said.

'I would've been guilty as hell, and I doubt very much he would've let go. He's a lousy loser. He still breaks rackets and you have to work at that these days.'

'If I hadn'ta cared about you, I would've taken you away and there wouldn't have been anything he or you could've done to stop me, could've or would've in your case.'

'Even when you were holding on you were also letting go.'

'You figure?'

'I realise now. Not then.'

'Get out of the car, will you please, Marion, now?'

'I understand you want to hurt me –'

'You don't understand the half of what I want to do to you. To *have done* is more accurate: to have done. Which is just about everything.'

'We don't even have a hotel,' she said.

'You don't have a hotel?'

'Why would we? He can find me at.'

'That's terrible. No *hotel*? That's way, way worse than giving up the love of your life for the sake of a couple of people who drop by a few decades later to say they made a little mistake after all and why don't we all go celebrate?'

'Nobody said anything like that.'

'No hotel,' he said. 'I'm going to leave you here and I'm going to go on home and tell Erica, if she's awake, because she does a lotta lotta sleeping, I'm going to tell her that you never showed. I only wish to Christ it was the truth.'

He was looking at her then, profile and full face all at the same time it seemed to her, and there wasn't anything else she could think to say. He was waiting for her to get out of the car and she did. All she wanted now was that he should say one more thing, no matter what, before he drove away. He drove away.

'What the hell kind of a pet name is Halifer?' she said, because that was what she had wanted to say and he hadn't given her the opportunity.

He drove with the tears running into his beard and working their way jaggedly among the spines and not quite getting through. His face was hot and pouting and only the wet eyes and the redness under them told him, when he looked in the mirror, that he was not deceiving himself about crying. He did not want the tears and he did not feel the pain that they seemed to respond to. He felt the numbness and, from the glances he gave left and right as he hit his own neighbourhood, people might have thought that he was smiling.

He hit Sequoia and turned into Maple and went all the way down the street to the Circle because, after all, that was where he lived and where else would he go? He parked the Honda behind some kind of a municipal truck with a lot of pipes folded onto it and got out and walked across the grass and it was a beautiful evening actually.

'Hey, Halibut!'

The E-type was right in front of the truck and Barnaby Pierce was getting out of it with a victor's smile on his face.

'Beat you to it, against all the odds. What happened to you?'

'Probably not enough,' Hal Pfeiffer said.

'Where's Marion?' Barnaby was bending down to look inside the Honda. 'What happened to Marion?'

'She got out.'

'Got out? Got out where?'

'Somewhere along the line.'

'But where? Why?'

'I told her to. She did.'

'*You told her to?*'

'Yes, and you're making it all worthwhile I did,' Hal said.

Erica, as it happened, was in the front garden. She had a low trolley which Hal had put together for her from an old baby buggy that allowed her to scoot her way along the flower-beds without having to keep bending down. They had spent a lot of money on her back, but it was still no better. There was a deaf-aid in her ear, but she must have switched it off, unless she was being tactful, because she never turned her head when she heard the men.

'Hal, come on, is she inside already or what?'

'She's not inside. I don't know where she is, and I don't care, do I? We got a divorce. She went her way; I went mine. Any business of yours?'

'Hal, where is Marion, please?'

'Somewhere . . .' He waved his hand. 'Unless she's somewhere else, of course.'

'What did you do to her?'

'At what point in our long history is this you want to know about?'

'Or say. Exactly. That she isn't here.'

'I said I loved her and she said she loved me, but that was long ago and far, far away and what I did to her was nothing I want to tell you about quite so much as I want to tell you what she did to me, which might . . .'

'One thing I never figured on,' Barnaby said, 'and that was you having that stupid beard. Did you have a fight?'

'I was really looking forward to this, Barnie, as a matter of fact, before we go any further. This was not . . . in the script for me.'

'This? What is this? Where's Marion, you prize bastard?'

'She's leading an independent life a little bit ahead of schedule. She got out the car.'

'We're on our way to our son's wedding, you jerk. Independent life! I need to find her. She doesn't know this city. Did she get out *voluntarily?*'

'We had said everything we had to say to each other, except goodbye, which we never actually said.'

'You're pretty damn pleased with yourself.'

'I take my pleasures where I can find them.'

'Do you so? Do you so?' Barnaby was nodding vigorously. It was as though he really and truly agreed with what pissed him off so much that he was looking up and down the street not sure if he wanted witnesses or he didn't. 'Should I maybe at least say hullo to Erica?'

'Say anything you feel like saying. She probably won't hear a thing. Much it matters. You made her miserable a quarter of a century ago, so she won't really expect you to make her happy today.'

'*I* made her? Excuse me: *I* made her?'

'You didn't even notice, did you?'

'*Erica?*'

'Was so in love with you . . .'

'Erica never even *liked* me.'

'What's that got to do with anything? You made her so miserable that maybe that's why . . .' Hal indicated what his wife was doing and also what she was not. 'She was so in love with you it hurt, and still hurts.'

'You're lying. You're making this up.'

'Think so? I don't think so. Her therapist neither. That's what I've lived with all these years. Not that . . .'

'Hal, where's Marion? Please.'

Hal did that thing with his face that he always did. 'So now you know it all, if you didn't before.'

'All I know is that you damn near wrecked my marriage. And now – '

'And now I'm wrecking your divorce, is that it?'

'I thought I liked you. I didn't; and I don't. She should've gone away with you. She should've gone the whole way, by which I don't mean . . . because I know all about that – '

'You don't really,' Hal Pfeiffer said. 'She did things with me she said she never did with you.'

'And my guess is, my guess is she wouldn't have ever wanted to think about you again. Instead of which, I was . . . weak. I was weak and frightened and she was . . . sorry for me, which . . .'

'Listen, go dry your eyes someplace else. Get out of my life finally, the pair of you. Because until you showed up, until I got the latest, I at least believed that I had given her up for something that was better, *righter*, than anything she could've had with me. Instead of which . . . oops, sorry! *Sorry!* All I meant to her was someone to rub your nose in, wasn't it?'

'Don't look to me for confirmation of anything, because I don't know anything.'

'She thought you'd married her out of pity.'

'She told you that maybe.'

'After the abortion.'

'She told you plenty, it appears.'

'And that was why I got lucky with my best friend's wife, purely for that reason. I got lucky accordingly with a hot little piece of ass and that's my *whole life* taken care of pretty well, except there's a kicker, isn't there? Because there was one more squeeze to be gotten out of me apparently and up you came to squeeze it. I have a joke for you.'

'I don't need jokes. I have a pension coming up.'

'Guy goes to his doctor and says "Doc . . ." This is one I was going to tell Marion, I was going to tell Nolan this one, but I didn't finally because of one thing and another, he says, no you ought to hear this, "Doc, I have a question, which is this: ten, twenty years ago, when I got a boner and I tried to bend it, and I tried to bend it . . ."'

'Pfeiffer, you are truly pitiful today, do you know that?'

'" . . . I absolutely couldn't, not even with two hands, whereas now, now, when I get one, I can bend it pretty well double just like that. So here's my question: how come I'm so much stronger now than I was ten, twenty years ago?"'

'OK,' Barnaby said. 'And now where's Marion?'

'She was the best I ever had, tell her that even if you don't tell her the joke. She hadn't really loved you so damn much I do declare she'd have sucked it right off one of those times. Is that what you wanted confirmation of? You have it.'

'My old friend,' Barnaby Pierce said, 'who I really, really thought I wanted to see.'

Zara

'Is she there, please?'

'May I ask who's calling?'

'All right, it's her mother.'

'*Zenobia?*' Marion could hear the girl calling and no one answering. 'Hullo?'

'She's not there.'

'She was. She maybe went to get something. Can she call you back someplace?'

'I don't know. How long will she be?'

'Well, there's something *I* don't know, because . . .'

'I'm in a booth,' Marion said. 'In Seattle. Outside Seattle. Truth is, I don't know where I am exactly. Which is why I needed to talk to my daughter.'

'Does it have a number at all, ma'am, where you are?'

'It has a number, but what happens if I give it to you? It's a booth. If you don't know where she is.'

'Maybe she slipped out to the library. But maybe, alternatively, she had a class to teach. I wish I could help you, but . . . she didn't say. Was she expecting you to call?'

'I'll try again later. In a little while. If she comes in, would you tell her that?'

'Are you all right, ma'am?'

'I'm all right. Tell her. She's not to worry. And I'll try again later. Probably. Is she all right?'

'Zenobia? She looked good the last time I saw her, five, ten minutes ago.'

Marion put the phone down and said 'Zenobia' and then she shrugged. What business was it of hers what kind of a name Zara

157

decided she stood for? It seemed sort of daring, and mould-breaking, to have a daughter called Zara after they had had one called Stacey, but was it? And if it was, god*dam*, what did it matter now? She knew it didn't matter and that was why her mind was racing through all the reasons, and the conceivably mistaken notions, which led up to something which couldn't be changed, because Zara was what Zara was. But Zenobia! Was she going to *publish* eventually as Zenobia Pierce? Maybe she was; maybe she should. Funny she chose *Greek* to do, when maybe what had made the name seem sort of brave (a statement!) was that movie *Z. Montand!*

Marion was not going to stay by the telephone, was she? She was already ashamed that she had tried to get Zara, which was more than Zara often did with her. She was even more ashamed about the face she had made when the girl, whoever she was, said that Zara looked good. She was glad that she was alone in the mall, with all kinds of people she could not possibly know and could never know her going up and down the escalators, because that face she made was something she never wanted a witness citing against her, and it surely would have been if anyone knew what brought it about.

What was she going to do? She was not going to panic, if she hadn't panicked already, which she probably had. What was Zara supposed to do? Make up the spare bed? How far was it to Santa Barbara, and what would she do there? Marion knew what had happened: she had been born prematurely, again. She was not ready for what she was supposedly overdue for. She was blue, but she was too old to expect anyone to notice or put her into an incubator and cosset her. Freedom was not supposed to make you frightened, was it? It was not supposed to come over you, like some viral condition, in a suburban mall somewhere inside/outside a city where the only person you knew was someone who actively wished you in hell and – if it wasn't ungrateful to say so, since there were no devils with toasting forks, only lukewarm piped music and plenty of everything – had already dumped you pretty well in it.

Was she hungry? She was thinking about being hungry, because that would give her something she definitely had to do. Everybody has to eat. Meantime, she was thinking about how she could find a way to let Barnaby know that he did not have to worry about her. It was tempting just to keep right on going. Why shouldn't he worry? He should worry; he *chould* worry. Even in his absence – his *welcome* absence, wasn't it? – she was arranging to allude to his little jokes and enrol them in her seductive armoury. Was it seduction or self-protection? What kind of a chameleon did a woman have to be, even now?

After Hal's push, after a prompt that *hard*, it was not easy *not* to keep right on going. But was it Barnaby's fault that she was now sore, and a little frightened (that was what she was sore about, the fear, which curdled freedom)? Whoever the hell's fault it was, she had to think about herself. She had to try. If she went back with him now, even temporarily, because she didn't know where the hell she was or where she should go, if she made contact with him when she was still in that state, how was she ever going to build a life on her own? She couldn't let him see her until she had her story straight. And when she had her story straight, that would be the time when she would see that she didn't need to see him.

But where was he? He did have things she physically needed. OK, she at least had her credit cards and stuff; she could begin again right there and then, but he did have things of hers she would have liked to have, definitely. The next thing she knew, he might cancel her cards. Did he have the right to do that? He had the number to call because she had insisted he be at least *that* responsible. But could he cancel *both* their cards? And if he did, could he cancel her numbers and not his, when they were – weren't they? – the same? How would he pay for his own hotel or gas or anything else? He wasn't going to cancel anything. Why did she experience that as a kind of treason too? Why *too*?

Either way, she did not have to take this one single opportunity or accept that she had blown the whole thing. Hal was incredible; she could not understand why he was doing what he did, but the funny thing was, she had been a little bit grateful, and even excited. He was not the man she remembered loving, or being loved by. Yes, he was too. He was exactly the man who had said that thing about a black man. There was something black about *him* when he was telling her to get out of the car. Implacable? Implacable. What was black about that? Plenty. There was something pitiless that made her glad to have seen the last of him and – admit it! – that made her want to see him again. She knew what it made her want, but she did not quite like to say it to herself (as if someone was listening, and wasn't she?) and that was: she knew precisely what she wanted. She wanted, but not really, to make him think that she was coming, that she was really coming, and then not say 'Oh no' (had she *really* done that?) but pretend to be, until the moment when he thought she was there, and then not be. That was precisely what she wanted, but not really.

There were not a lot of black men in the mall, or black women. There were almost no black women. Why did other people always know where they were going? She stood at the top of the escalator (it was always a *little* bit tempting to ride on up, wasn't it?) and everybody knew exactly what their destination was, even without looking at the store guide on the tilted slab with the gold letters behind the tinted glass. All the usual stores were there. You drove all the way across the country and you hadn't gone anyplace in particular at all. Barnie was right about that.

Barnaby wanted her to be the one. That was always his strategy. If they went on holiday, she decided where and then she had to do the packing and have the tickets. He'd say, 'Do you have the tickets?' as if that was the least thing she could do, as if she hadn't already, as he knew full well, done most everything else too. There was always a rush job he had to do when they were about to go anywhere or do anything and it was always the money from *that* was going to pay for the trip, regardless of what was already in the bank. Being too busy to help had to be something forced on him which he would sooner not have happened, when he had ten-to-one fixed for it to happen. There was nothing so terrible in that and she had never said there was, but no one was going to tell her that it wasn't true.

He might just get back in the car and head straight on down to

LA. Was he capable of a thing like that? Imagine Hal being as big a sonofabitch as he was certainly proved capable of being! Imagine that he was that vindictive. How much imagination were we talking about here? He *was* that vindictive. Imagine a man who had been in bed with her, been in love with her, been in her, and said that he would never never forget her, throwing her out of his car like that. He had loved her, he said, and she had . . . done all kinds of things with him that made her ashamed. Ashamed was silly; ashamed was true. What had they done that lovers didn't do? They were lovers and those were things that lovers did. Lovers did not forgive each other as well as not forget each other, and he had proved that all right. What was shameful was wishing – *almost* wishing – that Barnie had been there to see them. Love is Blue? She didn't really remember that one. She remembered it being around, but she didn't remember *it*.

She couldn't help it; the thought never quite left her that she had been punished. When what happened to Christopher happened, she thought right away of Hal. She didn't blame him and she didn't blame herself, she just thought: that was it, that did it. For years after Christopher, right up until she actually did it (because Barnie said do it), she wanted to call Hal. One time, she literally wrestled with herself before she didn't; she was alone and Barnaby was being heroically funny on the second series of whatever it was, but it wasn't to say that she loved him that she wanted to call. *Bimbo*? *The Stinkinsons*? And all that time Barnaby was being busy and funny as usual and she had told him to go on being busy and funny if he could; it was all right, they still had the other three, didn't they? Ha!

She had wanted to call Hal and say what? Tell him that she blamed herself and have him say that that was stupid? It was stupid, and also true; truth was stupidity, stupidity truth. Barnaby wanted it to be something to do with the damn car; he wanted to believe that Christopher wouldn't have had an accident in a car that went twice as fast as the Chevvy and was notoriously slithery on icy roads like the one that went down from Aspen, that Chris never got to take. Wasn't *that* stupid? And not true probably.

They left the Chevvy in the lot in the motel and never went to get it or have anybody get it. The manager wrote a few times and they never answered. Barnaby got so damn mad with the very polite letters the hotel wrote that he used to scrunch them up and jump up and down on them. She wanted to laugh but she didn't because she couldn't.

She went back down the escalator. She was not going to spend the evening in the mall, was she? It was not a gesture of independence to be marooned in a mall. Neither was it a sign of weakness to intend very seriously not to wait until Security was asking her whether she knew they were closing up and where her car was. She was playing hide-and-seek without being sure that there were any other players. Grown people didn't do that.

'Zara, that you?'

'Mother! I'm sorry! What's happening?'

'The silliest possible thing. I probably shouldn't have called you.'

'I've been so worried ever since Serena gave me your message.'

'Serena! Of course. I told her to say it was nothing to worry about.'

'She did. That guarantees you worry. You know that.'

'Not intentionally. I'm fine. What's happened is, I'm marooned in a mall.'

'Excuse me?'

'That's right. In or around Seattle, where I got left. Not by your father. By someone else.'

'You're not together.'

'We weren't at the time. So . . . I'm by myself in this mall, which is huge, which is like *gigantic*, and I need your advice. I'm on another planet. No one knows where I am. Me included.'

'You want me to beam you down, is that it?'

'If you can.'

'What are daughters for?'

'All I need is to ask you – How's the Greek?'

'This is the nature of your inquiry? The Greek. The Greek is fine.'

'I threw that in. To make you aware that this is not an emergency.'

'Just a routine call from another planet in or around Seattle where you happen to be marooned. As a consequence of what exactly?'

'All right: I had a lover. A long time ago.'

'OK. But . . .? And? Which? *Both? Both.*'

'And I just saw him again, after over twenty-something years.'

'Before I was born.'

'Correct.'

'He's not my father, is he?'

'I told you, this had nothing to do with Barnaby.'

'Mother . . . what are you telling me here?'

'Who isn't your father?'

'Your lover, you're not about to tell me that he's my natural father, are you, and that's why I don't have fair hair and a great figure like Stace's? That's why I'm kinda dumpy and ill-favoured but with lots and lots of personality and, better, application? Because, as everybody agrees, do I have application, and do I need to!'

'Zara, I don't know what you're talking about.'

'Then I must be close to home. I must be *hot as toast*; remember how you used to say that when we were looking for Easter eggs?'

'Zara, I need your advice.'

'Is this a postponement we have in being here? You decided to tell me something and now you've had second thoughts.'

'You're way way off, way way way. I'm calling to ask you, because I needed to ask someone . . .'

'Flattering! That's flattering.'

'Zara, please. Your father was not in the same car as me when this man . . .'

'Your lover.'

'Ex-lover. Very ex.'

'Who may well be my father. Who *is* my father?'

'I don't know where that idea came from. No. If you think you're not your father's daughter you must be deranged.'

'Why don't I look like Stacey?'

'Sisters don't always look like each other. I don't look like Vanessa.'

'You look just like Vanessa. Until she married Calvin you did. And if you don't, who's to say that she *is* your sister?'

'That's ridiculous: of course Vanessa is my sister. And you're Stacey's. As if I'd ever had a child with anyone except Barnaby!'

'People do. All the time. And they deny they do all the time. From way back. Look at Oedipus. Look at Moses.'

'Zara, what do I do now, please? Is why I called you.'

'You're going to do what I say you should do?'

'I didn't say that.'

'No. You were all by yourself and you needed somebody you could say no to when they said what you should do. You need Daddy.'

'I want to clear something up before we go any further: Hal *was* my lover . . .'

'And that was something that you suddenly had to call one of your children long distance to tell them because you've been in denial for *centuries* on the matter of fidelity and what Daddy means to you and this was the one time you *had* time and so here we are.'

'It's not that at all. In the least.'

'That's for the doctor to decide. And she's decided.'

'That's not what you're a doctor of.'

'But I've still decided. "In the least" is always a lie. That's a rule of thumb it's always safe to go by, and that's no lie whatsoever.'

'Zara, don't do this.'

'This is what she does, Mrs Pierce. This guy, he pushed you out of the car, was it like *moving*? Is he a gangster or something?'

'He's the editor of a newspaper. A bigger newspaper than I ever thought. He got mad and dumped me. Your father was supposed to be following us . . .'

'An *editor*? Like *the* editor, or *an* editor?'

'He's the editor of the *Herald-Examiner* I think it's called.'

'Meaning you know damn well. What was he when . . .'

'He was your father's best friend.'

'Your emphasis. What else?'

'I'm not emphasising a damn thing. I'm being truthful . . .'

'Which is a new experience for you.'

'Zara, this is your mother you're talking to. When did I lie to you? Don't say those things. I'm all alone here. I need to know what to do.'

'I'm sorry.'

'Well, OK. Let's get one thing perfectly straight. There has never been the smallest doubt in my mind who your father was.'

'In the least?'

'In the least.'

'Gotcha. But never mind, never *mind*! Never mind. What are you going to do?'

'Is my question to you.'

'Is he small and dark and smart?'

'Excuse me?'

'Whatsisname. Hal, is he?'

'He's bald,' Marion said, 'and he has a beard. You don't, do you?'

'He's small and dark and probably smart; editors can be.'

'He's average. Possibly a little above. A little above.'

'Thanks, Mother.'

'For what?'

'Average. A little above.'

'Nobody ever called you average.'

'And I'm not a little above *much*, am I now?'

'*Zenobia*? Since when is this?'

'Chelsea called me it and it stuck.'

'It would. It's sticky. Chelsea is who?'

'You know her as Serena.'

'She called herself Serena, when I called before.'

'That was for your sake. Station identification. She calls herself Chelsea up here now.'

'That was such a terrible movie.'

'*The Chelsea Girls*? It was also seminal.'

'I was thinking of something else.'

'Are you feeling better now, Mother?'

'I'm fine. You talked me down. I knew you would. Seminal?'

'Because like early next week I have things I have to do, like teach a class, and getting ready to teach one comes first.'

'Lucky class. If, *if* you were in my situation, i.e. in a mall somewhere outside a city you don't know, and you needed, supposing you did, to at least make contact with your husband, who has all your things in the car with him, and you didn't know how to get a hold of him, what would you do? That is my question. And why I called.'

'This is the Hal Pfeiffer that Daddy talks about all the time, am I right? Evidently.'

'How many are there? All the time?'

'At least I called him "Daddy" in there, in case you didn't notice. Looks like I too am back on boring planet earth. Do you have money?'

'Yes, I do. In the sense . . .'

'For a cab.'

'For a cab I have money.'

'You have Hal's address?'

'I'm not going there.'

'It was heavy?'

'It wasn't *that* heavy necessarily, but I'm not going to his house.'

'You could call his house.'

'I could, but what good would it do?'

'Maybe Daddy is there. Maybe both of my daddies are sitting in the same room drinking beer from the bottle. Not the same one, but . . . What do you think?'

'I don't see Barnaby sitting with Hal anywhere drinking anything.'

'You could call and find out. But you won't do that. You won't do that because you're too proud, Miss Pouter.'

'What did you call me?'

'You know that's what we used to call you. Christopher called you that first.'

'Christopher called me Miss Pouter?'

'When you used to gather yourself up and say "Now that's *enough*!" You're doing it now, aren't you? Sort of gathering yourself up like a pigeon. I can see you.'

'*Chris* called me that? I don't believe you.'

'He loved you. He loved it. He tried to provoke you so he could call you that. We used to giggle and try not to. Hands over our mouths. Where did you go that you met this editor in the first place?'

'We were all friends back East.'

'I mean like today. Where did you go to get in his car and where was Daddy?'

'Oh, OK: we went to his office and . . .'

'Go back there.'

'He isn't there. We were on the way to his house and Daddy was supposed to be following and . . . *Miss Pouter*?'

'Whoa, OK? It was a *character*; you were two people and one of them was Miss Pouter who . . . swelled up and pouted. Here's what you do, maybe, you go back to the newspaper office and you wait in the lobby. Better, you call up to Hal's office and get her to help you. There's always a her and she's always helpful and very resourceful, because if she wasn't she wouldn't last a minute with any editor I ever heard of. You wait there and let her organise the rescue party, which she surely will. Alternatively . . .'

'What?'

'Alternatively, think of a better idea, because I'm . . . about done here. You're coming to the wedding, aren't you?'

'If I can find a way out of Seattle, I am.'

'You go to the airport and you book a ticket. You have your credit cards, don't you?'

'Unless he's cancelled them. What's so funny?'

'Who's "he"? Daddy? Is he likely to cancel your credit cards for being pushed out of a car by Hal Pfeiffer? Come on! All else fails, and it won't, it certainly won't, you get a cab to the airport and you fly on down to LA and you call Benjamin in Burbank – you heard about the new job, right? – and he tells you which hotel to go to and you go there and you have your hair done and you come to the wedding, which is still happening you may be surprised to hear. I'll be the dumpy kid with the glasses and the personality you wouldn't believe. Goodbye, Mother.'

'Zara.'

'I thought you might say that.'

'You seriously think I should go to the editor's office?'

'No, Mother, I'm putting you on. I think you should right now sever all contact with people you normally call or see and begin a life of daytime dissolution and regular night classes and stay in Seattle until you're young enough to make contact once again with everyone who has stood in the way of your developing your full potential as a woman. That's what I *really* think you should do and never ever will.'

'Miss Pouter,' Marion said.

What Happened

'I tell you, I almost didn't come back. I never figured you'd be here.'

'I didn't know what else to do, where else to go.'

'I figured maybe it was providential. Or you'd take it to be, and I'd never see you again.'

'No such luck, huh? What happened to you in the first place?'

'Which was the first place? Which first place?'

'You were supposed to be following us.'

'Oh then! I stopped for a couple of girls. That can take longer than you imagine at my age.'

'I don't need to imagine.'

'They were very pretty,' Barnaby said, 'and I took my eye off the ball. Next thing I knew, you and Hal were in the motel.'

'Barnaby, could we possibly . . .?'

'Am I in serious trouble here? I thought this was shining armour I was wearing, but is it hell! Did I do something wrong? I went to Hal's house eventually and I waited, because you weren't there yet.'

'I was never there.'

'As I discovered. But since you were both in the same car, so far as I knew . . . At first, I was kinda amused that I got to Hal's house before he did. And then I wasn't, for reasons we don't need to go into. I waited in the car and he drove up and you weren't with him and, what with one thing and another, we proceeded to exchange extremely frank views on a range of topics. Quite a narrow range actually, but a range. He seemed *immeasurably* sore about something and, it quickly emerged, incurably too. What did you do to him, *bite*?'

'I think I said something about Erica, seemed to . . .'

'You and me both,' Barnaby said.

'And finally, which did not take very long, he pushed me out of the car.'

'That's incredible. I believe it. I believe anything. You know what he told me?'

'You found each other!'

'Oh, Lynn,' Marion said, 'you've been so kind! You remember Lynn, Barnaby, don't you?'

'Lynn, how are you?'

'Is there anything else I can do for you?'

'There is if you want there to be and that is, maybe not tell Mr Pfeiffer, OK, *everything*.'

'Darling . . .'

'I don't mean for our sakes. Our sakes are not likely to matter very much. I was thinking of Lynn.'

'You tell him whatever you want,' Barnaby said.

'I didn't want Hal to be sore with Lynn is what I was thinking.'

'As long as you're both OK now,' Lynn said.

'Don't give us another thought, Lynn,' Barnaby said.

'I think I'd like to get out of this building now, Barnaby, if that's all right with you.'

'You know something? For a fat moment back there, you were really pleased to see me. I mean, you were *pleased*. I just thought I'd read that one into the record, even if it never gets into the final draft.'

'I was relieved. I needed my things from the car. I'm not about to set up *house* in Seattle, am I, just because . . .?'

'Never set up anything in a city with a hostile editor. What exactly pissed him off?'

'Twenty-some years of frustration probably. He doesn't sleep with her any more. He hasn't since . . . a long time.'

'There must be other opportunities. Lynn?'

'He goes to Portland. He has this call-girl, once every six months or so.'

'That's kind of pitiful. You must be pleased.'

'I think it's as near as he can come to not existing at all. Why pleased?'

'Evidently it's you or nothing.'

'He has a hernia. Was the first thing he told me.'

'Everybody does.'

'You don't, any more.'

'A hernia or a scar. You know why men have hernias more than women do, *much* more?'

'It's nice to see the car again, I have to say that.'

'It's a nice car. And I won't push you out of it. Not until you want me to.'

'Why do they?'

'Are we leaving town or what are we doing? It's kinda late.'

'We can find somewhere along the way.'

'You seriously considered splitting, didn't you? Why didn't you finally?'

'We haven't got to finally yet.'

'"Tell him your plans", remember that one? How you make God smile. Great, great joke. It's because in the embryonic phase, a male's testicles descend through the wall of the abdomen before taking up residence in the scrotal region. It happens before birth but it has consequences for ever. Men are weaker than women on that as well as on other counts. And on the Anatomy Show *next* week . . .'

'I think I knew,' Marion said, 'about that. What did he tell you? You went to Hal's house and that didn't go too well, you said. He told you something.'

'Did you ever think she was in love with me?'

'Did I ever . . .? No. Erica? *No*. Was she?'

'He says that I ruined her life because she was madly in love with me. You don't have to laugh; my living doesn't depend on this. You don't have to laugh that hard.'

'I'm not laughing at that,' she said.

'It's Woody, is it, you're laughing at? When those old bombs finally go off . . .'

'You may not want to hear this.'

'In those circumstances, when did you ever wait to tell me?'

'If you knew . . .'

'I'd kill you? I'd love you?'

'He used to say how wonderful it would be if you and Erica . . . came to something.'

'Wonderful. That's what he used to say when? While waiting to calm down and slip quietly out of his lover's *lap*?'

'Boy! And to think I was glad to see you again.'

'You want to get your things out the trunk and be on your way? I can pull up. I won't push you. You tell me when you want to stop and that's what we'll do. And now he's decided that what he wished had happened really did happen and Erica, who actually despised me more than somewhat, secretly had the kinds of hots for me that scorched her panties.'

'It's possible. Maybe that was what he was trying to tell me.'

'Now or in the past? Erica never looked at me, to my knowledge, once things started happening between you and him, without a look of total disdain. She once even told me I was pitiful for letting you get away with it.'

'Which side is that evidence for, when you come to think about it?'

'I thought of it. I thought of it out of rage against you. And him. I thought of it because I used to lie there listening for the kids and I'd be fantasising I was over at her house doing all kinds of things to her, but it didn't have to be *her*, except to the degree that she was married to him.'

'In other words, you'd be doing them to him.'

'*For* him. Against him. It had nothing to do with wanting Erica whatsoever. It was a coward's fantasy and I mind admitting it.'

'You're not a bad man, are you, Barnaby?'

'And you can't quite forgive me, can you?'

'You'd like that to be so, because what would that make me?'

'Nothing too different from what you are, would it? So what did you do? When you weren't at the *Herald-Examiner*.'

'Did you ever hear Christopher call me "Miss Pouter?"'

'Christopher?'

'Was he to your knowledge in the habit of calling me Miss Pouter from time to time, if not more frequently?'

'Miss *Pouter*?'

'He was.'

'Was he?'

'Or why are you laughing?'

'Or? I'm laughing because . . . I never thought of that before.'

'You didn't think of it now.'

'Miss Pouter is fabulous.'

'Is it?'

'Want me to stop right here? You asked me.'

'You didn't have to . . . *laugh*.'

'Chris used to call you that?'

'They all did apparently. I was recently informed.'

'Yeah? How recently?'

'I called Zara.'

'How is she?'

'She's Zenobia.'

'That's OK then. And she told you this? Like today? How come you had occasion to call Zara?'

'I didn't know what to do.'

'And she did?'

'She talked me through a few things, a few scenarios.'

'She put it on a page and a half for you, did she? I wouldn't mind if I never had to do that again in my whole life.'

'You don't have to, but you will.'

'And one of these scenarios involved telling you that the kids used to call you Miss Pouter? You delved deep. But you need an idea; that can happen.'

'It just came out. I think she wanted to hurt me. Did you know?'

'Zenobia! If I had, and I'd known it would hurt you, would I have kept it to myself all these years? I had no idea. I can see why though, if that's any good to you.'

'*Good*? I don't pout.'

'You swell up. You bristle. You become . . . an authority.'

'Like a pigeon.'

'Very like a pigeon, without the feathers. Usually. I have seen you with feathers . . .'

'Stop it, Barnaby, please stop it.'

'Come on, Marion, you don't want to cry.'

'I never want to cry when I cry. Want to cry! You bastard.'

'I know what you want to have happen because it always does and you know it does.'

'They never even liked me,' she said.

'They loved you and you know it.'

'You can't love Miss Pouter. Write a book in which *anyone* loves Miss Pouter.'

'They loved Jean Brodie, didn't they? I didn't, but they did. You did. They were kids.'

'And you didn't know?'

'I was working.'

'I bet you wish you were working now. We're going to be out of Kleenex.'

'Some people stop for gas, we stop for Kleenex. Boats against the current, us.'

'You are a bastard, aren't you?'

'How was Zara?'

'What do you mean?'

'What do I mean, how was Zara? Zenobia. How complex a question is that?'

'She suddenly got the idea that Hal was her natural father.'

'Are you a total bitch or what?'

'What kind of a reaction is that?'

'It's the reaction . . . are you seriously asking me that question? "She suddenly got the idea"? You mean by that that you put it into her head. You called and told her that. Is it true?'

'Of course it isn't true.'

'They can run tests. If we can get hold of some of Hal's blood. Or maybe his sperm. Does he still *have* sperm?'

'Cheap. Zara is your daughter and you know it and if you don't, I'm telling you. Unequivocally.'

'Great adverb. Great. Figures on my twenty best list, year in year out. Unequivocally.'

'I know what you're doing, Barnaby. You're making a play, aren't you, for me?'

'Can you think why?'

'Because until you've got me again, you don't want to lose me. Am I right?'

'Could you be wrong? Miss Pouter is just wonderful.'

'No, it's not. Barnaby, it's not, OK? I'm going to wish I never told you.'

'Are you ever? Are you ever!'

'I called Zara for her advice and, that one thing aside, she was very supportive.'

'You must've hated that.'

'What did you do?'

'What did I do?'

'You went to a bookshop.'

'Did I?'

'What did you do?'

'I drove around a little bit.'

'And then?'

'What would you like the truth to be? Looking for these two chicks who had given me the eye. Just the one, but it was a beauty. And I didn't find them.'

'You found me.'

'But not for – what? – two, three hours, did I? And you hadn't been there too long, to judge from Lynn, so where were you meanwhile?'

'What did you think and why did you go back to Hal's office finally?'

'I thought I'd let you suffer some and I thought you'd certainly let *me* suffer some.'

'No.'

'These are my thoughts, Miss P., and you have no right of veto.'

'Don't call me that, Barnaby, please. Please, don't. But then what made you . . .?'

'I figured that you'd probably, on balance, eventually but unequivocally . . .'

'Barnaby . . .'

'. . . want your things. Which you did. So I then wondered which square square one would be, and the *Herald-Examiner* was like the only one in town.'

'Like I always do.'

'Home base is home base, wherever it is. So I thought I was damned if I would be there when you got there, but I guessed where it would be, and it was, and I was.'

'Why were you?'

'Because I like to think about being a shit – like I thought about the things that Erica might deserve to have done to her – but that's about as far as my shittiness goes, on the whole and in practice.'

'You're a nice man.'

'Dr Jekyll always was. Did you buy anything? While you were in the mall, did you make any purchases?'

'I had a sandwich.'

'But you left most of it.'

'Yes, I did.'

'I was thinking of her. I mean, shouldn't we give something specifically to her?'

'I'm going to give her that ruby ring my grandmother had.'

'Are rubies OK as wedding presents? That's a nice idea. I'd love a ruby wedding present when I get married but . . . isn't there some kind of a . . .?'

'I don't think so. She has black hair. She should look good with a ruby ring.'

'Is she still called Imogen?'

'Of course she is, why wouldn't she be?'

'Zenobia,' Barnaby said. 'I'm glad to see you again, Sweets. I'm sorry to say.'

'I'm glad to hear you call me that again.'

'Funny about names,' he said. 'You find that with characters: the Networks always want them to have amazing names – not memorable characters or ideas or personalities, just memorable names. Names are personalities these days. Have you noticed something else?'

'What did you do?'

'The first names at least used to be easy, but now they're getting so they're more difficult to remember than last names. Vy vould zis be so? I will tell you vy: because in our culture, to use a reckless overstatement, we use first names so much more than last ones that we *have* to have striking and original ones. I mean, who is Joan or George today?'

'For three hours.'

'I drove around some, because I had an idea that if I went straight to where you were, and found you there, which would be logical, that would prove something. That we were . . . still wired psychically, so I went to a local mart and we evidently weren't.'

'Which annoyed you.'

'Which annoyed me. Which gave me the feeling that you were deliberately making yourself unavailable, so I drove into town, thinking all the time that I should be heading on down to California. I wanted to and, if it hadn't been that we're going to this wedding, I maybe might've, but how was I going seriously to arrive in LA and explain how you weren't with me? There are always practicalities in my life. No one else's: only mine. So I decided to punish you and hang around.'

'That was my punishment, for what?'

'What've you got?'

'You did too go to a bookshop.'

'OK,' he said, 'I went to a Pussycat Theater.'

'A Pussycat Theater?'

'I went to a porno house.'

'You never did.'

'I did a few times and I did again. Sure I did.'

'*Why?*'

'To see movies of people having sex. No, actually, to be accurate, to see movies of girls having sex. I have never been interested – and we won't analyse this – in seeing men having sex, although people who make porno pictures, except the lesbian ones, always think that's what men want to see. I don't imagine they cater too much for female audiences, although there were a coupla women in the audience. The great thing about porno houses is, number one, they are never, in my experience, crowded and, number two, which follows, is no one comes sits near you and no one *ever* talks during the picture. The other thing which is interesting, is that it is always quite exciting when you walk in there – the primal scene, I guess – and then, after quite a short time, you begin to feel a little foolish and then a little bored and then quite contemptuous, and yet at the same time *relieved*, lonely. No: alone, and yet, OK, comforted . . . is what I feel, more than stimulated, unless . . . You asked me what I did.'

'You seriously . . .'

'Have you never really been to one of those places?'

'How would I go to one of those places?'

'You have a car, you have feet.'

'And why?'

'Curiosity. Desire. What do I know about why you'd do something?'

'Unless what you were about to tell me.'

'It doesn't matter. Unless they show a movie that's been made, OK, *seriously*. Dare I say with art? Nearly always, they're kind of jokey. Maybe because that's the only way the performers can get themselves to believe they're not . . . betraying something.'

'You're a puritan, Barnaby, deep down.'

'I don't think I necessarily *go* deep down. There was one movie in the show . . .'

'How many did you see?'

'They're never too long, and it was made with skill anyway. Knowledge of what voyeurism is really about, i.e. what the audience wants and doesn't want, which is, above all not to be ashamed of itself.'

'Meaning they usually are?'

'Or I usually am. You want there to be a secret, something unrevealed, something terrible somewhere, at the point where pleasure and – no, not pain – *ritual* converge.'

'You never told me you went to one before.'

'Why would I tell you? I probably wouldn't tell you, would I normally?'

'If you weren't angry with me.'

'I'm not angry.'

'If you weren't what with me? Because why tell me now? Because you're sore with me.'

'You always know the answers, you could spare me the questions. I am not sore. You want the truth? I wanted to be possibly. Sore. I don't deny it. You and Hal got into that car and . . .'

'You wanted me to go with him.'

'I thought you wanted to.'

'You wanted me to go with him, Barnaby. You would've been disappointed, and impossible, if I hadn't of gone with him.'

'I don't deny it. It was like being back then. It was like I hadn't changed, even if I was driving a fancier automobile than we had then. Like being young again. You don't want to hear this.'

'You're totally mistaken.'

'In those days, when you were with him, when I knew you were with him, I never imagined, tried imagining, the two of you. It hurt too much. That's OK. I know I wasn't supposed to be jealous. You told me not to be. That was meant to be a kindness on your part, or was it? Maybe it was a deprivation. Even that little luxury was something I wasn't to raid the icebox for. Maybe it was just you exercising all the power you could, which was pretty well limitless just then. You can purse your lips all you like.'

'I was just trying to tell you that . . .'

'This was something that didn't concern me. OK. Even now, if you want the truth – and it's very, very clear you don't – I don't *really* believe that you fucked Hal Pfeiffer. Not really, really fucked him. And by not really believing . . .'

'Go ahead. Go ahead.'

'. . . I mean that I never dared to visualise it. No: never *managed* to visualise it. I could never make a blue movie I could run convincingly in my head in which he was actually in you, even in the most natural possible position . . . Let alone . . .'

'OK,' she said.

'It's so nice to be able to embarrass you.'

'I'm not embarrassed. I'm . . .'

'Yeah?'

179

'Listening. I'm listening. I'm . . . being educated here. About you. So?'

'So?'

'You did what? You went to porno houses.'

'Now you want to despise me. No, I did not. When he told me that about Erica – that she was supposedly in love with me – that made me realise something, which was that what I wanted to do to her when I knew he was with you was like my own . . . *that* I *did* visualise, very specifically at times, and yet I felt nothing, *nothing*, for Erica personally, in the flesh, even though it was unquestionably her, and no one else, I had these fantasies about.'

'You imagined her instead of us.'

'You saying "us" like that, Sweets, you can't imagine how that still goes through me. After all this time. Makes me want to kill you, and keep you for ever, so I can keep doing it.'

'You ought to be happy,' she said, 'I ruined that poor bastard's life.'

'We did,' he said.

'Which should give you some quiet satisfaction.'

'Was I being quiet about it? As a matter of fact, but only after thinking about it, it seems pitiful to me. To have taken so much trouble confounding – that's a nice word rarely used in prime-time dialogue – *confounding* somebody who wasn't really worth the expenditure involved.'

'Expenditure?'

'Energy, imagination, *thought*. Expenditure. I mean, the guy is probably fine when he's not being exposed to . . . I *understand* what threw him and I guess it was tactless of us to . . .'

'*Tactless!* It was brutal. I didn't realise how brutal it was, but seems you did. You talked me slap bang into it, right?'

'Slap, bang! That covers a lot of it. I never consciously foresaw any of it. I thought I was being generous. I even thought maybe you and he . . . because, truth to tell, I blanked Erica totally out of the equation. I knew she still existed, because we hadn't heard any different, but I assumed that she was going to be, OK, negligible finally. You want me to tell you something despicable, because that'll seem credible? I maybe, *maybe*, thought I'd make myself young again by going back to the crossroads; I thought I'd be the age I was when I was hurting.'

'You're really something, Barnaby.'

'Think so? Check my credits.'

'Because I can see where this is leading, with the kids, with everyone: I wrecked your life and I wrecked your marriage. Barnaby Pierce, saint and martyr.'

'Think so?'

'*You* think so. I missed out hypocrite, naturally, because I know you will.'

'I never made the claim and don't talk that way to me, please, as if someone else was here agreeing with you and you were appealing to him. Let's not be doing some things, shall we, here, before – ?'

'When are we going to do those things?'

'In any kind of a marriage, there are things you don't do which are part of what you do, which are *positively* not done. Not doing something *is* doing something.'

'Spend the afternoon in a porno house and listen to him!'

'Don't call me a hypocrite, please, Marion, OK? The hypocrite went to a bookstore. They're full of shit and you know it; in some ways – and this isn't something we're going to elaborate on – porno movies are the most honest form of art there is in this country.'

'Upfront,' she said. 'The most upfront. As you might say.'

'At times. Is a thesis I could defend.'

Silence came over them. They had been talking and then they were not talking and Barnaby was driving and Marion was looking at the scenery as if she were pretending to look at it. He was aware of her knees and after a while she moved them slightly, but very together, towards the door her side. The shine of light on them made it seem as if they might have been sensitive to Barnaby's glance and had shied from it. Marion's head stayed in the exact same place.

Finally he said, 'Would you care to drive?'

'I don't like to drive this car,' she said. 'You know that. And you don't like me to drive it. I haven't touched a stick shift in years. You know that too.'

'I'm a positive fountain of knowledge,' he said.

'Thank you for being there,' she said.

'That comes out like it was a bone in your throat you managed to dislodge finally.'

'We ought to call Mrs Biebel,' she said.

'*Ought to?* I don't feel the compulsion or the obligation.'

'You hung up on her.'

'I know I did. I don't like her.'

'She's trying to sell the house.'

'Do you sense a link possibly? I just might go back and live in that damned house.'

'Yes? Do it.'

'I love that house as a matter of fact.'

'Paula would be very happy.'

'Paula means nothing to me, whatever you say.'

'Unless I'm around.'

'I'm afraid that's it. And so do you love it.'

'Yes, I do. Did. So who has to be around for me to matter?'

'You're different."

'Neither did Erica, right? That you made movies with.'

'You're jumping and you're also . . .'

'Not really. You'd really like to have sex with a woman that didn't mean anything to you. You might even prefer it.'

'Either you're stupid or you're playing with me, and you're not stupid. So you know very well that what I said about Erica, and what Paula, OK, actually was, was all about you. If you're not there, or threatening to be there, Paula would be more a deterrent than a lure. Much more. I don't want to make her happy. And in Erica's case at least, I never wanted to have sex with her in any practical sense.'

'You wanted to rape her is what you wanted to do.'

'Not even quite that. Brutalise her without hurting her, would be the truth, if I was insane enough to tell it.'

'I was no different from any other woman.'

'Would be very convenient, if it were true. Which makes it true for you. But not for me. You were all the women in the world.'

'I don't think so.'

'He'll always be around, that sonofabitch, and you know it. He pushed you out, you'll never push him out, and he knows it. You think things change, but do they? *Can* they?'

'Nobody else thinks like you do.'

'Nobody else fucks like you do is what we all believe, until we see they do, give or take a reel or two. Is that depressing or is it reassuring? Both, of course. *And* it makes no real difference to anything. What was the guy's name in *Psycho*?'

'The guy's name in *Psycho*.'

'Norman. He had a motel; we could use one. The woods made me think of him. *Bates*?'

'"That kid gets no tip from me."'

'Right. The joke trumps the real thing, and the real thing was a joke too.'

'Because it wasn't real.'

'Which brings us back to marriage, doesn't it?'

'I wanted to be strong enough to walk away right then and I wasn't. It was a humiliation, Barnaby, really.'

'I didn't do a thing. If that's not enough to make you hate me for ever, what is?'

'Not hate.'

'Resent.'

'Is nearer the truth possibly. Resent intermittently. You know what we need?'

'A meal, a bottle of good red wine and a warm room to be grouchy in.'

'You want to be the good guy, don't you, *so much* in this?'

'I'm the only guy. Which imposes quite a strain. I have to play all the parts. It's OK, that's the bit I really like quite a bit.'

'You don't have to tell me,' she said.

'You want me to dump you in the woods?'

'I already got dumped. That's not remotely funny.'

'There's always a temptation, especially at this point in the proceedings, to prove you can do something that no one thinks you can. Look at Tolstoy.'

'Really?'

'Because he got up off his deathbed just to prove to his wife what a disaster their marriage had been. The same guy who wrote *Anna Karenina*, in which his character, Levin, was so shy he couldn't even *say* what he felt about the same girl who . . .'

'Maybe he couldn't say it because what he said wasn't what he felt. He knew all along it couldn't ring true.'

'Sincerity,' Barnaby said, 'how often does it?'

'Sincerity,' she said. 'Isn't the thing about sincerity that it always misses something out?'

'Which is?'

'Something you know about: the dark side, the unsaid. It leaves that out, which is fine, but pretends it doesn't. Sincerity is a form of politics, not of feeling, if you ask me.'

'Did I ever tell you I really admired you? I really admire you.'

'And what does that do to you in the desire department?'

'Plenty, and I'll tell you why, because – that's the dividend of this, whatever it is – desire is a way of – do you want to hear this?'

'Beats Highway Information,' she said.

'And by what score?'

'Of course I want to hear it.'

'Because desire enjoys doing things to admiration. I can't put it better than that, but then I haven't been paid to. Desire equalises.'

'Male desire does more than equalise. Male desire does things to equality, even when it pretends not to, even when it's being . . . subservient. Or sincere, you might say.'

'You never trusted me, even in bed.'

'That's what I liked,' she said.

'You made me up, Marion. I guess any wise person would.'

'And what did you do with me?'

'Thought how lucky I was. How lucky and what a thief. How about that? My own wife. You were something a little bit, not

entirely, illicit. Imagine if that was what Prohibition had prohib-
ited! I'm tired; I think we should stop.'

'This?'

'Stop, as in for the night. It's been a funny, funny day.'

'And what effect will that have on the night?'

'That's true,' he said.

'Bearing in mind that you went to the movies,' she said, 'and I
didn't.'

Welcome to LA

They were waiting to check in, when this voice said, 'Barnaby Pierce, can it seriously be?'

'Gary!'

'You're still *working*?'

'Low guy, low blow. Have you heard something I haven't?'

'What are producers for?'

'They've finally discovered something? My wife, Marion, whom I don't believe you ever met except on the telephone. Gary Pereira I used to work with. Once.'

'Marion, how are you? You look great.'

'Gary produced a pilot Stan and I did back in the old days. That never lived to fly.'

'Crash and burn. Can be a living sometimes. I'll tell you something funny.'

'There's always a first time, Gary. Sometimes.'

'Seriously, are you out here on an assignment?'

'For tax purposes we are. The bagel has landed. Our son is getting married end of the week.'

'For tax purposes? Do you want to have some coffee? We could go to the coffee shop and have some coffee.'

'We haven't checked in yet.'

'So?'

'We can't put it on the room.'

'I invited you to coffee, would I stiff you?'

'You've changed?'

'When did I ever stiff you?'

'Then how about that final payment on *Sherlock Holmes, Sniffer Dog*?'

'Barnaby, I'd really like to get our room straight and go on up, so . . .'

'Excuse me, excuse me, Mrs Pierce: I'm being very thoughtless. Goes with the territory. I said it before he did.'

'No, no, it's just that we just came a long way and – '

'He was being very thoughtless. Tell you what, Gary, give me your number.'

'And you can take great pleasure in not calling me.'

'You don't have any deals?'

'I have deals.'

'Why wouldn't I call? Because you only work with quality writers. Suddenly.'

'You two guys go and have coffee and fun,' Marion said, 'and I'll check us in and go on up to the room and . . .'

'Come on down and join us when you're ready,' Gary Pereira said. 'Coffee and fun. I like that. If only we could.'

'You still have the smile,' Barnaby said.

'For selected customers, nothing is too much trouble.'

'I don't come down,' Marion said, 'you come up, Barnie, OK? Once you've closed the deal, of course.'

'Pleasure, Mrs Pierce. Another time, I hope. So: welcome to LA, not for the first time.'

'It's been a while,' Barnaby said. 'But it doesn't change. I mean, aside from wrecking a perfectly good hotel, which this used to be, by turning it into a tasteful symphony in beige where you wait all day at the desk before some goddam clerk doesn't recognise you and has no trace of your reservation because nobody can spell Pierce any more. P,e,a, they had us filed under.'

'Dumb, dumb, dumb. This isn't really a place to stay any more, you want to impress people.'

'That's why we chose it. We're here for our son's wedding, Gary, like I told you. I don't want to impress people. What're you doing in here if it's off-limits to A-listers?'

'Japanese stay here,' he said. 'They like to stay here. They have a quality Japanese restaurant here now. Seventeen out of twenty for a place with no chairs.'

'*Adios compañeros*,' Barnaby said. 'I always regretted that.'

'Don't you believe it. You can still get *great* gourmet Mexican. I don't remember *Sherlock Holmes, Sniffer Dog*, do I?'

'That was Stan's title for it. It never got out the kennel.'

'*Sherlock in Manhattan*. Did we really hope that would go?'

'Do you remember the last payment? That's what I remember. Absence leaves a lingering taste.'

'You're putting me on.'

'I'm putting you on the stand, Rico.'

'I don't remember any payments. What kind of coffee do you want?'

'I'll have a regular *cappuccino*,' Barnaby said, 'but hold the chocolate, if you were even thinking about it, please. Stan died.'

'Stan . . .'

'Tarlo. He died. Did you ever see him do his Eddie Cantor imitation?'

'I don't even remember what he looked like.'

'He made like eighty million dollars importing food and wine from Europe. He started with Greek yoghurt, which he had out there and couldn't get in the US, and from there it mushroomed. His last venture was this *prêt-à-manger* line of gourmet foods.'

'Eighty *million*?'

'His company is now quoted at.'

'Kind of a small guy, very dynamic, with this way of – he had sort of rubber legs, he used to do this number with. I remember Stanley. He *died*?'

'He died in front of our eyes as a matter of fact. End of last week.'

'My wife serves it sometimes to people, *prêt-à-manger*. That was a clever campaign they ran, wasn't it? The pretentious guy going out into the kitchen to congratulate the chef in *French* and she's the hostess's kid, twelve years old. That was clever. He *died*.'

'We were passing through Chi and . . . called in and . . . next thing he was dead.'

'And it's not even as if you were writing his show. Stan Tarlo made eighty million dollars. I'll be a sonofabitch.'

'It pays to like Greek yoghurt,' Barnaby said, 'if you get the timing right. But you can still die.'

'Are you planning to see people while you're out here?'

'No, just hoping to bump into them in lobbies and places. I'm having a little vacation and thinking about writing my memoirs.'

'Be advised: don't. Unless you screwed a lot of famous names. Or swindled people, like real bad, i.e. real well. In which event take legal advice. I still see your stuff here and there. Your residuals must give you a healthy cushion.'

'Is why I'm thinking of changing my life a little bit. I'm tired of kids fresh out of college or someplace telling me what's wrong with my scripts, not because they particularly think there is anything wrong but because they think someone else might, or –'

'Alternatively.'

'Because they think someone else might *not* and they want to sneak past them on the inside by proving how smart they are when it comes to twisting writers' necks. I'm sick of people who work with people and *to* people and who assist people and people who say he isn't here right now but can I help, or hinder, in any way because I just got this job by fucking some asshole and I don't know shit about it or you so imagine what I can do to your project unless you make like eight million changes that don't make sense.'

'Barnaby, you're tired of *life* as we know it is what you're tired of. Did you ever like Gothic?'

'Gothic. Architecture?'

'Because I'm planning a series of Gothic tales, OK? Halfway between Edgar Allen Poe and Hawthorne with a smidgin of the Addams family in there someplace. *Son of Frankenstein* meets Hester Prynne in *The House of Usher*.'

'And has thirteen kids, all of them exactly forty-eight minutes long. Good luck.'

'I want to get some quality directors who really want to do something a little bit . . . imaginative."

'That's code for small budget.'

'Were you always this cynical? I don't remember you this cynical. It's code for low budget.'

'The directors get nothing and the writers get proportionately less.'

'There's a little money. I thought of you when I thought of Hawthorne, I don't know why.'

'We have the same colour flowers,' Barnaby said.

'You have the same colour flowers has to be it. You know his stories?'

'Some.'

'Because take your pick.'

'And shovel, and go to work?'

'I didn't say that.'

'But you're capable of it.'

'I have my days.'

'And how are your nights?'

'You have to meet Karen, who I'm very close to.'

'Is that code for thirty years old? That's code for thirty years old.'

'Thirty-four. But bright? My God! How long are you in town?'

'We're staying for the wedding, Saturday, and then we go our ways. Not often you get a chance to say that.'

'How about co-producing with me?'

'What'll Karen say?'

'Welcome aboard.'

'Don't twist the kid's arm, Gary. That's not nice.'

'She's a nuts and bolts person.'

'Gary, you don't need me. I'm not here really. And if you're feeling guilty about that payment . . .'

'Do you want me have my bookkeeper check it out?'

'This was a century ago. This was before you could talk seriously about blow-jobs with people in prime time. No, I'm sorry: the *problem* of blow-jobs you can talk about.'

'I never see those programmes. I remember that pilot now and it had Gothic elements in it is why I thought you might be interested.' Gary Pereira was talking to the air now because he had seen somebody he wanted to see him and, when she did, he ticktacked that they had this date noon. The enthusiasm of his fingers was truly eloquent. 'Marsha Kapinski,' he said.

'*Gesundheit*,' Barnaby said.

'Write your goddam memoirs, Barnaby, if you have to: you are still sharp as a tack.'

'Comes of being sat on so often.'

'Who ever sat on you for very long?'

'Is my point.'

'You sound bitter. Why? You have achievements to kill for.'

'To kill *myself* for,' Barnaby said.

'And even when you're doing it, you'll be auditioning for the part of Chris Carry. Marsha is about to be Head of Development, movies, for TV, at Gayley.'

'That explains why you go down on her in public.'

'*Barnaby*. Please, this is my town. I'm doing a remake of *Rebecca* with her, also *The Birds*, with a totally different concept, much more ecological. I don't remember you like this.'

'I wasn't always drunk at this hour in the old days.'

'You have a problem in that direction?'

'West Coast air. Is there a cure? Must do it to me. Good to see you, Gary. Give my regards to Freda.'

'Karen.'

'Karen. What is she, the third?'

'Fourth. Fourth *marriage*.'

'Of course.'

'You know what else I'm doing? That's a projected comedy series about a lady officer in the Marines. *An Officer and a Lady*, we're thinking of calling it. Did you catch up with *An Officer and a Gentleman*?'

'A lady officer in the Marines. I have to go.'

'Apologise to your wife for me.'

'Why, what did you do to *her*?'

'Excuse me?'

'You didn't steal her purse, did you? I can cancel those cards, you know, like that. No, like *that*, I can cancel them.'

'You should see a doctor.'

'When I can see a shit?'

'Now wait a minute.'

'There's more?'

'You want to be careful.'

'But I do find it increasingly difficult.'

'Oh my God,' Gary Pereira said. 'Oh my God. Oh my God.'

'Burst into prayer by all means. It's a free country and it's a free coffee, because I'm paying for it. Cash. Is how I feel.'

'My new series has *nothing to do* with *Sergeant Bimbo*. Kathie is an *officer*.'

'Maybe I'll sit back down and have a Danish. Marsha Kapinski, is that her name?'

'Yes, it is. Why? This series is about a *marine*. When did I ever steal an idea?'

'Whenever you had a good one, didn't you?'

'Get out of here.'

'Right.'

'Get out of here right now.'

Barnaby put a hand up in the air and then he went a couple of tables along the narrow coffee shop and stopped. 'Marsha Kapinski.'

'Hullo,' she said.

'You have an appointment at noon.'

'I know.' She was confirming it to Gary Pereira, who still looked worried.

'With a thief.'

'Excuse me?'

'With a thief. So next time he goes down on you, watch your purse, OK?'

'Now wait a minute.'

'You have that long?'

'I'm going to call somebody.'

'Call them. Tell them.'

'You must be insane.'

'Barnaby . . .'

'Hey, *Gary*, long time no see. Are you out of the joint, does this mean?'

'He's drunk,' Gary Pereira said. 'Or something.'

'Lotsaluck, you guys. Gothic! Great, great idea. Maybe you should be the one wears the black mask over your face, Gary. It would help people recognise you.'

'Who was *that?*'

'Marsha, do you remember – you wouldn't – a guy called Stanley Tarlo. Comedy writer.'

'Tarlo?' Marsha said. 'No, I don't.'

'Friend of mine,' Gary Pereira said. 'Worked for me.'

'Unlikely combination,' Marsha said.

'He just died, worth eighty million.'

'Who *was* that?'

'Stanley Tarlo.'

'Said that to me about you being some kind of a *thief*.'

'He's a psycho. I was being kind to him, trying to be, guy used to be in the business. Out here panhandling, I guess. I forget his name even.'

Mother and Dad

'You're where? At the hotel?'

'Room 415,' Marion said, 'with the all-plastic décor and the view of the kitchen roof. Wait till your father gets here.'

'I told them to give you a real good room. I actually went in and saw somebody. I wore a suit too. Dad isn't there?'

'He's cruising a job in the coffee shop. You know your father: a producer has only to fire a shot across his bows and he's already hove to. Heaved to? Whatever, that's what he is.'

'He wants a job, I can find him one fast enough.'

'I'll have him paged.'

'You heard I got a new job?'

'But not what. What?'

'With an outfit called Gayley TV, over in the Valley. I'm solely responsible for developing movies for TV together with an exceptionally bright girl called Marsha Kapinski.'

'Solely responsible *with*?'

'The two of us are solely responsible. We have the right to make decisions up to the two million mark. Which is not much, but it's something.'

'It sounds like something to me. Congratulations. How is Imogen?'

'Imogen is perfect.'

'You can't improve on that.'

'You haven't worked in TV. Perfect is what gets notes. Pages of them.'

'You sound like your father, Benjamin.'

'Do I? You guys are . . . in what kind of shape?'

'Still talking,' Marion said. 'Walking and talking. Which will make a welcome change from driving and talking. I have a bad case of sititis, really.'

'Imogen had it coupla times. More than a couple. Eight.'

'*Sititis*,' Marion said.

'Oh, OK. I'm longing for you to see the house. I hope you're going to be seriously worried for my sanity, because it's like on *stilts*, with a great, great view. Imogen found it. Right on top of San Isidro, if you know where that is.'

'It'll have to be there whether I know or not, because . . .'

'Where Billy and Constanza lived when you were living out here, only way, way up.'

'Expensive?'

'More than that. But we figured we both were working and how often do you get the house of your dreams?'

'Rarely to wake up in,' she said. 'Very. Here's your father just walked in the door after prolonged work on the easy-to-open lock. It's Benjamin.'

'You talk,' Barnaby said. 'I'm going to throw up.'

'He'll be right out. Is something wrong?'

'You talk,' Barnaby said, 'I'll be there in a minute.'

'Benjie, did you talk to your sister Zara recently?'

'Sure.'

'So you know what happened?'

'Of course. Chelsea finally moved in with her. I wish I was totally happy with that.'

'To me.'

'Something happened to you?'

'She didn't tell you how I got lost in Seattle and panicked? She will. I called her and she gave me sane advice. Finally after what?'

'She left her live-in and moved in with sis. And I wish I was happy.'

'Why wouldn't you be?'

'Wait till you meet her, then ask me. If you still need to.'

'She sounds very, OK, capable.'

'And then some,' Benjamin said. 'Don't get me wrong . . .'

'It's not going to be easy, is it?'

195

'She has something. Zara thinks she's totally brilliant. And maybe she is.'

'You sound like your father suddenly. What does she do?'

'OK,' Benjamin said, 'she's some kind of a holo-therapist, is what she is.'

'Hollow therapist?'

'H,o,l,o. The whole ball of wax is what she aims to play with. Reshape. Whatever. I don't see too much of them since I somewhat questioned one or two of her premises. She's also been a nurse.'

'Benjamin, I didn't ever know I was called "Miss Pouter". Did you?'

'You did too, you must have.'

'You did. I did not.'

'Chris started it. Affectionately.'

'All right. How many bedrooms does the house have?'

'Three. There'll be room for you because there's also a separate space over the garage, bathroom and studio. Until we have a chauffeur, that is.'

'Is everything all set?'

'Set as it can be. You found the press pack? I left a press pack for you. How to get to the church, which you won't find difficult, in Brentwood, which is right near where Imogen's folks live. You'll like Brian.'

'Is that an order?'

'You will. Dad especially.'

'An admiral called Brian.'

'Vice-admiral. Retired. He won't be in uniform. He's now vice-president of an electronics company, if that's easier to believe. They want you and Dad to come to dinner Thursday. I hate to say this, but I have a stag night on Friday, which I fought against like crazy.'

'Have they actually invited us?'

'It's all there in the press pack they should have at the desk for you. I'm going to get Jack to call them as soon as I hang up. Correction: I'm going to get him to call before I hang up. JACK!'

Marion covered the phone and said, 'Better get your sea legs over here, Barnaby, and talk to your son. Duty dinner with the admiral and his lady, Thursday.'

'I'm not doing the hornpipe,' Barnaby said.

'After what happened to Stan, don't you,' she said and then uncovered the mouthpiece. 'Here's your father.'

'Hi, Dad.'

'Hey, hotshot! How's the new job?'

'Pretty well like the old one, but much better paid.'

'I like the new one.'

'I'd like you to come out and see the set-up. Admire my view. I can see clear into Burbank Studios script library.'

'Shit on shelves. I can hardly wait. How do I get out there?'

'How was your flight? You had to stop over in Seattle?'

'We had to stop over in Seattle. No, but we did. We wanted to see some old friends.'

'So, you need to hire a car.'

'Don't worry about that,' Barnaby said.

'You know how to get to Burbank.'

'If I lose the way, I'll take off the blindfold.'

'Tomorrow? We can have lunch in the Commissary.'

'And then go and find something to eat.'

'You sound in great shape.'

'I'll get over it. It's the warhorse syndrome. I get out here, hear the sounds of battle and I have a natural tendency to run like hell.'

'I know more people who are fans of *The Stinkinsons* . . .'

'Don't introduce me. I won't be here that long. Looking forward to meeting Imogen again. Last time, she was but one of many.'

'Think Mother will mind?'

'If – ?'

'You come out to the Valley without her.'

'She can always call Zara. When's she coming to town?'

'I don't know. We haven't communicated in a while. Stace gets in Saturday morning. Pretty typical.'

'Is she coming with Clifford?'

'Clifford. I think she is. Yes, she is. Come to the Studio gate and I'll leave word so you can park where it feels exclusive, OK?'

'Barnaby.'

'Gotta go, Benjamin. Your mother . . .'

'And I'll swing by the hotel tonight round six-thirty, seven, OK, to see Mother.'

'Got it,' Barnaby said. 'She'll be here. Not that I speak for her.'

'They want to give us an upgrade,' Marion said. 'They're here to move us. And I just took everything out of the bags.'

'That's Jack,' Barnaby said. 'He's someone gets things done evidently.'

'Barnaby Pierce,' the bellboy said. 'Would that be *the* Barnaby Pierce?'

'If the money's right,' Barnaby said, 'anything's possible.'

'Who also wrote *The Stinkinsons*.'

'I can hide,' Barnaby said, 'but I can't run.'

'Only among my five totally favourite shows of all time. Why don't you leave everything right where it is, Mrs Pierce? I'll take care of it. Imagine putting you in here in the first place!'

When they were in the junior suite and everything was demonstrably in the closets, the bellboy absolutely didn't want to take the ten bucks, but he did. They looked out over the back of the hotel. There were still rows of towelled chairs beside the pool but no one much was sitting in them. There was no sense in risking skin cancer in order to be paged, the way people were in the old days. With mobiles, no one had to *be* paged any more and besides, who was around to be impressed if you were?

'I think Benjamin would appreciate seeing you alone,' Barnaby said. 'Or so I gathered, slightly, from the way he spoke.'

'You're unduly sensitive about not being wanted,' Marion said.

'How did that come about? Care to hazard a guess?'

'You know what's wrong with you, Pierce?'

'You have the test results?'

'One thing you can never manage and that's letting go.'

'I let go of the novel,' he said. 'Of more or less the same title. I had no problem letting go of *that*.'

198

'You duck, you weave.'

'If only it was a living.'

'What's wrong with you, since you can't give me a straight opportunity, is that you can only ever remember what consolidates your idea of yourself as some kind of a martyr.'

'It's the Jewish grandmother in me. Old Sadie.'

'Save that stuff for the bullshit hour,' Marion said.

'Two, three hours in LA and you're showing signs of settling in already.'

'What about last night?' she said.

'Last night,' he said.

'What about that?'

'It was . . . exceptional. Eighteen out of twenty.'

'What do we have to do to get all the way?'

'Sex is asymptotic. Ask the panel. It tends to perfection but of its nature can never quite get there. If it did, no one would ever do it again, which is not the manufacturer's intention.'

'One thing I want to know from you: why doesn't anything good that happens count towards the meaning of anything?'

'That's a question we don't have time for. Here's one we do: are you going to have your hair done before Benjamin gets here?'

'What's wrong with my hair?'

'I always liked it,' he said. 'Whichever way it was. Or is. Don't look at me that way, Marion, OK, because who does your question apply to if not the both of us? And it may even lean very slightly towards applying more to you than to me. Is how I feel about it, rightly or wrongly, of course. You're the one wants a new life, a clean sheet . . .'

'And after last night,' she said, 'also a dry one.'

'Maybe you should write the goddam *Stinkinsons*,' Barnaby said. 'Maybe you should get that bastard Gary to commission a new series. You're crisp, you're shameless.'

'You can't be *embarrassed* surely, can you?'

'You'd be amazed what I can be.'

'When roused? When roused you can be extraordinary. Why does that embarrass you?'

'It makes me angry, if that helps, more than it embarrasses me.'

'You were *angry* last night is what you're telling me?'

'Who knows what I was? But I know one thing about it, which is naught for your comfort, or anyone else's, and that is, whatever it meant or didn't mean or even clocked on the Richter scale, which I hope was in the high sixes, it's never anything that *adds* to anything in my experience. In fact, although this is not commonly admitted, least of all by you . . .'

'I hate this kind of a build-up coming from you.'

'Your privilege,' he said.

'What do I not commonly admit?'

'Giving someone pleasure almost counts against, OK, me, in most instances. Making love seldom makes love, is what I'm saying in simple terms.'

'Those make a sweet change, even if nothing sweet is said in them. Am I someone?'

'Now you're sore, is that the size of it?'

'Resigned. I don't know what size that comes in. Because whatever happens, it seems your mind's set on . . . having a grievance. And I don't want to get into why.'

'You want to sell my house,' he said. 'You want to advertise to the world that I'm a failed husband, dull at best, and that your life with me has been something you absolutely have to do better than before it's too late and yet you wonder what my problem is.'

'No one thinks you're a failure. And if anyone's dull, I'm dull. I'm never going to get hired to write the stinking *Stinkinsons*. Don't get my hopes up, because all I'll do is, I'll fall and break my stupid neck.'

'We really have to have dinner with these people? His name is Brian, what's hers going to be?'

'I suspect Nancy,' Marion said. 'Don't ask me why. I don't think Benjamin wants to see me alone particularly.'

'I do. I'm not being . . . ornery. I seriously do. I'm seeing him for lunch tomorrow, was what he fixed first, only, I suspect, because he didn't want to hurt my feelings.'

'Maybe he's coming by the hotel so's not to hurt mine.'

'All things are possible,' Barnaby said, 'once you forget about happiness.'

'I was a stranger is the truth, isn't it?' she said. 'Last night, and that's why you're embarrassed today.'

'And what was I? I won't say who. I probably know who, don't I?'

'You never understood the first thing about Hal and me. You certainly don't understand the last thing, which is why he threw me out of the car. He hated me.'

'You should've seen him with me. I never touched Erica, never so much as indicated the smallest interest, and without difficulty, because I never *felt* the smallest interest. And yet . . .'

'Why else was he so sore? You made it clear to him that you thought his wife was totally unattractive. Now you want marks from him for that?'

'OK,' Barnaby said. 'But he still thinks I stopped him being happy with you, and so do you, don't you, all these years?'

'I'm not doing any more of this, with you, with anybody. Least of all ahead of the vice-admiral.'

'You know something, Marion, despite everything, I'm still very, very nearly crazy about you.'

'When I sound like you you are.'

'There goes the ball game,' he said. 'And be it clearly said: you're the one what threw it.'

'It wasn't you, it wasn't me,' she said. 'Last night. Is the curious thing about it.'

'Strangers in the night. Suppose it counted for something, what would it count for?'

'You're a little bit of a bastard, aren't you, sometimes?'

'I'm a bully and a brute,' he said, 'and that never comes cheap.'

'You think you're kidding.'

'Is but part of the service,' he said.

'Telling me what finally about what?'

'I wanted you to be sorry,' he said. 'If I hadn't wanted you to be sorry, I don't think I could have been the man I was, if I was.'

'I think the evidence will show you were.'

'The more this goes on, the more you can observe what's happening. On my side of the fence anyway. Talking of evidence.'

'Anger,' she said. 'On top of that movie, of course. We

shouldn't forget the movie, should we? And what's this about me selling *your* house?'

'Appetising or not, it's an undoubted giveaway. What I'm going to do is, I'm going to go call a coupla people, including Raymond Laserowitz . . .'

'Who you distinctly said you would never speak to again under any circumstances.'

'You heard about new leaves? I'm turning one over. I hate to think what I'll find underneath.'

'You're not seriously calling that . . . that . . . He always called me "dear". Ten, fifteen years and he never learned my name. *Why?*'

'He represented me when I was working with Gary. I'm going to get him to press for that last payment on *Sherlock*, and then I'm going to talk to a lawyer about injuncting Gary Pereira for breach of copyright and anything else that'll squeeze a buck out of him. Rich is happy, remember? And the reason? It never upsets your digestion or leads you to ask yourself questions about whether you deserve to be loved. You're rich, you do. The bank loves you. Get your hair done. It's perfect the way it is. One thing I ask above all, and that is, don't tell Ben about the car. I want that to be a surprise. So don't let it out, will you, inadvertently?'

'Would I?'

Benjamin had left his car at a meter on Beverly because, he said, the hotel's Vietnamese valets took upwards of twenty minutes sometimes to get it back up again and then expected a tip on top of the totally excessive rates. So he had to walk a block and a half. He called up to the suite and cruised the lobby till Marion came down. She didn't like the idea of having drinks out of the minibar, still less opening complimentary champagne. There were plenty of empty tables in the Celebrity Room, so they went in there and had to wait to be seated. Marion ordered a Margarita; Benjamin settled for San Pellegrino.

'You had your hair done already.'

'Already is none too soon. Do you hate it? Will Brian?'

'It looks fine. Don't get yourself . . . You'd never guess he was a vice-admiral.'

'I'll never have to, will I?' she said. 'Is something wrong?'

'Nothing I know about. Did you pick up the press pack?'

'Brian and Elsie,' she said. 'I guess if she hadn't been Elsie he might have made full admiral.'

'You'll like her.'

'Or else, is that?'

'That's probably true.'

'As if it mattered,' Marion said.

'It matters to me, quite a little bit.'

'I won't let you down,' she said.

'Tell me a time you ever did and I'll be surprised.'

There was a piano player. He was a little loud and he leaned back and scanned the company more than his competence justified. They took their drinks to a more distant corner and the Captain brought them nuts and olives. It seemed he knew who Benjamin was, or thought maybe he ought to. Benjamin had decided style: the subtle suit, the Rosetti loafers, the ring.

They sat and leaned slightly forward over the pool of silence between them, as if it too were some kind of an appetiser. It was maybe deep; it was maybe shallow. Benjamin sniffed *out*, it seemed, as he looked at his mother again, and said it wasn't important, in the sense of anything he wanted to influence anybody over, but what was going to happen to the stuff in the house, if and when they sold it?

'We didn't make any plans,' Marion said.

'Is it up for sale contents included? You must know that.'

'We're open to offers, I guess is what it comes to.'

'Including our things?'

'What do you take us for?'

'Us? Is that what you still are?'

'Anything you want us to ship out to you, we'll do it.'

'I was thinking principally of toys. I was also thinking about, OK, some of Christopher's . . . Not that I covet them. I just don't want them to go out with the garbage. I covet them, but only for any kids we might eventually have. Is that coveting?'

'It's very natural.'

'Is coveting?'

'Has to be. Why else would it be forbidden?'

'What are you going to do, Mother, truly?'

'Enjoy this week. Make sure everyone does, so far as it's within my power. I'm sorry if we didn't make it clear about your things, or other things, unless one of the girls wants them. It wasn't callousness. Quite the opposite.'

'What is the opposite?'

'Squeamishness, isn't it? It could just be that – are you old enough for this? – it's not your father I want to be ... distinct from: it's what happened in the house. Or happened while we were in it.'

'We're talking about Christopher.'

'Which is not something your father and I ever do too much. Doing it at all, to be accurate, was doing it too much. Because I feared two things, which are cousins, if not twins: talking of nothing else and talking it, in the end, into being nothing, something we were just *tired of.* You know what I remember, and never told you about, and that's being so, so afraid to be happy again, afraid to smile, afraid to forget. I wanted the pain so much I got numb with it. And at the same time, I knew I had to pretend to smile, for you, for the girls. And so it got to the point where I doubted my own sincerity, about just about everything, including my own secret feelings. I faked to myself too. Or thought I did. And it was something I was just a little proud of doing. I'm sorry . . .'

'No, that's OK. I probably need to hear this.'

'I don't think you do. I doubt anyone does. Is she pregnant, are you telling me?'

'Imogen?'

'Who else?'

'No, no; no one is pregnant.'

'Stace is.'

'That I knew.'

'And her new man, you know about him?'

'Clifford? I know who he is.'

'Everybody does,' Marion said. 'Except your dumb mother. She thought he was a hockey player. You do want kids though?'

'Assuming Imogen can go on with her career, we do.'

'She's right to want to. Is there some reason you wanted to see me?'

'You're my mother,' Benjamin said. 'Dad, how are things with him?'

'Aren't you going to ask him,' she said, 'when you see him?'

'I imagined he'd be here now. How come he's not?'

'He imagined something different,' Marion said. 'He does a lot of that, when he has the time.'

'Zara's bringing Chelsea to the wedding,' Benjamin said.

'And? But?'

'Which I hope is a good idea. But what could I say?'

'Zara sounded fine when she and I spoke. Quite up in fact. Zenobia I should say.'

Benjamin said, 'You know the Jaguar.'

'I do.'

'What're Dad's plans there? Is he aiming to sell it?'

'He loves that car. I can't see him ever selling it, can you?'

There were beautiful flowers in the suite, with very warm feelings from Brian and Elsie, when Marion went back up there. Barnaby returned not long afterwards and she asked him how the movie had been and he said 'Movie?', as if he didn't get the point right away. They went up to Century City and ate corned beef and coleslaw and stood in line for some movie which everyone had told them how good it was and of course it wasn't. By the time they got down to the car park, most of the cars were gone and Barnaby took her arm and walked tall to the isolated Jaguar.

Barnaby rented a red Toyota to drive over to the Valley the following day. He was afraid that Benjamin would see the Jaguar, however tactfully he parked it. Gayley Productions had a cottage on the back lot. Benjamin was walking towards him, in loafers, cotton pants and a collarless shirt, when he turned the corner by the water-tank.

'Come on back and meet my partner,' Benjamin said, 'and then we'll go wrestle with some pastrami.'

The cottage had three rooms, which had not yet been organised.

Pictures were leaning against the wall and there was plastic on the couch and the matching chairs. Jack was a black man in a tartan shirt. He had a shaved head and an earring and black-rimmed glasses. Barnaby reached and shook hands with him and said, 'Thanks for the upgrade.'

'Thanks for all the pleasure,' Jack said. 'I studied you in film school.'

'And you can still talk about pleasure?'

'Most certainly.'

'This is me,' Benjamin said, 'and through here is Marsha.'

Barnaby looked at Marsha Kapinski and she looked at him and both of them said, 'Aw-aw!' at the same moment and then they were laughing and looking a little shy all at the same time and then Benjamin was the reason they were laughing and they were not shy at all.

'Your father is a crazy man,' Marsha said. 'He says terrible things to people in coffee shops.'

'He says terrible *true* things,' Barnaby said.

'That's what's terrible.'

'What is this? You two already know each other?'

'Intimately,' Marsha said. 'Your father confided to me that Gary Pereira was a thief.'

'When was this?'

'When was this? As long ago as yesterday morning.'

'I'm a little embarrassed actually,' Barnaby said. 'Not about what I said, which was . . . I sort of assumed that you and Gary were . . . which is clearly not the case.'

'It's totally not the case,' Marsha Kapinski said, 'and there's nothing whatsoever to be embarrassed about.'

'Didn't Gary explain that I was this sad old lush by the name of Pierce?'

'He said he didn't know who you were.'

'Bless that loyal old heart of his!'

'Gary Pereira? He's the worst.'

'I've known worse, but who's counting? He said he didn't know who I was.'

'The scandal is, I didn't. Or is that quite true? I had this feeling that I should've known. You have Benjamin's . . . *trenchancy*.'

'And he has mine, of course.'

'Whose else's?'

'He gave the impression, Gary, that he was doing a lot of things with you.'

'He's *hoping* to,' Marsha said. 'Which is surely his right.'

'What made you say he was a thief, Dad?'

'He's doing some comedy series about a female officer in the Marines. Which is not, if you think carefully about it, a thousand miles from *Sergeant Bimbo*.'

'You know something? It never occurred to me.'

'With which he was briefly associated on the production side. It didn't occur to you because you didn't create *Bimbo*.'

'*Bimbo* owed something to *Bilko*, finally, didn't it?'

'And it acknowledged it did. In so far as it was a Service comedy, but . . . am I defending myself here? Do I need to?'

'Absolutely not,' Marsha said. 'We're throwing out the charges anyway, aren't we, Benjamin?'

'You're implying I lifted the idea for *Bimbo*? Where did I get the one for *The Stinkinsons* from? Do you have a bill of particulars on that one conceivably too?'

'Come on, Dad! This isn't a remake of *All in the Family* we're doing here possibly, is it, right here in the barn?'

'I talked to the *Bilko* people. I cleared it with them. We had to. It was a homage, but I didn't steal a thing. Ever.'

'Dad, I was kidding. He kids; we can't. House rules.'

'Pretty soon there won't be a house,' Barnaby said.

'I bet there'll still be rules though.'

'I doubt if there'll be much of anything.'

Marsha said, 'It's really amazing to meet you. You seriously can't imagine what kind of a shadow you throw.'

'On a good day,' Barnaby said, 'I can precipitate one hell of an eclipse.'

'We ought to get your father to do something for us.'

'Show me a hoop,' Barnaby said, 'and I'll stumble through it.'

'I'll keep my eyes open,' Marsha said.

'Pity not to when they're as beautiful as yours.'

'He is your father,' Marsha Kapinski said, 'definitely.'

'You too are a phoney and a flatterer?'

'But I don't throw your shadow yet. How about some lunch, get that shadow filled in a little bit?'

'Are you coming to have some lunch with us, Miss Kapinski?'

'I have something fixed unfortunately. Another time, why don't we?'

'I can't think of a single reason. Yes, I can though: Gary Pereira, he's there, I can't be.'

'Such a pleasure,' Marsha said. 'And let's find something to do together. I'm serious about that. Wouldn't that be great, Benjamin, to have your dad do something for us?'

'I'm up for it,' Benjamin said, 'any time.'

They walked back past the water-tower towards the Commissary and Benjamin raised his hand quite a few times at people who frowned at Barnaby as if to say who's *that*?

Barnaby said, 'She's very nice.'

'I gathered you thought so.'

'Was I out of line?'

'Absolutely not. Funny you two guys having met already.'

'She was truly very nice about it. I must've embarrassed her quite a bit.'

'She's a very bright girl.'

'But nothing goes on between you.'

'What kind of a question is that? I'm getting married Saturday.'

'It's impressive,' Barnaby said, 'is what I meant. To be partners with an attractive woman like that and not have any problem with it.'

'Happens all the time these days. All the time. Has to.'

'OK,' Barnaby said.

'She's in a relationship herself. Was. Will be again soon, no doubt.'

'She's never been married?'

'She's been married. How old do you think Marsha is?'

'Thirty-three.'

'She's thirty-three. Of course she's been married. To an actor who now has a restaurant. She was married to Hank Mead. *Ready When You Are*, his place is called. Marsha is a free spirit. And bright.'

They went into the table-clothed room at the back of the Commissary where there was waitress service. The tables were further apart and it was a tradition that people didn't table-hop unless evidently desired. They waved a little bit, but that was it. Barnaby stirred pepper and a very little salt into his Virgin Mary; Benjamin's drink was San Pellegrino, Chantal, please, as usual.

Benjamin said, 'Would you ever think of coming out here again to work?'

'I don't honestly know,' Barnaby said. 'I don't know if I would, if I could or if I'd want to. I wish I could be the person who came out here to work, but not because I want to do what I did again, or even something different, more because that would take me back to a time *before*, a time when I was in the club, I wasn't wondering if I could do things, or should've done them, or shouldn't which is worse. If I came out here again it would be because I thought a new pair of sneakers and a different haircut could set the calendar back, which it can't.'

'You're thinking about Christopher,' Benjamin said.

'Maybe I am. Not consciously. But maybe I am. Maybe I am. I'm ashamed to tell you that I was *consciously* thinking about me. Who I'd be if I had my chance again. Which is probably pathetic and unworthy and *certainly* unproductive. You don't want me out here.'

'You seriously don't know whether you're selling the house? It's for sale, isn't it?'

'Yes, it is. But we don't have an offer in from anybody and even if we did, who knows whether finally we'd take it? Is the situation. Is the unsatisfactory situation. Everything is on hold, but whether it *can* hold, and for how long . . .'

'You don't have a script,' Benjamin said, 'is what you're telling me.'

'We don't have a script.'

'Can I say something?'

'Go ahead.'

'Because, forgive me if I'm wrong . . .'

'I'll even forgive you if you're right,' Barnaby said, 'but that's as far as it goes.'

'Dad . . . if you and Mom are *not* parting at this point, why have we got to hear about it? Why did this have to become public property at this stage exactly?'

'We probably talk too much,' Barnaby said. 'We thought we were being upfront about things, because you were all adults now and we didn't want to spring anything on you.'

'But that's exactly what you did do. And then you tried to . . . go back on it.'

'It was badly handled,' Barnaby said. 'I give you that. It was not intentionally . . . Why are you so concerned?'

'You think it doesn't matter to me? It matters to all of us.'

'You've spoken to the girls about this?'

'Of course. Not at length, but . . . of course I have.'

'And they feel the way you do?'

'I don't know exactly how I do feel, but we all feel . . . *disturbed*; we certainly all feel that.'

'Stace seemed very calm about it, very . . . understanding.'

'Oh Stace,' Benjamin said.

'So what it comes to is, you feel threatened by the uncertainty.'

'Is that so damned unreasonable? Fuck it.'

'It's very reasonable, and I'm very sorry. I wish I could say something definitive.'

'Oh when did you ever?' Benjamin said.

The pastrami came with chopped salad but without the cole-slaw. Benjamin was very patient with Chantal and they waited for her to correct the order.

'I would be very happy personally to go on living in 5764. I'm not saying that it's all your mother's *fault*, but it's certainly her idea that we should make a change, and maybe a big one.'

'You don't love each other any more, is that it?'

'Not exactly I don't think. I'm not blaming her when I say this, because doubtless if I have to blame anybody it's me, but what we don't seem to love . . . what doesn't seem to *be loved* any more, or not too much, is being together. I have no *reason* not to love your mother, the mother of my children; I also admire her and respect her . . .'

'You don't have sex any more?'

'I don't want to talk about those things with my children, Benjamin, however dated that may be of me.'

'Meaning you don't.'

'Meaning can we please not be having this conversation, because I find it aggressive and obnoxious.'

'On my part.'

'Since you initiated it, I guess I can't say no to that and be honest with you.'

'Obnoxious,' Benjamin said.

'Let me say something here, which is that I think you look great; you evidently have an excellent job and you handle yourself real well out here. I'm here to celebrate your wedding and your happiness and nothing is more an occasion for pride and joy than to be doing that. I'm sorry, on quite a different plane, if my and your mother's . . . tensions – let's call them tensions – '

'Oh that reasonable tone of voice!'

'Fuck it, Benjamin, if you don't mind me saying so in my turn, and in the nicest possible way. If what's happening in my marriage disturbs you, I'm sorry, but by Christ it also disturbs me and it wouldn't hurt you to have a little sense of that, please. Thank you.'

'Push it back in the bottle and hammer in the cork. The old recipe, which I hoped a little bit we might do without.'

'What's this all about, Benjamin? Are you worrying about this marriage of yours?'

'Do you hope I am?'

'I'm your father and that's what you say to me? Shame on you, for that.'

'You have to be the hurt one. I've seen you do it with mother. I've seen you do it with everyone.'

'That's a lot of people you've seen me do it with then.'

'Yes, it is. I am not worried about getting married in any way whatsoever. I want to marry Imogen because I love her and she loves me and I don't want anyone to have doubts on that score in any way whatsoever. Why are you looking at me like that?'

'That's the way I look.'

'That's the way you look when that's the way you look. Christopher.'

'Christopher?'

'Is what it's all about. Is what everything is about, if you ask me.'

'I don't understand.'

'Even that. Your dishonesty.'

'You think I'm a lot older than I am, Benjamin, sometimes, by which I mean – I'm going to explain all right – by which I mean you assume that I have some quality of, if nothing better, *endurance*, solidity, which you don't think you need to have yet, which you think you'll acquire over the years. You won't. You won't, because no one does. No one does. What you acquire, and you blame me for acquiring at the same time as absolutely insisting that I don't let go of it, is a kind of weary hardness, a kind of wary refusal to spend more and more of what you don't have too much left of, getting . . . getting involved with emotional wrestling from which no good can come. Call it resignation; call it what you damn well please, because I'm not about to try and work out, for the ten-thousandth time, what I really feel or what I really might have felt or anything along those exhausting lines, because I simply do not have the time left. There's nothing wrong with this pastrami.'

'Dad . . .'

'What?'

'Christopher. Can we please talk about Christopher, and not because I want to blame you for anything or have you talk about anything you don't want to talk about. Certainly not for its own sake, if you know what I'm trying to say. But doesn't it all come down to Christopher, go back to him, or whatever?'

'All is too much to talk about, always. Christopher's death was certainly, to say the least, catastrophic. It twisted everything ways they would, to say the least, never have gone, if I . . . it hadn't've happened.'

'I know,' Benjamin said. 'I know that.'

'I can't and, rightly or wrongly, I absolutely won't, as I have said, try to distinguish what was and wasn't the result of what happened.'

'I don't ask you to.'

'Thank you.'

'I just wish you could see the accusation in your eyes.'

'The mote and the beam,' Barnaby said. 'We were taught all about that and I guess we were among the last.'

'Try not to let what . . . we said before . . . enter into this, but when you first heard the news, what did you hear exactly?'

'You have some kind of an agenda here, Ben, which it would be a kindness to let me in on.'

'I truly don't.'

'I don't know what kind of an answer you want, like do you imagine I have some kind of a transcript I've been keeping back?'

'All right,' Benjamin said, 'all right, let me ask you this: when they called from Colorado to tell you there'd been an accident, what precisely did they say?'

'They said there had been a bad accident and that . . .'

'I'm sorry.'

'I'll be OK.'

'I'm real sorry.'

'What do you expect of me when you do this?'

'This wasn't meant to be a painful . . .'

'We were going to . . . what? Laugh? I'm all right. Don't look around. I'm all right. Are those people you work with?'

'It's not important. We should maybe have gone someplace else.'

'It's not too late,' Barnaby said. 'I can get out of here without disgracing you, if that's what's bothering you. Alternatively, I can put it to you squarely right here and now and in front of whoever and ask you to tell me what the *fuck* you want to hear from me.'

'I guess I want to hear what I don't want to hear, is what I want to hear.'

'Which is?'

'They said somebody was dead, didn't they? Did they tell you that?'

'Am I going to have to make a speech at this wedding? I don't have to do that, do I?'

'I don't believe so. The bride's father says something, doesn't he, but no one else has to. You can if you want to.'

'They said there had been a fatal accident and that . . . yes, they said that they were afraid that our son was . . . involved, is what they said, as well as I can recall. I should never have let him take the Chevvy without insisting he use the chains. It's my fault. You know, I almost wish it was. It would be more . . . dignified to be guilty than just to be . . . would dead suit you?'

'I hate to be doing this. I truly do. But I started something . . .'

'Oh you started something,' Barnaby said, 'did you ever!'

'Which is this. You didn't know, did you, when it happened, which one of us it had happened to.'

'They said the driver. You weren't driving. You were fifteen years old. Christopher wouldn't have let you drive. Why are you doing this? On the flat possibly; snow and ice, never.'

'You have to know.'

'I have to know or you have to know?'

'You have to know that I have to know. And I do know, don't I?'

Barnaby said, 'Oh Ben. Oh Ben, for God's sake.'

The table was huge between them and he couldn't reach across somehow. He sat there gulping and his hands hanging at his sides. Benjamin wanted to move closer to his father but the chair might have been too heavy for him, because he sat there and worked his head a little as if he hadn't been able to move it for a long time and it took him at least a minute to work his face round so that he could look directly at his father.

'I always wished I could ski like he did,' Benjamin said. 'And I always knew you wished . . .'

'That's totally untrue. You don't know what it is to be a parent. You don't compare your children like that.'

'You compare them. Of *course* you compare them. I heard you and Mom sometimes.'

'Not in the way that's in your head, I swear to you. They said it was the driver and I knew right away it was Christopher.'

'They said your son and for a moment . . .'

'That's your . . . let's say that's your way of mourning, your way of being guilty. That's what survivor's guilt is, Ben; it has nothing to do with what you think we thought, or might have thought. That's too convenient, if I can be brutal for a moment, if only to be . . . unambiguous. Unambiguous, Jesus. Christopher is dead. Not a day passes but I don't wish it wasn't so, and for some of the reasons you maybe suspect, that your mother and I might've, I don't know, had a different take on things if he wasn't. But he is, and here we are. I don't believe a single damn good thing came of it. I haven't come to terms with it. I don't want help; I don't want consolation, because there is no consolation. And I don't . . . whatever you may sort of hope or fear, if that's what's happening in your head, wish . . . what you imply I might wish, or have wished. We have you and we're very, very glad we do, and I don't want to talk about this any more, but I will if you seriously insist.'

Barnaby had his elbow on the table now and his hand came up at an angle towards Benjamin, who could put his elbow on the table too and his hand in his father's. They might have been about to elbow-wrestle, but they didn't do that. They just sat there like that until Chantal came by and wanted to know if they cared for any dessert today.

'Just coffee,' Barnaby said, and then he had to be stirring his coffee before he said, 'You know that Jaguar I had?'

Benjamin said, 'I don't believe it.'

Barnaby lifted his other hand and there were the keys, which he pushed like a pawn with one finger. 'It's back at the hotel,' he said. 'It's yours. Drive carefully, won't you? For God's sake.'

'I don't believe it,' Benjamin said. 'I don't believe it.'

This Man and This Woman

Imogen and Benjamin came out of the church with the short shadows of early afternoon. They smiled and defended themselves as the air whitened with the rice that rattled and bounced on the sidewalk and made some of the older women step carefully and hold on to their husbands while they waited for the limos.

The service had been prompt and cheerful. The ceremony had paused only in that brief, attentive moment when the preacher asked if anyone knew any just cause why Benjamin and Imogen should not be joined in holy matrimony. During it, Marion had scanned the friendly faces, many of which she had never seen before, for fear that some crazed objection might come from the back of the bright church to humiliate them. Her certainty that there could, in truth, be no valid impediment seemed almost to contribute to the smiling dread she felt. She found time to wonder, during that small hiatus, whether it was not she herself who she feared would call out, with mad plausibility, that she knew something to prevent the wedding of her son.

Imogen seemed to be a very nice girl. If the white bride was not at all the same smart girl who had been at dinner with Vice-Admiral and Mrs Brian MacWilliam, there was something generous in her parade of virginity. The resumption of innocence gave the day a laundered brilliance which justified Barnaby's suit and Maron's wide hat and the deliberate wardrobe of all the people who crowded onto the sidewalk and filled the suburban street with optimistic chatter. Drive-by smilers waved and some clapped.

Clifford was in a slim blue suit and wrap-around shades and he was famous enough for everyone to act as if they had known and liked him for himself for quite a time. Stace was more of a stranger than her man; the attention he won made her an outsider among her brother's friends. Marion went through the smiling people and embraced her daughter and was worried about that white face and the lostness that seemed to be shared by the unseen child in her daughter's belly.

'Mother, I don't get it, where's Zara? Did you hear from her?'

'I talked to her last night,' Marion said, 'and she said it was going to be a little tight for her, but she'd certainly be here.'

'"Tight" meaning? Did she seem peculiar at all?'

'I don't think peculiar,' Marion said. 'Nervous maybe.'

'She is peculiar,' Stace said, 'still and all, not showing at her own brother's wedding.'

'She said she'd be here. They probably got lost.'

'Lost? They live out here. Nobody else got lost.'

'Nobody we know of,' Marion said.

'I think you should go call. Maybe something . . .'

'Let's not even say it,' Marion said. 'The word accident today. They'll probably turn up at the hotel. Maybe there was a lot of traffic coming into town and they cut to the hotel. That would be logical.'

'Does that make it probable?' Stace said. 'I feel strange about this.'

'Pregnancy,' Marion said. 'That makes you feel strange going in.'

'I haven't seen or spoken to Zara in quite a while,' Stace said. 'But I've been feeling marginally uncomfortable about her.'

'Benjamin says she's fine. She's into this stable relationship apparently. She'll be there at the hotel. I bet you.'

'Brian!' Barnaby said. 'So far so good, would you say?'

'They're a handsome couple, Barnaby. More than handsome, because you know what I feel about your son? I feel that he's a good man. A man, and a good one. It doesn't hurt too much giving our daughter, all right, into his keeping. You know what surprises me, or did, and that's that he was never in the service. I'm not saying he should've been; it's just my guess he would've had a really good time.'

'Did you, sir?'

'Personally? I had a helluva good time. I saw the world. I saw men under pressures of various kinds and it was strange, to say the least, to see the kinds could take it and the kinds couldn't. I saw a lot of bravery and I saw a little bit of cowardice too, I guess, and the cowards weren't always the ones who cracked in the face of physical danger, they were more often people that just didn't trust themselves. What the hell are we talking about this for at a time like this? Are you planning on making a speech at the reception?'

'You're looking at one of your cowards right this minute,' Barnaby said, 'because they tell me I don't have to and I am certainly not about to volunteer.'

'Never do anything so foolish,' Brian MacWilliam said. 'That's something you learn on day one. It's just that I know you're a man who knows how to make people laugh and I'm someone more used to making them stop. What I need is a good joke.'

'Everyone does,' Barnaby said.

'Do you know the one that a friend told me in the office that I never heard before, about the young guy went to the doctor and the doctor said he was sorry to tell him this but he only had six months to live . . .'

'There are quite a few of those,' Barnaby said. 'I've just realised something, my other daughter, Zara, she's not here.'

'. . . and the young guy is understandably distressed and begs the doctor, who maybe has previous experience of how to deal with this kind of a situation, to give him advice how to make the best of the six months he has left . . .'

'She was meant to be.'

'And the doctor says, "Well, son, I'll tell you: Marry a Jewish girl and go live in Kansas – it'll seem like a lifetime." I can't tell that one, Barnaby, can I?'

'No, sir, I don't think you can.'

'Lawyer colleague of mine at Acutronics, Gabe Fohlmann, told me that when I was looking for a story, but I can't tell it, can I? That's Gabe over there. He could tell it. You heard it before?'

'And I'll no doubt hear it again,' Barnaby said. 'It's one of the best.'

'The worst cowards were the ones who lied. Just lied. About what they had done or, more often, just what they had said. And they were often the clever ones. I don't mean to say that clever people are cowards, but the clever ones knew how not to get caught very often. They felt the temptation. What the hell are we talking about this kind of thing for on a day like this? Let's get to the French champagne. Where are those damn cars?'

Benjamin said, 'Well, Mother?'

'Imogen,' Marion said, 'you are more than a picture and I know I'm not supposed to say that kind of thing any more, but are you ever?'

'Thank you, Mrs Pierce.'

'Marion, wasn't I going to be when we last talked?'

'It's the veil,' Benjamin said, 'it puts the clock back.'

'I love it,' Imogen said. 'I know just why they always did it. I resisted, as I expect he told you, but now I know *exactly* why girls dreamed about their wedding days, because why wouldn't they? I feel . . . magical.'

'You can tell she's a lawyer works in advertising, can't you, Mother?'

'You're not supposed to say a word against me for at least a week,' Imogen said.

'I don't believe I ever will,' Benjamin said, and Marion had to smile while Imogen lifted aside her veil and, with one hand up by her ear, had Benjamin kiss her.

Marion said, 'Finally!', because the first limo was coming round the corner and Imogen was saying 'Whoops' because her heel nearly turned over on some rice while she was ducking and smiling and getting into the car, quite as if she had a dozen things to do all of a sudden in order to do something so simple.

Barnaby said, 'Elsie, do you think I might have the pleasure of escorting you to the hotel?'

'That's so gallant of you, Barnaby, how could I ever refuse?' Imogen's mother was wearing a shiny blue silk suit and a tight hat with seed pearls sewn into its half-veil. 'Have you seen the house yet?'

'We were by there yesterday,' Barnaby said.

'A million and a half dollars,' Elsie MacWilliam said, 'and at their age the admiral and I were living in married quarters in Seattle we rented for, oh, two hundred dollars a month can it have been?'

Barnaby said, 'I don't know what we were doing. I think we were living in a walk-up on the South Side. But happy.'

'Do you think it's safe?'

'Safe.'

'The house. I wouldn't want to be living way up in the air like that necessarily. They don't have slides up there like they do in Pacific Palisades, but still and all . . .'

'I think it's pretty OK,' Barnaby said. 'Those stilts go in pretty deep and, as you say, they've been there quite a while, those houses.'

'He's not going to tell that story about the Jewish girl, the admiral, is he? Because I don't think that would be in at all good taste, do you?'

'He isn't,' Barnaby said, 'because he told me he wasn't.'

'I don't like those kinds of jokes too well at any time,' Elsie MacWilliam said. 'To tell you the truth.'

The cars backed up at the hotel and some people got out in the driveway and walked on up while the doorman blew his whistle and urged drivers into tight spaces or signalled them to keep going on down under the palm trees and have people walk back. There was an easelled notice-board in the foyer with CONGRATU-LATIONS IMOGEN AND BENJAMIN on it that Marion could have done without even if she smiled at it as she walked on through with Brian MacWilliam. She thought she saw the back of Zara's head, but she couldn't be sure. The dark hair gleamed for a moment under some hooded light from the ceiling of the atrium and then it was gone behind a pillar someplace.

It took a few minutes before the receiving line was established to the admiral's satisfaction and then the bulging crowd of guests began to come in and shake hands and make their happy noises.

They spilled through the narrow doorway like grains of sand in an hourglass and what suddenly happened did not seem to happen suddenly at all, but to be happening for a while before it had any effect or anyone quite knew what was going on or quite knew that it was anything but part of the celebrations. What was sudden was the realisation that the two women who were handing sheets of paper to the people who were going for their champagne or preferred beverage were not offering something to supplement the joy of the afternoon, because, for a few minutes at the least, no one much looked at what was printed on the pages and even then did not really have eyes for what was written on them.

There was something about Zara which meant that Marion either did not really appreciate who she was or that she was so alien, so different from what her mother hoped or expected that Marion refused to see who it was or to register that she was doing something that was not just unexpected but terrible. The only indication of strangeness, at first, was the snap of the paper as each sheet was detached from the stack and handed, as if it were an order, to guests who accepted it with more indulgence than interest. It was not a time for reading and a lot of the older people did not have the right glasses with them.

What followed was that nothing unusual seemed to be going on and yet it was. There was no explosive moment but rather a slow, steady, chilling of the room, as if someone had lowered the temperature and people were not willing to admit that they were feeling chilled. As the chill fell on the company, the guests divided between the people who felt it almost at once and shuddered and wondered what they were supposed to do and the people who, with their glasses and their appetisers and their determined happiness, grew a little bit louder and more cheerful as the silence worked its way into the room like ice forming on a pond. Even when the spreading silence was undeniable and speech turned into resistance to something which the speaker acknowledged by refusing to give in to it, people were looking here and there, conscious that a blight had struck the afternoon but not sure where it came from or what could be done about it. The sheets of paper advertised the origin of the contagion, but very few of the guests had set themselves seriously to read them. They had taken them as you might take a napkin, with no immediate plans for its use. And when they did start to read, the message was so stark and so dense and so inappropriate their horror took the form of a smile: they read on as if, while they got deeper and deeper into the brutal detail, the specific charges, they hoped and expected, or hoped that they expected, that they would come finally to the bottom of a page and be able to explode into hectic laughter because, of course, the whole list of charges was a joke and they had been well and truly had.

Marion and Barnaby and Elsie and Brian and Elsie's mother, Mae, began to sense, along with a lot of other people, that something unscheduled was taking place, but they were locked into their routine and could only wonder, until the last guests had spilled past their smiles and kisses and handshakes, whether something was wrong with the food or what the matter was.

Stace read the thick paragraphs as if she had guessed what they contained. She scanned the accusing pages and then she went right up to her sister and said, 'Get out of here and get that woman out of here. Both of you get out of here.' She made no effort to keep her voice down, but it was as intense as a laser, as if the words were bound tightly together and beamed into Zara's brain.

Chelsea was wearing blue jeans and platform-heeled white slingback sandals and a grey, natural cotton top. She was only a little taller than Zara but wider. Her face was bracketed by cropped, light brown hair and it was lightly freckled and had the complexion of unplaned wood. She had stood by Zara as she handed the sheets of paper to the guests and Stace sensed that it was her will which forced her sister's hand. It seemed that Zara was taking the responsibility, but she was not responsible.

Chelsea said, 'Don't pay any attention to her. Do what you have to do. You have to do it. Do it.'

Stace said, 'I'll never forgive you for this. Never. I want you both to get out of here and never, never get in touch with any of us again.'

'You're in this yourself,' Zara said, 'and you know you are.

You were right. Chelsea said you'd deny it, you'd be on their side, at least at first, until you allowed yourself to remember.'

'What exactly is happening?' Brian MacWilliam said. 'Is something wrong?'

'I'm afraid so,' Barnaby said, 'and it seems to have something to do with my other daughter, whom you haven't had occasion to meet.' He heard his own voice like that of a stranger and it was using words that came from some source that was not his own.

'That girl is your daughter?'

'The one in black is. The other one is a friend of hers that we don't know at all.'

'What're they doing exactly?'

'I don't know. I'm standing here same as you are, Brian. I don't know what's going on. What's going on?'

'What's she giving everybody?' Marion said. 'What's on that paper?'

'Have I seen it?' Barnaby said. 'I haven't seen it any better than you have. What is this craziness?'

'Is it conceivably a joke?' Brian MacWilliam said.

'I don't hear anyone laughing,' Barnaby said. 'Do you?'

He was beginning to be angry, and frightened, though he did not yet know what exactly he feared, which was why he feared it, because behind all the niceness of the day were all the things which divided and individualised these people who had agreed to be very much alike and any of them might be, or have done, enough to change niceness into some kind of a hell, and that was what was happening more and more every second and there was nothing he knew to do about it except to be angry. Specifically, but for some reason he could only dread, Zara was going to ruin the day, had evidently *planned* to ruin it, was *there* to ruin it. What seemed to be happening was going to get much, much worse, so much so that, bad as it seemed, it had hardly happened at all yet. He felt such violence ready in him that he was already short of breath. The violence was a kind of helplessness; all he could think was, he was going to explode about something, that he was perhaps not going to live much longer.

Marion said, 'Zenobia, can I see you alone please?'

'I don't think that's a good idea at this juncture.'

'I'm talking to my daughter. Can she possibly answer for herself?'

Stace said, 'Just let's get them out of this room. Let's collect this *shit* and get them out of here. Can't we call Security? They must have Security.'

'You see,' Chelsea said, 'how entirely right I was when I talked about denial? This is denial a thousand times over.'

Stace said, 'You're an evil, evil person. Don't ask me how I know. I know.'

'You know that this is the truth your half-sister is telling and that you've always known it and you don't want to know it.'

Stace called out, 'Will everyone please tear up these pieces of paper right now. Don't read them, don't look at them any more, they are all *shit*.'

There was a gasp at the loud word, as if Stace's use of it licensed an expression of the shock which had been loose in the room, without anyone knowing how to admit it, for however long it was since people began to be uneasy and then stupefied by the paragraphs they held in their spare hands and had glanced at, at first, with the suspicion that they were some kind of amateur poem in honour of the newlyweds which they were expected to admire and might even have to applaud if its author got up and recited it, might have – God forbid – to sing along with. At least some of the readers, especially the local crowd that had been at college with Imogen, thought they recognised an outbreak of creative writing and only after those several minutes of plunging temperatures did they realise that the thing was neither a joke nor a tribute but, OK, an indictment of, principally, the bridegroom's father and, secondly, his conniving wife.

Marion managed to say, although only the husks of the words came out between her dry lips, 'Did I hear half-sister? Is that what I heard from the person responsible for all of this, as I assume her to be?'

'That's the person primarily responsible for all of this, standing right there in the blue suit and seemingly puzzled by what is going on, when what is going on – and everybody needs to come to terms with this – is that finally, and only perhaps in time, the truth is coming out in a certain family.'

'Half-sister,' Stace said. 'Half-sister?'

'You didn't know, Stacey? You knew. You knew. Because think about it and you'll know you always knew from as far back as things can go, and perhaps further, because if you read Zenobia's evidence, which has the undoubted status of something recovered from . . . if you like beyond the cradle, from inside the womb itself, where there are no influences aside from the cosmically true . . .'

Benjamin said, 'I want you outside. I want you out of here before something uncontrollable happens. You're destroying my life. You're killing something that's in the process of being born.'

'Sit down quietly, Benjamin Harold Pierce, and read the evidence.'

'What is half-sister supposed to imply?' Stace said. 'I want an answer.'

'And you shall definitely have one. It implies the truth, which is that these two people, principally him but also her have been living a deeply evil and complicated lie and that, as she will sooner or later have to have the courage to confess, the perfect mother is an adulteress who may, just may, have been involved, partially due to him, in a Satanic cult of almost incredible deviousness. You should sit down quietly and read the evidence, everybody should, and that's why we have gone to the trouble to boil it down, to render it clear enough to be undeniable.' Chelsea turned to the girl beside her and snapped her fingers and said, 'Zenobia.'

Zara said, 'Are you going to say that you never had a lover who impregnated you?'

Brian MacWilliam's voice was saying, 'Friends, friends, everybody, I've arranged for us to go into another room, just along from here, and I suggest we all do this, with one or two clear exceptions, right away.'

'You can throw away the evidence, you can pretend things

haven't happened that have happened,' Chelsea said, 'because that is exactly what you are pretty well programmed to do and certainly that fulfils our total expectations. I can show you a piece of paper written long before today in which exactly this kind of reaction is predicted. Zenobia.'

Zara said, 'You can go or you can stay, you can deny it until your dying day, but I know in my body, in every orifice of my being . . .'

Barnaby came over, he didn't know how, and stood there, right in front of the two women, with his hands braced either side of a space he seemed powerless to compress and his mouth was cluttered with words he could not emit. It seemed to him that he filled the whole room, or the room filled him, and he was blown up like a balloon, huge and about to burst, swollen with emptiness, a person without personality who could never come back to the smallest kind of normality. He towered above the girls and should have had the strength to make them vanish, but he had no strength at all and then he was sitting on the ground with his steep knees in front of him and his hands over his ears and he could not tell, from the sounds he heard inside himself or outside, whether he was sobbing or what he was doing inside or outside of the shell of himself.

Zara was saying, 'Look at him, the man who abused me because he knew I was never his, the man who thought that he had the power to hide it for ever and ever, look at him and tell me, tell me, you who have the courage still to be in here, if he isn't guilt itself. This is what guilt is, the head-shaking, the palpitations, denial in the form of confession, this is *exactly* what Chelsea predicted and can be verified to have predicted.'

'God damn you to eternal hell.' The words came dry from Marion's lips and seemed to cost her all her breath to deliver. 'Damn you to hell, you're not my daughter.'

'Wrong, Mrs Pierce: she is not his daughter. Is she the devil's daughter, is that the truth you ought to be telling us today?'

Benjamin said, 'I have to take Imogen away from this. I have to get her away from this.'

'You were there,' Zara said, 'you were there and you're the

witness and you know the pain you've lived which is coeval with the pain you've denied and wanted to believe was love, you were there when the coven condemned their son, your brother, because he knew the truth.'

Barnaby was sitting on the red and russet lozenges of the wool and nylon floor and it seemed to him that his buttocks were pointed, that they were in like pickets, down to the boards below the carpet. He looked up at Benjamin, tall and tapering above him, and he held up one hand, not for assistance, not to be helped, but as if he had a question that needed to be asked. Benjamin looked down at his father and then he was crouching beside him and saying, 'She's crazy and I know she's crazy. I told you there was something . . .'

'Love the truth more than appearances,' Chelsea said, 'or you'll never come through this. Let them go. Distance yourself or you'll continue to be contaminated. Dare to be braver than you have ever had to be in your whole life or go down to the pit with the people who have ruined it so far and could ruin it for ever. Zenobia.'

Brian MacWilliam said, 'Marion, I want you to come with me now. Barnaby, get up from the floor. Take my hand. We're leaving this place.'

'He knows that I'm telling the truth,' Zara said. 'You can see it in his eyes. I was abused and abused. I was abused in the womb by the unconscionable things that they did and conspired to have done and when my brother Christopher found out, they feared what he knew so badly that they fixed for him to die.'

Clifford Wordsworth said, 'I'm going to take care of Mr Pierce, Admiral, with your permission. You're coming with me, Barnaby, and you're going to be all right doing it. This man is a good man and I know it. This man is a man I like and trust and you people are going to have to live the rest of your lives in the knowledge that you are sicker than anybody could ever expect to be.'

'Uncle Tom too has his agenda,' Chelsea said. 'And don't we all know it. Uncle Tom sides with the devil because he cannot accept himself for what he is any better than the woman who needs him because he will black out for ever the light which she fears will shine on her and what happened to her alongside her half-sister. We have the evidence and you can run but you can't ever ever hide from it; the evidence is in the vagina and the anus and the mouth and in every aching bone of this sacrificial victim. And it can be verified clinically. It can be verified clinically. I myself have begun the verificatory process and it is undeniably so. This is not a matter of opinion, this is a matter of fact and will soon be a matter of law, because there are consequences here, and reparation to be made. This is not the end of something, or if it is, as I hope it is, then it is also the beginning of something very, very other.'

Barnaby said, 'Where are we going? Where are you taking me?'

'We're going outside,' Clifford Wordsworth said, 'and look at the world out there which has not changed one bit since we came in out of it and you're going to take some breaths of that air out there, good or bad, and so am I, because this kind of craziness only gets dispelled by getting air into those lungs and steadying down and recognising shit for what it is.'

'Why do people say those terrible things?' Barnaby said.

'OK,' Clifford said, 'mainly because they are terrible people.'

'Did Stacey hear about this before you came out here?'

'Not that she told me.'

'Would she tell you?'

'Who would tell who what?' Clifford said. 'I don't know, and I doubt anyone knows.'

'I feel like I ruined my son's day.'

'That's because you don't want her to have done it. You prefer to hate yourself than admit you hate your own daughter.'

'That woman,' Barnaby said. 'That woman. Why?'

'I don't like them,' Clifford said, 'between ourselves.'

'After what she said, why should you?'

'It's a power thing,' Clifford said, 'and when people who have no power want to have it, there isn't anything they won't turn to. You should see some of the letters I get, hear some of the calls, and I'm talking about from black people here, which could include some Hispanics, but not too many, because the black situation is pretty well something all by itself, and you can't get it right, Barnaby, is the truth: you succeed, you're out of your league, you fail, you have to hide it from yourself, or blame it on somebody. With those women, it's what? It's they want to be accepted, want to be natural, and they also want to be compensated, and in this case, it looks like she's found a way to make that compensation something they can get from you. In other words, and don't dislike me for saying this, this was a stick-up. This was a stick-up in there this afternoon and one you couldn't think about using a baseball bat on, a stick-up that didn't concern a black guy in this instance or someone you knew had nothing imaginable to do with you. There was no way you could be a hero in there today, which is what made you flip out.'

'I was never a hero,' Barnaby said, 'and I don't know what the crazy girl was talking about because I may be all kinds of things but I never even had a *thought* about my daughters, not a thought. I had thoughts about my wife, and a few other women in my life, from time to time, but my daughters *never*.'

'She was schooled, Barnaby; she was scripted in there. You could tell that, couldn't you? She was *cued*. You heard; you saw.'

'A woman I never so much as met before, never even spoke to, could dream up something that diabolic? How?'

'You have to go back and back and even then you don't know, but this happened at a wedding. They bided their time in there and they sprung this thing at a wedding, at something they could despise and envy and didn't know which was which. I know, you think I shouldn't say that kind of a thing about your daughter . . .'

'The idea that she isn't mine! That's a fantasy.'

'Fantasy is what they think is real, because then they control it. I knew athletes thought they'd been put under spells, thought I'd put them under spells, because they didn't measure up and didn't have the balls to admit as much.'

'I am totally innocent,' Barnaby said, 'and here's my question, to which there can be no answer: How do you defend yourself when you're totally innocent? Because there's no possible defence to being innocent that I know of.'

'My God,' Marsha Kapinski said, 'you're not leaving already? I didn't miss the whole thing, did I? I can't have. I got here as soon as I could but my mother had a suspect heart attack, would you believe it, in Sherman Oaks, and . . .'

'This is Clifford Wordsworth,' Barnaby said. 'Marsha Kapinski my son works with.'

'Clifford Wordsworth!' Marsha said. 'Now I'm going to have a heart attack! You better call my mother.'

'Is she all right?' Barnaby said. 'I gather she's all right.'

'She has them,' Marsha said, 'especially when I'm slated not to be there when she thinks I should be. Parents and children, that's an old, old story that's never going to go out of style. Clifford Wordsworth.'

'He's with our daughter, Stacey, at the moment,' Barnaby said, 'in Minneapolis they've come from.'

'Are you all right, Mr Pierce? I'm not seriously too late am I, for the celebrations?'

'I've come out into the sunshine because I needed to, Clifford thought, rightly no doubt.'

Marsha frowned at Clifford and all of a sudden they had a pretty good understanding together. 'I saw you play a few times,' she said, 'in the flesh, I mean. Walk on air, you really did.'

'That was then,' Clifford said. 'Why don't you go on in and see people?'

'Is he sick, is that it?'

'No, no, he's just a little overwhelmed.'

'I'm a dead man,' Barnaby said. 'Remember today, Marsha, because you talked to a ghost on Wilshire Boulevard and that has to be something to remember, doesn't it?'

Marsha said, 'Did something go wrong?'

'Apparently; apparently something went wrong.'

'There was an incident,' Clifford said, 'inside just now. A crazy person . . .'

'Two crazy people,' Barnaby said.

'Came in and . . . caused some disruption, which I hope has now been taken care of.'

'They didn't come out,' Barnaby said. 'It's still happening in there. I can't get away from it like this. It's here with us now. It always will be.'

'What the hell kind of an incident? He's seriously distressed,' Marsha said. 'He should possibly even be sedated. So what kind of an incident?'

'You're a beautiful girl, Marsha,' Barnaby said. 'So maybe you shouldn't be talking to me or something.'

Marion was under the canopy of the hotel, looking up and down the bright sidewalk and her eyes seemed not to see Barnaby until she came back to look at him and Clifford and Marsha again and then she came over and said, 'Barnie.'

He looked at her and he smiled, with just his lips, no teeth showing, and the corners of the mouth quivering a little bit, and defiance and surrender were the same things with him, and then he looked at Marsha and said, 'My wife,' and that was the last thing he ever said.